"Looking for someone?"

Even before Simon spoke, Laura sensed his presence behind her. His hand touched her bare shoulder, and beneath his fingers, her skin burned with awareness. Butterflies went wild in her stomach as she turned to meet his smoky gaze.

But the look he gave her was oddly daunting. There was something different about him tonight. He looked taller and tougher. His eyes were cool, his voice remote, and his long study left her shaken . . . almost frightened.

"I thought you weren't coming," she said breathlessly. She stared at him, mesmerized by the grave, intense look deep in those gray eyes.

"Obviously. But now that I'm here, I think you and I need to have a little talk."

Dear Reader,

Spring is on its way in at last, but we've got some hot books to keep you warm during the last few chilly days. There's our American Hero title, for example: Ann Williams's *Cold, Cold Heart.* Here's a man who has buried all his feelings, all his hopes and dreams, a man whose job it is to rescue missing children—and who can't get over the tragedy of failure. Into his life comes a woman he can't resist, a woman whose child has been stolen from her, and suddenly he's putting it all on the line all over again. He's back to saving children—and back to dreaming of love. Will his cold heart melt? You take a guess!

Mary Anne Wilson completes her "Sister, Sister" duet with *Two Against the World.* For all of you who loved *Two for the Road,* here's the sequel you've been waiting for. And if you missed the first book, don't worry. You can still order a copy—just don't let Ali's story slip through your hands in the meantime!

The rest of the month is filled with both familiar names—like Maura Seger and Amanda Stevens—and new ones—like Diana Whitney, who makes her Intimate Moments debut, and Dani Criss, who's publishing her very first book. I think you'll enjoy everything we have to offer, as well as everything that will be heading your way in months to come. And speaking of the future, look for some real excitement next month, when Intimate Moments celebrates its tenth anniversary with a can't-miss lineup of books, including Patricia Gardner Evans's long-awaited American Hero title, *Quinn Eisley's War.* Come May, Intimate Moments is definitely *the* place to be.

Yours,
Leslie J. Wainger
Senior Editor and Editorial Coordinator

OBSESSED!

Amanda
Stevens

Published by Silhouette Books New York

America's Publisher of Contemporary Romance

SILHOUETTE BOOKS
300 East 42nd St., New York, N.Y. 10017

OBSESSED!

ISBN: 0-373-07488-3

First Silhouette Books printing April 1993

Printed in the U.S.A.

Books by Amanda Stevens

Silhouette Intimate Moments

Killing Moon #159
The Dreaming #199
Obsessed! #488

Silhouette Desire

Love Is a Stranger #647
Angels Don't Cry #758

AMANDA STEVENS

knew at an early age she wanted to be a writer and began her first novel at the age of thirteen. While majoring in English at Houston Community College and the University of Houston, she was encouraged to write a romance novel by one of her instructors, who was himself writing a historical. Her first romance was sold to Silhouette Intimate Moments in 1985. Amanda lives in Houston, Texas, with her husband of seventeen years and their six-year-old twins.

This book is gratefully dedicated to S.J.A.,
for heroically rescuing
the story

Prologue

Key West, Florida

Laura Valentine awoke abruptly with the terrifying realization that she'd heard a noise she couldn't identify.

Pushing back the covers, she slipped out of bed and padded across the carpet to the balcony doors she'd left open to the balmy night air. A light rain had started to fall, turning the street below into a mirror.

She stood for a moment, peering out into the wet darkness. A sheet of lightning flashed across the sky, illuminating the garden below and the street beyond. A muffled sound, like a cough, drew her gaze to the sidewalk in front of the house.

For the instant the world was lit, she saw a man standing beneath the sagging branches of the banyan tree. He bent his head to light a cigarette, shook out the match, then casually strolled on.

The lightning faded, and the yard below grew dark again. Laura listened for the sound of the man's footsteps on the sidewalk, but all was silent.

She stared down at the spot where she had seen him as she tried to tamp down a sudden spurt of fear. She was all alone in a house that had at least a dozen entrances. There was no one to call. No one to hear if she should scream.

It was times like this—with her heart pounding, her pulse racing, her stomach churning—when she realized just how alone she truly was. It was at times like this when she realized that her impulsiveness almost always got her into trouble.

She chewed her thumbnail as she anxiously peered into the darkness. The wind shifted, blowing a leaf across the street. The sudden movement startled her, made her jump. Calling herself nine kinds of a coward did little to alleviate her fear.

She should have waited for Jake. She realized that now, but it was too late. In spite of the mansion's elaborate security system, she should never have come early. For all she knew, the man outside was a crazed ax murderer who preyed on insecure cartoonists, in which case, she was a prime target.

Come on, Laura. Don't panic. Use your head for once. Just take a deep breath and try to think like Vicki. What would her cartoon heroine do in a situation like this?

Actually, Vicki would probably go down and confront the man, but for once Laura preferred to use her own logic.

Okay. There were probably a dozen good reasons why a man would be walking past this house, after midnight, in the rain. Someone who couldn't sleep perhaps? Someone who had his own private demons to wrestle? Someone who found his bed the loneliest place on earth in the middle of the night?

Someone a little like her, perhaps?

For just a split second, Laura felt a strange sort of bond with the man outside, as though somehow his loneliness had melded with hers. Comforted somewhat, she secured the glass doors, then climbed back into her bed and huddled under the covers.

But in spite of her own reasonable assertions, she couldn't shake the uneasy notion that the man was still out there somewhere, watching and waiting.

But for what?

Gentry stood huddled under the dripping limbs of the giant banyan tree that stretched across the sidewalk in front of the MacKenzie mansion. It had started to rain a few minutes after he'd first arrived, and now he was soaked and miserable. He took a long drag from his cigarette and idly watched the glowing orange tip in the dark. He stifled another cough.

Damn. He'd gone for months without a cigarette. He thought he'd licked the craving, but this had been one hell of a day. The urge had returned full force. He was weaker than he liked to admit, he guessed.

Throwing down the half-smoked cigarette, he watched it sizzle on the wet pavement, then die. Hell, nothing was fun anymore.

His gaze slid back to the upstairs window he'd been watching for several minutes. Had she seen him? And who was she?

His reports all indicated that Senator Jake MacKenzie and his entourage weren't scheduled to arrive in Key West for at least another day. He'd had no indication that someone would be coming ahead, but the figure he'd glimpsed on the balcony a few moments ago proved that someone had. A woman.

In the flash of lightning, he'd had tantalizing impressions of long, flowing blond hair, of a tall, slender body encased in a white, satin nightgown. He'd seen her only for a second, that was all, but it was enough to make him want to see more.

Fool. Don't wish for things you know you can't have. If he'd learned anything in his forty-one years, it should be that.

He went back to his original question. Had she seen him? He cursed softly. He was losing his touch, getting careless. After all this time, the hunt was wearing on his nerves.

But it would all be over soon. The case that had tormented him and driven him relentlessly every waking hour for the past three years was coming to a close. The traitor he sought had finally messed up, trusted the wrong person. A fatal mistake. He'd slipped through Gentry's fingers for the last time.

Gentry closed his eyes briefly, letting his mind wander back to that night three years ago when he'd first been drawn into this case. An agent had been dispatched to hear the statement of a young woman named Cassandra Chandler who was in hiding in a motel on the outskirts of Washington. When the agent had called in, his voice had been almost frantic with excitement.

"I'm convinced she's telling the truth, Gentry. What she knows, what she *saw* is a matter of national security at the highest level. I'm bringing her in, but she'll have to be protected. Her life wouldn't be worth a plug nickel if he found her."

But the agent hadn't brought her in. He'd died in the crash when their car had been forced off the road. Cassandra Chandler had survived, but her memory had been wiped clean. Gentry had been faced with the challenge of a witness who could not remember her own name; and someone—someone with enough power to have eyes and ears in the Bureau—had wanted her dead.

Through the course of the lengthy investigation, one name had turned up time and again. Senator Jake MacKenzie, a man with top-priority clearance and an unlimited access to classified information; a man who had close ties to Key West, Florida, where the information was being filtered out of the country; a man who had been both a business and social acquaintance of Ellen Mason's, his witness's cousin and a known traitor.

A man who had eluded Gentry for three long years.

His gaze went back to the looming mansion in front of him. In two days his nemesis would be in that house. A cold-blooded murderer and traitor who aspired to be the next president of the United States. A man who had been a little smarter, a little faster, a little more deadly than Gentry had been. But not this time.

His gaze strayed back to the balcony window.

God help anyone who got in his way.

Chapter 1

A storm brewed at sea.

But far to the east of the darkness, the *Valhalla* still basked in light, pristine white, gleaming in the sun, the floating symbol of Senator Jake MacKenzie's wealth and power.

Gentry trained his binoculars on the yacht as he fished in the cooler behind him for a beer. With one hand, he popped the top on the icy can and lifted it to his lips. Damn, it was hot today. He'd already been out here for hours, and the relentless heat made him feel edgy and impatient.

Which was unusual for him. Surveillance rarely bothered Gentry. The endless waiting and watching, the hours of killing boredom played havoc with some agents' nerves, but not his. He was used to the solitude. He liked it. It gave him a chance to think and to plan his next move, because he never acted on impulse, never threw caution to the wind.

Not anymore he didn't.

That's why he was still alive.

At the corner of his vision a flash of apricot distracted him momentarily from MacKenzie. A woman had detached herself from the crowd around the senator, and moved to the railing, where she stood alone. With a minute adjustment, Gentry brought her in closer, so close, it created the illusion that he could reach out and touch the lustrous tumble of wheat-colored hair that fluttered lightly on the breeze. So close, he could almost smell the tantalizing scent of the suntan oil that glistened on her gorgeous, long legs.

As Gentry stood staring at her, a strong premonition of danger washed over him. It had nothing to do with the mission, he realized, and everything to do with the woman. He committed her image to memory, vaguely disturbed by the persistent notion that they had met before. Had she been the woman in the mansion two nights ago? he wondered uneasily. Was she one of *his?*

Gentry grimaced. She looked the type, unfortunately. Blond. Beautiful. Classy. And dangerous. Dangerous, because women like that almost always held a fatal fascination for men like Gentry. It was the classic "look but don't touch" syndrome that irresistibly drew them like a moth to flame.

Thank God he'd learned a long time ago to curb those baser instincts. He'd had to.

"Anything happening?" His partner's muffled voice broke into his thoughts as the younger agent stirred from where he'd been dozing in the sun. Greenwood yawned noisily and stretched as he came to stand beside Gentry.

"Chopper brought MacKenzie on board a little while ago. I'm surprised the noise didn't wake you."

A boyish grin split Greenwood's handsome features. "I'm a sound sleeper, Gentry. Comes with a clear conscience."

Maybe that explained why he seldom slept more than a couple of hours a night, Gentry decided. Unlike the younger man, his conscience hadn't been clear in almost fifteen years. His continued failure with this case only added to the old torment. Maybe that's why he felt so compelled to solve it, to make sure Cassandra Chandler, three years in the Federal witness protection program, remained safe and alive. He'd failed once before, a long time ago, and some-one else had paid the price.

He lifted the binoculars again and scanned the decks. "Looks like they're finally getting ready to go ashore," he commented, watching MacKenzie's party climb down the steps to the motorboat bobbing beside the yacht.

"It's about bloody time. We've been out here for hours," Greenwood complained. "Are they all going?"

"I count nine," Gentry said slowly.

"That's one more than's allowed on a vessel that size. What do you say we have the Coast Guard pick 'em up?" Greenwood grinned again as he popped the top on a beer and took a long swig.

"You're real cute, Greenwood," Gentry muttered dryly, focusing the binoculars on the motorboat. "Someone's missing." Mentally he called roll: MacKenzie, his two bodyguards, his secretary, two aides and three bathing beauties. He'd counted ten people on board.

"The blonde."

"What blonde?" Greenwood asked, his curiosity imme-diately quickening.

"The one on board. She's not leaving with the rest of them."

"Kind of screws with our little plan, doesn't it?" Green-wood asked with a frown. "The crew's below, but with her on deck . . . I don't know, Gentry." He shook his head as he scratched the back of his neck. "I'm not sure broad day-light's the right time to try this."

"That's just what MacKenzie'll think, too. After dark, that boat will be crawling with guards. Now's my chance. We've only the woman to worry about, and I can handle her." He hoped.

He handed the binoculars to Greenwood, and the younger agent gave a low wolf whistle as he adjusted the lenses.

"Whoa, Gentry, no wonder you're so anxious to get aboard that yacht. What a pair of—"

"Just tell me what she's doing, Greenwood," Gentry commanded sharply.

"She's going up on the sun deck, but don't tell me you didn't happen to notice her...considerable attributes, Gentry. Even a man with ice water in his veins has to appreciate a woman like that."

Unaccountably irritated by Greenwood's correct assessment, Gentry slipped into his diving gear without comment. But as he stepped overboard and the water closed over his head, there was a little niggling worry in the back of his mind that fate was about to get in his way.

The breeze fluttered the pages of her sketchbook as Laura sat back against the padded lounger and contemplated her dilemma.

She needed a man and she needed one fast.

Not just any man, of course. A hero. A soul mate for her comic-book heroine. After years of struggling in relative obscurity, Laura's *Vicki Love* had become what the critics called "an overnight success." A movie deal was in the works, the first issues of the comic book had suddenly become collectors' items and several pieces of original cover artwork would be premiered at an exclusive exhibit here in Key West this week. Her career had suddenly sprouted wings, it seemed.

But with the success had come a fair amount of pressure. Readers had been clamoring for months now for a new love interest for Vicki, and Laura's editors at Action Comics had even conducted a contest, letting the readers vote on the hero's name—Richard Manley. He had a name now, but still no face. That part was up to Laura, and so far, she'd been appallingly uninspired.

Well, she'd known it wouldn't be easy when the editors had first approached her with the idea. Villains were easy, a dime a dozen, but heroes were always hard to find.

Speaking for yourself, or for Vicki? a little voice in the back of her mind asked.

Maybe it was the thrill of her first gallery showing that had blocked her creativity, Laura mused. Maybe it was the excitement of seeing Jake again, or all these luxurious surroundings—so opposite to that of her tiny studio in Washington. Maybe it was simply the fact that her last relationship—which had ended so disastrously—had made her attitude toward men cynical at best these days.

Heroes just didn't exist in the real world, Laura concluded a trifle wistfully. Instead of wasting her time searching for a role model, she'd do just as well to take the first man she saw—a total stranger—and mold him into a hero for Vicki.

Maybe that's exactly what she would do, Laura decided, as her pencil flew across the page of her sketchbook, adeptly adding finishing touches to Vicki Love's mane of blond hair. She'd pick a man—any man—and use *him* for a change.

The notion gave her a perverse sense of power as she automatically supplied the facial features to her heroine—features as familiar to her as the ones she saw in the mirror every day.

And with good reason. Vicki Love, superspy extraordinaire, was not only Laura's creation and occupation, but also her alter ego...sometimes her nemesis. The perfect woman.

Now that she was starting to get recognition, Laura realized the folly of modeling her heroine—at least in looks—after herself. People, especially men, expected her to *be* Vicki Love. It was a strange paradox, and one that could actually be quite useful at times—because when she pretended to be Vicki Love, Laura Valentine and all her problems could quietly fade into the background.

But no matter how much she pretended, how much she fantasized, Laura Valentine knew she could never really *be* Vicki Love. Vicki was perfect. She was not.

Gentry surfaced in the shadow of the yacht, hugging the line of the ship as he removed his mouthpiece and shoved the mask on top of his head. Above him somewhere, rock music blasted from speakers, which was good, he decided. The racket would cover any noise he might make boarding.

Inside a waterproof pouch strapped to his belt was a tiny but extremely sensitive listening device he hoped to plant in MacKenzie's stateroom. Gentry knew MacKenzie ordered frequent sweeps for bugs, and this one would eventually be found. However, he had been instructed by the expert who'd designed the minuscule device just where to plant it for optimum security. Hopefully, they'd get lucky before the device was discovered.

What he had to worry about now was the blonde. It'd be a damned shame to have to deck someone that gorgeous, but, hey, if push came to shove, he'd do it. With deadly resolve, Gentry knew he was prepared to do whatever he had to to get Jake MacKenzie.

His tank bumped against the metal steps with a loud clang. Above him, the music was silenced. Gentry froze. Had the woman heard him?

He clung to the ladder, holding his breath as he waited for the blonde to make her move. His glance scanned the looming hull of the yacht. Overhead, from one of the lower decks, a metal diving platform protruded over the sea. Gentry's heart banged against his rib cage as he watched the woman walk to the edge of the platform and look down, as if gauging the distance to the water.

He gauged the distance himself, calculating rapidly whether he could make it to the top of the ladder before she surfaced. The heavy air tank would be a hindrance, but he couldn't abandon it. She might see it, and besides, he'd need it to swim back to the launch without detection. The last thing he wanted was to be spotted near MacKenzie's yacht.

The girl stretched, lifting her arms high overhead as she prepared for the dive. At the last minute, too late, she hesitated, as though losing her nerve. But she was already off balance, and for a breathless moment she seemed to hover on the edge of the diving board. Then her arms flailed wildly as she slipped. Her head banged sickeningly against the metal platform as she fell in an ungainly sprawl toward the water.

It seemed to take forever for her to hit the water. Without even being aware of his actions, Gentry adjusted his mask and mouthpiece and slipped beneath the surface, searching.

The sun filtered through the bottle-green water in sporadic patches, and for a moment, he didn't see her. When he spotted her, his heart seemed to stop.

She was plunging toward the bottom, face first, arms and legs limp and lifeless. Her long hair streamed behind her like some golden, gossamer cloak as a sun ray suspended her in light. Even now, with her life hanging by a thread, Gentry was struck by her ethereal beauty.

The deep, underwater current was carrying her swiftly away from the boat, and Gentry kicked harder, his stomach knotted with tension. When he reached her, she was completely unresponsive. A thin stream of red from the cut on her head swirled in the water around her.

Grasping her with one arm, he pulled the cord to inflate his buoyancy compensator and they were propelled quickly to the surface.

Like a giant sea monster, the *Valhalla* towered above them. Gentry knew there was no way he could drag her up the ladder to the lower deck. Instead, he maneuvered them toward the low-riding ski boat moored at the starboard side of the yacht.

Gasping and cursing, he managed to haul her over the side of the boat and climb in behind her. Laying her on the floor, he knelt in the cramped space between seats and felt for a heartbeat. Shoving his mask on his head, he bent and put his ear to her chest.

Relieved to find the rhythm steady, he pushed back the wet bangs to locate the cut on her head. His gaze quickly scanned the rest of her, looking for further damage, but the golden expanse of skin left bared by the apricot bikini appeared untouched. Perfect, in fact, he thought with a flicker of grudging admiration. MacKenzie had outdone himself this time.

Her breathing deepened, and the delicate rise and fall of her breasts irresistibly drew his gaze. A sea breeze ruffled across her skin and beneath the thin fabric of her swimsuit, he saw her breasts unconsciously respond to the chill. In spite of himself, something responded inside him.

That's what happens when you do without for too long, Gentry. Overreaction to just another pretty face.

Right.

And the *Valhalla* was just another boat.

With a muttered oath, he tore his gaze away and returned his attention to the cut on her head. The wound was superficial; the bleeding had already stopped. But she'd probably have one hell of a headache, he thought with a glimmer of sympathy that annoyed him.

Lying there so still and pale, so damned fragile-looking, she had the air of a woman who badly needed someone to take care of her, and he had too strong a desire to be the one doing it.

Beneath his bold stare, she stirred, her long, golden lashes fluttering as lightly as butterfly wings against the porcelain skin. She groaned softly and tried to shove his hand away. His reaction to the sound of her voice startled him. He cursed again, recognizing temptation when he saw it.

Not here, he thought savagely. *Not now.* And certainly not with her. He didn't have to know who she was, didn't have to know anything about her to realize she spelled trouble. She was with Jake MacKenzie, and that fact alone told Gentry more than he wanted to know.

He'd make sure she was all right, then he'd get the hell away from her as fast as possible. The bug would have to wait. He couldn't afford to hang around here much longer. His internal warning system was going crazy as it was.

As Laura slowly opened her lids, a face floated above her
eyes. She blinked once, then again, as she tried to bring the
man's features into focus, but everything was blurry and
inconsistent. She felt herself grow panicky.

"Jake?"

"Hardly." The voice was deep and edged with annoyance.

The sharp pain in her temple drew her fingers to the cut,
and she winced when she made contact with the wound.

The stranger peeled her hand away. "Leave it alone," he
commanded in a tone that was forceful, yet oddly gentle.
"Just lie still for a minute."

"It hurts," she protested groggily.

"I'm not surprised."

His hand was still around her wrist, and as Laura's head
began to clear, her first instinct was to pull away. The
warmth from his fingers seeped inside her skin, lulling her
into a sense of security and well-being she didn't dare trust.

But as she tried to tug her hand away, their eyes made
contact for the first time. Laura's heart plunged to her
stomach like an elevator with its cable clipped.

He had the grayest, sexiest eyes she'd ever looked into,
and the way they were looking at her now—half warily, half
seductively—made her flesh come alive with an awareness
that took her completely by surprise.

Six weeks ago, when her wedding had been called off,
when she'd found out at the last minute what a miserable rat
her fiancé was, she'd sworn off men forever, especially men
she couldn't trust. And she had absolutely no reason in the
world to trust the man glaring down at her, even if he had
rescued her.

But he *had* rescued her. That had to account for something. It was strange, Laura mused, because he really didn't
look like a hero at all. His face was far from handsome, but
there was both strength and character in his features, which
made her think he just might be someone very much worth
knowing.

He was still kneeling over her, but she could tell he was tall and thin, with a sort of innate toughness that belied his lean physique. His face was slightly sunburned, emphasizing even more the deep creases around his eyes and mouth, the thin scar over his right eyebrow. He had the distinct look of a man who had been tested, maybe even battered, by time and experience, but had so far managed to come out on top.

By all appearances there was absolutely no reason why he should take her breath away, but she *was* breathless. No question about it. Dizzy, light-headed, breathless.

"Who are you?" she whispered.

He ignored her question and said, very unheroically, "What the hell were you doing going into the water alone? A five-year-old knows better."

His tone made her suddenly defensive, made her heart beat even faster. She gathered her thin veneer of sophistication and lifted her chin haughtily. "I was swimming before I could walk. I've won medals in both swimming and diving."

He said, unimpressed, "Medals don't help much when you're coldcocked before you ever hit the water. Lucky for you I decided to go diving today."

"I don't believe in luck."

His face remained implacable, but his mouth thinned slightly in a line that hinted at displeasure. Some men found her long, blond hair, wide green eyes and tall, slender figure attractive, but whatever the stranger saw in her features apparently only irritated him. His eyes were as dark and threatening as a rain cloud as he glared down at her, and the deep furrows across his forehead only enhanced the stormy image.

Laura winced inwardly, more from embarrassment this time than pain. *Idiot!* she berated herself mercilessly. Vicki would never had done anything so asinine, so utterly stupid, and if she *had,* she certainly wouldn't be lying here now as helpless as a beached fish.

With that thought, Laura struggled to sit up. His hands, strong and capable, grabbed her shoulders and pushed her back down.

"Just take it easy now. You've had a bad shock, but you'll be all right."

His tone soothed Laura in spite of herself. There was something about him, a quiet air of authority, that made her want to listen to him. In fact, everything about him appeared calm and controlled, but with a startling flash of insight, she knew the emotions were there, simmering beneath the surface, where they were usually the most dangerous.

She wondered suddenly what it would take to bring those emotions boiling over. Exploding bombs. Crashing planes. A woman? When his gaze swung back around to hers, her heart fluttered against her chest like a leaf caught in a whirlwind.

"You'll be all right now," he said again, as if to reassure himself. Then he added grimly, "I'm afraid I've done all I can here."

He stood and readjusted his equipment, but just before he stepped over the side of the boat, he paused and turned back to her. A spark ignited in his eyes like lightning before a storm. Like an invitation to disaster. Like a preview of what was to come.

"Do me a favor, will you? Stay out of the water. Esther Williams you're not."

Then he stepped over the side and was gone with a splash that shattered the golden light dancing on the surface of the water.

"Wait a minute!" Laura called out, realizing she'd just let Richard Manley—Vicki's hero—slip through her fingers. She scrambled to her knees to gaze over the side of the boat, but the only thing remaining were the air bubbles from his tank, rising like tiny silver coins to the surface.

"Who's Esther Williams?" she asked softly, her heart sinking with disappointment.

Chapter 2

Sun diamonds danced on the shimmering blue swells that gently rocked the pleasure cruisers, fishing vessels and motorboats dotting the shimmering bay. The horizon, where sea met sky, displayed an endless turquoise blue marred only by specks of green haze, where islands were misted by distance.

It was one of those days in paradise that could almost make Gentry believe he was in Key West for nothing more than a vacation—except for one small detail. He didn't take vacations. Not anymore he didn't.

Vacations were for relaxing, and Gentry never relaxed. Vacations were a time for hardworking men to spend quality time with their wives and children, but family was a concept he had given up on a long time ago. Vacations were a time for lying in the sun, long walks on the beach, making love under the stars. Murderers didn't track you down while you were on vacation, while you grew complacent, while you'd let down your guard. They didn't stalk you, didn't blow your world all to hell with one, perfect shot.

Your wife didn't die in your arms because she'd been the target of a madman's revenge against *you.*

But that had all happened years ago, a lifetime ago, and it was better not to reflect on what had been ... except that that aspect of the past was still very much alive for Gentry. In some ways, every case he'd worked on since then had become a part of his own personal vendetta. That was why this case was so damned critical. He'd failed Caroline, and she'd died. He couldn't afford to fail Cassandra Chandler.

Gentry lifted his binoculars and scanned the bay again. The picturesque view before him included MacKenzie's private dock and a glimpse of the garden and pool area, where a midday party was in full swing. He wondered absently if the woman he'd rescued yesterday was there today, then he cursed himself for even so momentary a lapse of control. He couldn't afford to get sidetracked, even for an instant. Not while Jake MacKenzie still walked free.

He'd waited too long for this.

Besides, the blonde was about as far out of his league as the Queen of England—the porcelain skin, hair the color of sunlight, a body that was lush and long-legged and made for seduction—everything about her shouted money and class and breeding, and Gentry knew her type a little too well. She was exactly the kind of ''perfect'' woman MacKenzie liked to surround himself with. Women who lived capriciously, with no regard for consequences, no thought for tomorrow.

And if there was anything Gentry respected, it was living long enough to see tomorrow.

He got up from the bench and backtracked toward the street, toward the telephone-repair truck parked in an alley a couple of blocks from the MacKenzie mansion. He jumped lightly over a wooden fence, coming up on the rear of the van. He knocked twice, then once, and the door swung open. He stepped inside and closed the door behind him.

''Got anything yet?'' he asked.

Greenwood removed his headset as he spoke to Gentry in a low tone. "It's a little hard to tell at this point, boss, but when we go back and separate the voices on the tape, we may pick up something in the background. Right, Doug?" The other agent in the van nodded as he munched on an apple. Both of them looked so damned young, Gentry thought absently, so unconcerned.

He said gruffly, "I appreciate what you two are doing, giving up your vacations for this."

Greenwood smiled disarmingly. "Only for you, Gentry. Only for you."

"Yeah, well, I'll owe you both. Let me know as soon as you hear anything, you got it? I don't have to remind you, this assignment is a matter of life and death."

Greenwood grinned. "It always is, Gentry. That's why we like it, right?"

Right.

And the blonde he'd rescued yesterday was only mildly attractive.

He glanced back at Greenwood. "Are you all set for tonight?"

"No problem. I recruited a female agent from the local office, a real looker. We shouldn't have any problem getting into the club. I didn't fill her in on any of the details except to dress flashy and look interested in me. Should be a breeze evening for her." He grinned again, but Gentry knew he was dead serious. If there was anything the younger agent did not lack it was confidence.

To be that young again, Gentry thought grimly as he stepped from the van and closed the door.

And to have the knowledge he had now, but had needed years ago.

The incident on the yacht yesterday almost seemed like a dream to Laura, an image straight from her own fantasy world, except for one small detail. She couldn't get the gray-eyed stranger out of her mind.

Telling herself he was too hard, too old, too *real* for the man she needed did no good. Reminding herself that heroes looked more like, well, like Senator Jake MacKenzie—with his Nordic blond hair and blue eyes, his old-world charm and charisma—did not keep her mind from plotting a new story, either.

Lounging poolside at the mansion, dragging her feet through the crystal-blue water, Laura idly watched the crowd gathered around Jake MacKenzie, her former stepbrother and sometimes mentor, as he held court under the shade of a blue-and-white striped awning.

At forty-seven, Jack was still the dashing man she remembered from her childhood. Fit, handsome, bronzed and blond, he reminded Laura nothing so much as one of the proud, ancient Vikings for which he'd named his yacht. An errant sunbeam made a soft halo of his golden hair, and for a moment he looked almost saintly in the filtered light. But the image was lost as he dipped his head to say something to the brunette on his left. Her feminine laughter rippled across the terrace like the soft clanging of a ship's bell.

Reclining against her elbows, Laura watched the charade with growing amusement. It was all an act, of course. A carefully staged performance that Jake had honed to perfection. He was the consummate politician, the ultimate actor. Laura only wished her own performances were so flawless.

Across the terrace, he caught her eye and smiled, raising his crystal goblet in salute. He excused himself from his fans and rose gracefully, then sauntered across the flagstones toward her.

As Laura watched him approach, she marveled as always at his potent physical presence. He exuded a kind of power and charisma that seemed an almost tangible commodity, and yet for some reason she couldn't understand, she had failed time and again to capture his unique essence on canvas.

Jake sat down beside her and draped a casual arm over her shoulders. He made a slight signal, and instantly another Baccarat crystal flute of champagne materialized at his side. He handed the glass to Laura.

"What are we celebrating?" she asked, reluctantly accepting the chilled wine.

He smiled enigmatically. "The sunset, of course. It's a tradition here in Key West."

"Sunset is hours away."

"But there *will be* a sunset," he assured her, clinking his glass lightly to hers. "Trust me. The sun always shines in Key West."

"I suppose I'd better drink to that then." Laura lifted the glass to her lips and took a tentative sip of the Dom Pérignon, trying to hide the inevitable grimace. She'd never liked champagne, much less in the middle of the day. A glass of tea or even a cold beer would have tasted much better, but somehow Laura didn't think Jake would appreciate the fact that she'd acquired a taste for beer. Champagne was a way of life in his camp. There was always something to celebrate.

"We could also toast your success," he suggested, lifting his glass and watching the millions of bubbles spiral upward.

"That's a little premature, as well," Laura said with a frown. "Suppose no one shows up at the premiere? Suppose no one buys any of my pieces? Suppose no one bids on the ones we're donating to the auction this weekend?"

Again he smiled mysteriously. "Have a little faith in your own abilities, my dear. You *will* be a success. Trust me."

"You keep saying that."

He laughed again, draining the last of his champagne. "Maybe one of these days you'll believe I only have your best interests at heart. I know I may have bullied you into this showing, but sometimes you have to take a chance, a risk. After all, that's what makes life worthwhile, isn't it?"

That's exactly what Vicki would say, Laura mused.

Jake said softly, "Do you know what I was thinking about when I first saw you sitting over here by yourself? I was remembering that first summer you and your mother lived here. Crystal and Dad had gotten married that spring, and I'd just come home from Vietnam, remember?"

Laura smiled. "How could I forget? You were a hero. Everyone adored you."

Jake grinned again. "Including you."

"Especially me. It was all pretty dazzling to a seven-year-old."

"You were such a shy little thing. Stayed in your room most of the time. I never could quite figure out why. Were we that frightening?"

Laura's smile was wry. "You were a bit."

But that wasn't the reason she'd stayed in her room. She'd stayed in her room because her mother had told her to. The first day they'd arrived at the mansion, Crystal had taken Laura upstairs and shown her her room.

"This is where I want you to stay until I tell you you can come out, do you understand? I want you to keep out of the way. William doesn't like kids, and I don't want you ruining this for me."

The obvious conclusion for a seven-year-old had been that if she had the power to ruin this marriage for her mother, she must have somehow done something to ruin the last one. It must also have been her fault that her father had left them, her fault that he never called, never came to see her.

Laura had spent hours and hours of isolation in her room that summer, agonizing over what she had done, what it was about her that made people want to run away from her. And then one day, quite unexpectedly, she'd learned the truth.

The revelation had changed her life forever.

Crystal had been having a garden party, here on this very terrace, and she'd summoned Laura for a very brief appearance to show her guests what a proud mother she was. As always, Laura had endured the torture of their scrutiny without fidgeting, but instead of going back to her room after the performance was over, she'd hidden just inside the French doors of the library, watching the party, admiring her mother's cool elegance and beauty from a distance.

"Crystal, my word, how did you ever produce such an ungainly, backward-acting child? She hasn't a bit of personality, has she? And those poor, scrawny legs—they'd look more appropriate on a stork than on a little girl!"

Laura had frozen, paralyzed with humiliation at the speaker's cruel observation. An awkward, loaded silence had followed during which Laura had waited, her chest heaving with horror, to hear her mother rush to her defense. Instead, she'd heard Crystal's laughter ring out across the garden.

"She takes after her father, poor thing."

With tears of humiliation and despair flowing down her face, Laura had turned and fled back to her room. No wonder no one loved her! Even her mother thought she was ugly and stupid!

Wiping away the tears with the back of her hand, she'd grabbed her sketchbook and frantically started drawing one figure after another until her labor produced the image of what she thought was a perfect little girl. Over the years, that perfect little girl had evolved into the perfect adolescent, the perfect teenager, the perfect young woman. Laura hadn't known it at the time, of course, but *Vicki Love* had been born that terrible afternoon.

But even *Vicki Love* wasn't good enough for her mother. In spite of Laura's success, Crystal never missed an opportunity to let her daughter know how disappointed she was that Laura wasn't a *real* artist. No matter how many times Laura told herself it didn't matter, even at the age of twenty-seven, she still found herself craving just one word of praise from her mother.

"Hey!" Jake snapped his fingers in front of her face. "Where did you go?"

Laura shrugged, trying to dismiss the heaviness her memories had created. "I was just thinking about that

summer so long ago. Jake...do you think Mother will come
to the premiere?''

"When she called this morning, she said she was trying to
clear her schedule.''

"She called this morning? She...didn't ask to speak with
me?''

Jake's large hand closed over hers and squeezed sympathetically. "I'm sorry. Do you still mind so much?''

Laura bit her lip, shaking her head slightly. "I should be
used to it by now. Of course, I know why she's doing this.
She's punishing me for calling off the wedding. I embarrassed her in front of the guests, mostly *her* friends. You
know what stock Mother puts in appearances.''

"Well, never mind her. You did the right thing," Jake
assured her. "Kendall didn't deserve you. He's a user,
Laura. Don't take it personally.''

Right. Except it *was* personal, extremely personal, when
someone tried to marry her to get what he wanted, Laura
thought bitterly, when all he'd been interested in was how
your association with a senator could further his own political ambitions. But she'd learned her lesson this time, and
learned it well.

No one would ever use her again.

"You're coming to the club tonight. I absolutely will not
take no for an answer," Jake said decisively as he stood to
leave.

Laura grimaced. Discos were hardly her favorite hang-
out, but it sure beat spending another lonely night in that
bedroom.

A line had formed—as it did every night—in front of the
ritzy Club Kenya, but entry into the underlit, overpriced
disco was limited to only the most elite of patrons—the very
rich and famous or the very young and beautiful. Unfortunately, Gentry met neither requirement.

Seated in a wicker chair in the alfresco bar across the
street, he sipped his drink and watched with wry amuse-

ment as the bouncer—a dark-haired Hulk Hogan type—
stood in front of the garish purple door and passed down
judgment as each hopeful stepped forward in line.

Greenwood and the female agent were inching toward the
front. Dressed in a dark, double-breasted Armani suit, a
flashy gold Rolex adorning his wrist, and the chesty brunette adorning his arm, the younger agent blended perfectly with the jaded, international crowd around him. Once
inside the club, Greenwood's mission was to keep an eye on
MacKenzie's comings and goings.

Casually Gentry lifted his drink, but the glint of steely
determination in his eyes contradicted the laconic movement of his hand. He scanned the street, then returned his
gaze to the club.

The agents stepped forward, laughing and talking with
bold confidence. The bouncer made a light movement with
his head toward the street. Gentry could see Greenwood's
outraged gestures as he argued with the bouncer.

Gentry groaned. If there was anything he'd learned about
the younger agent in the years they'd worked together it was
the fact that Greenwood sometimes had a hard time with the
concept "maintaining a low profile," a concept Gentry
considered his particular specialty.

Maybe that was why their partnership had worked out so
well. Neither of them stepped on the other's turf. They each
had their own strengths, their own weaknesses. Greenwood
had enthusiasm, Gentry had maturity. Greenwood had his
confidence, Gentry had his obsession. Together they could
be a formidable, dogmatic team.

He watched anxiously as the bouncer's thumb jerked
through the air toward the street, a gesture no one could
misinterpret. Gentry released a sigh of relief when both
agents gave up and turned away, stalking across the street.

They seated themselves at the table next to his and placed
their drink orders before Greenwood spoke.

"You saw?"

Gentry never glanced in his direction. "Nice going."

"Hey, is it my fault that clown has no taste?"

Gentry stood and tossed some bills on the table. "I'll give it a shot."

Greenwood's gaze ran a quick appraisal of Gentry's blue jeans, open-necked shirt and sport coat. His brow lifted in a smirk. "Dressed like that?"

"That thousand-dollar suit didn't do much for you, now did it?" Gentry asked, then chuckled at Greenwood's crestfallen expression.

The line in front of the club had diminished considerably as Gentry sauntered across the street and took his place behind two men dressed identically in lavender suits. When the bouncer waved the couple inside, Gentry's gaze shot heavenward. He didn't have a prayer.

Nevertheless, he stepped forward and looked the bouncer straight in the eye. The man returned his gaze with cool indifference, but whether he would have nodded toward the door or toward the street, Gentry never found out. The man's gaze moved past him, and Gentry also turned to look. Then he froze, a sinking sensation in the pit of his stomach.

He recognized the legs first, long and golden and smooth as silk as they swung from the open car door of a white Corvette parked at the curb. The white pumps encasing her feet were tall and sexy, and she wore them with an airy disregard for her height. As she got out of the car, Gentry's gaze traveled upward, slowly, enjoying the trip.

She wore white leather that did wonderful things to her curves. The short skirt snugly rode her hips and stopped just above midthigh. The matching jacket crossed over her body and snapped at the waist, leaving a low V at the neck that made Gentry wonder what, if anything, she wore beneath it.

Her face yesterday had been pale, her eyes huge with shock. But now her features were vividly alive, her golden lashes darkened slightly with mascara, her luscious lips glossed with red. She looked beautiful and regal, and about as far removed from the near-drowned woman he'd seen yesterday as he could imagine.

Her gaze brushed him briefly, then danced away without a glimmer of acknowledgment. Odd that he should feel disappointment, he thought in annoyance. He should be counting his blessings that she *hadn't* recognized him.

The line miraculously parted for her directly behind Gentry. She looked neither right nor left, but as she passed by, she said over her shoulder in a gut-wrenching, sexy voice, "He's with me, Tony."

The air quivered with a sort of stunned silence. Gentry wasn't sure who appeared more startled, him or Tony. But he collected himself rapidly, and strode through the purple door behind her.

Laura was truly thankful for the murky atmosphere inside the club because the man beside her couldn't possibly see her pounding pulse, her sweating palms. A trickle of perspiration followed a precise course down her spine. Leather hadn't been such a great idea, she thought dismally. Not in this heat.

She took a deep breath and glanced at the man beside her. Could she actually pull this off? she wondered anxiously. Could she actually pick up a complete stranger and keep him interested long enough to get what she needed?

When she'd first seen him standing outside the club, she couldn't believe she'd found him again so easily. Inviting him in had been a lark, a hunch, a gamble that maybe, just maybe, he was indeed the man she'd been looking for. There was only one way to find out.

Beside her, she heard him murmur a expletive as he took in the surroundings—the trophy heads mounted on the walls, the loinclothed waitresses. His expression ranged somewhere between dumbstruck and disgust—an opinion that mirrored her own.

She flashed him a cool, knowing, Vicki Love look. "I don't particularly care for it, either."

His brows soared in surprise. "Why are you here, then?"

She shrugged wearily, striving for a bored look and praying she'd succeeded. "I was supposed to meet some people here."

"Was?"

"And now I've met you. Let's dance," she invited casually, moving toward the dance floor.

He caught up with her and said at her ear, "Couldn't we find a table and talk instead? I'm not much of a dancer. Two left feet."

"I somehow doubt that," Laura murmured, her gaze raking him up and down. Everything seemed in the right places to her. Maybe that's why her heart was pounding so uncomfortably. Maybe that's why her face felt so flushed. She gave him another Vicki Love smile, sucked in her flat stomach and took his hand.

Mercifully for Gentry, the rock number ended and the obnoxious deejay spun a slower song. Without hesitation, she drifted into his arms, and without hesitation, he closed them around her. She danced close, but not seductively so. She didn't talk, either, but merely followed his lead, smiling when their eyes occasionally met.

She seemed so different tonight, Gentry reflected. So confident and bold. He almost wondered if she were indeed the same woman he'd met yesterday. Beneath his hands, the white leather felt warm and supple, as though a reflection of her body's texture. Her fragrance swirled through his senses. No light, floral fragrance this, but a deep, heady musk that smelled dangerously like sin.

Dear God, how long had it been since he'd held a woman like her in his arms? She was undoubtedly the most beautiful, the most desirable woman he'd ever met, and for a moment, as their bodies moved rhythmically together, he found it almost too easy to forget who he was and who she was and why they were both here.

But as they turned, his gaze scanned the tables near the dance floor, and his eyes locked with Jake MacKenzie's. In spite of the noise in the place, MacKenzie was talking into a portable phone, but his gaze, for that one split second, shot through Gentry like a well-timed bullet.

Gentry casually glanced away, but his heart pounded against his chest like a jackhammer. It all came rushing back to him—his job, his mission, his destiny.

Abruptly he stopped dancing.

"Let's sit down," he said and led her off the floor, selecting a table directly across from MacKenzie and his entourage.

"I want to ask you a question," he said, watching her facial expressions closely as they both took seats. "Exactly why did you do that?"

She shifted the candle in the center of the table, casting the light directly on his face. "You mean dance with you?"

"No, get me in here."

She lifted one shoulder. "I thought you wanted to come in."

His gaze narrowed. "Didn't you think I could get in on my own?"

"No," she answered with brutal frankness. "But I don't mean that as an insult. Quite the contrary. I don't consider it much of an accomplishment to be welcomed into a place like this." She smiled as a passing waitress greeted her warmly.

"For someone who has such a low regard for the place, you certainly seem to be well-known around here."

"I've been here before," she admitted, almost reluctantly it seemed. Her gaze flickered away from his. "With friends."

"The same friends you were meeting tonight? I wouldn't want to keep you from joining them—"

She leaned her forearms on the table and bent forward. Her hair glinted like gold in the candlelight as her clear, direct gaze took his measure. "If I didn't know better, I'd say you were trying to get rid of me."

"Not at all. But I'm not sure Senator MacKenzie's happy with the arrangement. Aren't you supposed to be with him?"

The elegant brows lifted. "How did you know—you recognize me," she finished ironically. "It all happened so quickly yesterday, I wasn't sure you would."

As if he could forget, Gentry thought, not pleasantly. He hadn't slept well last night, and now it suddenly dawned on him just why. He seldom slept the night through, often waking to take long walks in the dark or to stare mindlessly at the television screen until his brain simply shut down from exhaustion. But last night the old memories, the gnawing guilt, the endless waiting for revenge, had not made him restless. It was a new memory, a new face, a new awareness that he was still human, still a man with needs and demands that had raged for attention.

Which was stupid, he knew. He couldn't afford any kind of involvement with this woman, for both personal and professional reasons. Fortunately for him, a woman like her would lose interest quickly. He was a novelty right now. He'd saved her life, and because of that, they shared a bond, but only a momentary one. It could never be anything more than that.

His expression turned slightly grim as his gaze reluctantly slipped over every perfect feature of her face. He realized now that his assessment of her yesterday had been way off target. She no more needed someone to take care of her than did a charging rhino. She had the air of a woman who knew exactly what she wanted, and wasn't afraid to go after it.

Question was, what exactly did she want?

At the moment, Laura wanted desperately to sketch him. His features were so elusive, she knew she could never remember all the details that made him so unique.

He was younger than she'd originally thought, probably somewhere around forty. But he still wasn't the kind of man she normally looked for. His hair was that nondescript shade between blond and brown, and his hairline was slightly receding. But rather than trying to disguise the fact with an unattractive hairstyle, he'd swept it back, rather carelessly, as though he didn't give a damn.

All in all, his eyes were the most truly remarkable thing about him. While his face remained expressionless, a myriad of emotions swam in those murky depths, pulling Laura deeper and deeper into a fantasy world that had eluded her for too long. This man, her reluctant hero, had secrets. Dark ones. And because of that, he might very well be the man of her dreams.

A waitress bent over the table and placed a chilled glass of champagne in front of her. Laura looked up quickly. "I didn't order this."

"Compliments of the senator." Laura lifted her gaze and met the stranger's, sensing the familiar quickening of inter- ست. She smiled weakly and shrugged.

"Can I get you something from the bar, sir?"

"Bourbon," he said, his eyes never leaving Laura's. There was something about the way he looked at her, studied her, that made her uneasy. It was almost as though he wanted something from *her,* she thought with a frown.

When the waitress disappeared, he turned with a half smile, his tone slightly ironic. "Under the circumstances, I feel I already know you, but maybe we should introduce ourselves anyway. I'm Simon Hunter."

She extended her hand across the table. "Laura Valentine."

"Pretty name for a pretty lady."

Laura caught the brief flash in his eyes, the flicker of some indefinable emotion, but what intrigued her more was how quickly he let go of her hand, as though perhaps he'd felt the same little jolt she had.

She'd almost convinced herself today that she'd imagined the blast of masculine power, the intenseness, the blatant sexuality that had captured her fantasy. Not so. Every time their eyes collided, tingles raced up and down her spine.

The almost overpowering sensual awareness disturbed her because, after her debacle of a wedding, she should have known better.

Down, girl, she advised herself sagely. *He's not for you, remember? Just talk to him for a little while, commit his features to memory and then use him. Flirt with him, flatter him, do your very best Vicki Love imitation, so that when you ask him if he'll pose for you, he can't possibly refuse.*

It sounded so simple. So why was her heart thrashing, her pulse skipping, her stomach quivering? For all her bravado, Laura suddenly had the very disturbing notion that the stranger sitting across from her could see right through her charade. Unobtrusively, she wiped her damp palms on a cocktail napkin as she gave him a brilliant smile.

She lifted her drink. "So here's to your daring rescue yesterday."

Simon lifted his own glass. "And to being in the right place at the right time." He smiled a sudden, swift smile that almost knocked her breath away. The transformation was nothing short of miraculous. The edge softened, the years melted away and Laura had the vague premonition that the tremors in her stomach were merely the prelude to an earthquake.

She sipped her champagne and tried to think of something clever to say. *What would Vicki say?* she prompted herself urgently. "Speaking of being in the right place at the right time, I've been wondering what you were doing yesterday, diving so closely to Senator MacKenzie's yacht?"

A flash of annoyance flickered in his eyes, but his voice was casually disinterested when he answered. "A buddy of mine here in Key West owns a deep-sea salvage company. He recovered the wreck site of a Spanish galleon in that vicinity a few years ago. He was showing me the location."

"How fascinating," Laura said, captivated. "So is he rich and famous now?"

"He's no Mel Fisher, but he's doing okay." His gaze had been lazily scanning the dance floor, but now his eyes swung back to hers, and they seemed oddly intense. He hesitated a moment, then said, "How well do you know Senator MacKenzie?"

Some of the warmth in her gaze faded. "We have a business relationship at the moment," she replied carefully.

Simon's glance dropped to the champagne in front of her, then back up. "Does he always conduct business on board his yacht?"

"As often as not."

Their eyes met again, and a subtle challenge, one Laura didn't quite understand, drifted across the table between them.

"What line of work are you in?"

"I'm an artist. Senator MacKenzie has generously arranged for some of my work to be shown at a local gallery here in Key West, and then I'm donating a few of the pieces to the International Art Auction on Saturday. I owe him a great deal."

Simon scowled slightly. "So you're an artist," he mused.

"That's right. Has anyone ever told you, you have an interesting face?"

He laughed, a short, startled burst of sound. "An interesting face? I've been told a lot of other things, but never that."

"But it's true," she insisted. "I'd love the opportunity to draw you."

He stared at her, as though not quite believing her sincerity. "I don't think so," he said slowly.

"Why not?"

"I'm the impatient type. I wouldn't be able to sit still long enough."

"Oh, but it wouldn't take that long, really. Just think about it, okay? I've been looking for someone like you for a long time." *Oh, God, tell me I didn't say that,* Laura moaned inwardly.

But if Simon Hunter thought her comment strange, he chose to ignore it. His finger traced the rim of his glass. "Have you ever drawn Senator MacKenzie?"

"Why do you ask?"

He shrugged. "I thought that might be part of your... business relationship. You know, painting his portrait or something. All heroes want to be immortalized sooner or later, don't they?"

"I guess not," she said softly. "You just turned me down."

His eyes glinted with some obscure emotion, a mere shadow, but she felt the renewed stirrings of a vague uneasiness. He set his glass on the table with a loud thud.

"Believe me, I'm no hero. What I did yesterday was no more than anyone else would have done. We just got lucky, the both of us."

"I don't believe in luck."

"You said that yesterday." He leaned forward, his voice edged with double entendre as he took a slow, steady regard of her face. "Tell me what you do believe in? The MacKenzie mystique?"

She eyed him shrewdly over the rim of her glass. So that was the game. He *did* want something from her. An introduction to Jake? An entrée into his circle? A story, maybe?

She set her glass down on the table, and the crystal toppled threateningly. His hand shot out and steadied the glass without spilling so much as a drop of the champagne. Even in her growing anger, Laura marveled at his quickness.

"What's the scam?" she asked coldly.

His brow lifted guilelessly. "Scam?"

"The gig, the angle." She leaned toward him and said with sarcastic succinctness. "What do you *want*, Mr. Hunter?"

"I don't know what you mean, *Ms*. Valentine."

She stood abruptly and leaned over the table. "Then let me spell it out for you. I'm on to your questions. If you want to know something about Jake MacKenzie, I suggest you ask him, not me." She paused for a moment, gathering steam. "Just who are you anyway? A tabloid reporter looking for some sleazy story? Is that why you were so *conveniently* near the yacht yesterday? Is that why you're here tonight? You used me to get in here, but that'll be the last time, I assure you."

She turned to stalk away, but Simon's hand snaked out to wrap around her arm. She spun around, glaring at him stonily as she tried to shake off his grasp. "Let go of me!"

"Not until we get a few things straight," he said, very quietly. "Sit back down."

"Oh, sure. And let you pump me for more information? Not bloody likely, Mr. Hunter—if that's even your real name. Find yourself another source. I'm not available."

Simon stood, too, but he didn't release her arm. Instead he drew her closer, so that they were standing toe to toe, eye to eye. His voice was deadly quiet, his eyes darkly intense. "*You* were the one who pulled that stupid stunt yesterday. *You* were the one who invited me in here. *You* were the one who wanted to dance, remember? Maybe you should wait to be asked once in a while. Maybe then you wouldn't feel so threatened."

Laura wanted to protest in outrage, but her tongue felt like lead all of a sudden. A strange weakness invaded her knees, a traitorous warmth stole up her arm where his fingers touched her skin.

Something's happening, she thought, almost in panic. *Please, not again. Not him.*

In that brief moment, with their eyes locked, Gentry recognized one important fact about Laura Valentine. She was more dangerous than he could have imagined. She made him remember too clearly a past that was best forgotten. She made him remember with aching loneliness all that he'd had and all that he'd lost. She made him remember dreams and innocence and first love.

He had a gnawing sensation deep inside his gut that made him realize she could all too easily make him feel again.

Damn it, she wasn't even his type, he tried to rationalize. He didn't like forward women.

But there was something about her...

He dropped his hand from her arm immediately. "I'm sorry. I shouldn't have said that. I didn't mean to offend you. I'm not a reporter, I promise. I was just curious, that's all. Please sit down, and let me buy you another drink."

She seemed to waver with indecision for a moment, then she sat down heavily, as though her legs had suddenly folded.

"More champagne?" he asked.

Laura shook her head. She looked a bit dazed, a bit shaken by their encounter. "I'll have what you're having."

His brows rose slightly in surprise, but he didn't comment. "Two bourbons," he told the waitress who answered his signal. "Make one a double." Then he said to Laura, "Look, I really am very sorry. No more questions, okay?" His eyes met hers again, and she smiled weakly, the full lips curving upward in a way that threatened his rigid control.

"I... overreacted a bit," she admitted, her smile turning wry. "I've had a bad experience or two with people wanting to get to Jake—Senator MacKenzie—through me. I'm a little gun-shy at the moment."

"Let's talk about a safer subject then," he suggested. "Tell me about yourself. Where're you from?"

"Washington?"

"D.C. or the state?"

"D.C. How about you?"

"New York. I'm an attorney with the firm of Wyndam, Ford and McConley. We've a pretty good reputation in D.C. Perhaps you've heard of us?" The lies slipped out as smoothly as a twig gliding into backwater.

She was shaking her head, a small frown flitting across her brows. "An attorney," she said ironically, not pleased. "I'm usually pretty good at reading people, but I never would have taken you for a lawyer."

"Oh? And just what would you have taken me for?"

She gave him a long, steady evaluation. "If you're not a reporter, I would have guessed a cop."

He managed to hide his surprise behind a mask of wry amusement. "I'm not sure how to take that."

"It wasn't an insult," she said with a cool shrug. "I've nothing but respect for law and order."

"And lawyers?"

"Well, let's just say, I haven't had the greatest experience with lawyers."

He arched an inquiring brow. "Would you care to elaborate on that?"

She took a long, careful sip of her drink, grimaced and then set the glass back on the table before she answered. "Lawyers like to use people. I don't like users."

"I don't imagine anyone does," he said grimly, feeling a sudden stab of self-loathing because that was exactly what he was doing. Using her to gain information about MacKenzie. His gut instinct told him she wasn't involved, but something else told him the closer he got to Laura Valentine, the closer he got to MacKenzie. He'd been watching both of them all night, and whether Laura was aware of it or not, Gentry had the distinct impression that the senator had staked his claim.

So lost in speculation was he, that when she reached across the table and touched his hand, Gentry very nearly jumped out of his skin.

"Is something wrong?"

With a jolt, he realized he'd let down his guard. The mask had slipped, and that would not do.

"No, why do you ask?"

"You were scowling so fiercely there for a moment . . . that look in your eyes—" She broke off, searching his face for a moment. "It made my blood run cold," she said, almost to herself. She shook her head slightly, as though trying to dispel an unpleasant image. Then she laughed and tossed back her hair. "My artist's imagination running away with me, no doubt."

"I'm just a harmless attorney," he said innocently, but the lies that rolled so easily from his tongue suddenly left a bitter taste in his mouth. *The end justifies the means, Gentry.*

Yeah, right. It was damned poor timing to be developing a conscience now after all these years. The girl knew MacKenzie; very possibly she had information that would be helpful to the case. Gentry had an inroad with her. He'd saved her life. So what was the problem?

I don't like users.

He glanced at his watch, surprised to find how much time had slipped away. He hadn't checked in yet. "Would you excuse me?" he asked abruptly. "I need to make a phone call."

"At this hour? Don't you lawyers ever stop working?"

"I didn't say it was business, now did I?"

Her green eyes opened wide. "I think I'm jealous," she murmured, bringing a grin of masculine pleasure to Gentry's face in spite of himself.

From across the room, Senator Jake MacKenzie watched the exchange with cool, brooding eyes. What the hell did she think she was doing, bringing a man like that in here with her? He'd always suspected his former stepsister was a little lacking in the social graces, but that would all change soon, when he had her under his full control.

He sipped the perfectly chilled champagne—compliments of the establishment in appreciation of his patronage—as his gaze swept over Laura, remembering the exact moment when he'd become aware of her considerable womanly charms. Who would have thought that such a plain, clumsy child would have turned into such a beauty? She had blossomed almost overnight, it seemed. But then, he had a habit of losing track of the years.

Until a few months ago, he hadn't seen her in quite some time. Oh, he'd kept up with her occasionally mostly through Crystal, who called him from time to time when she needed a favor. Actually, Laura's showing at the gallery had been Crystal's idea, one of the few good ones she'd ever had. She'd pressed him to encourage Laura to concentrate more on her "serious" art. Having a cartoonist as a daughter wasn't exactly the image Crystal wanted, but a daughter traveling in the art circles—now, that opened up all sorts of possibilities.

Jake had halfheartedly agreed to look up Laura and see what he could do, primarily to get his former stepmother off his back and to keep her mouth shut. Unfortunately Crystal held something over his head, and Jake wasn't anxious to have gossip spread among the various cliques in Washington about the relationship he'd once had with Crystal MacKenzie—or whatever the hell her name happened to be at the moment—while she'd been married to his father.

He'd momentarily put the encounter out of his mind when he happened upon Laura at a political fund-raiser in Washington. She'd been with her fiancé at the time, but her eyes had eagerly lit up when she'd spotted him. He'd always considered the crush she'd had on him a minor annoyance, but suddenly her attentiveness stimulated him.

Three things had occurred to Jake almost simultaneously. One, the art exhibit Crystal wanted for her daughter could easily be arranged to coincide with the charity art auction in Key West. He already had one of her paintings—a surprisingly good one—that she'd given him a long time ago. It was a romantic piece featuring him as a knight on the proverbial white steed, with a complicated background that would be perfect for hiding the series of microdots he'd recently acquired.

Two, as Laura's benefactor and a champion of the National Endowment of the Arts, his presence beside her in Key West would not be questioned. The auction would provide the perfect coverage for smuggling the top-secret Pentagon file, code name Hawkwind, out of the country. All he had to do was let his buyer know which painting he had to acquire.

And three, Jake discovered rather quickly that he wanted Laura for himself. A few whispered rumors here, a dropped innuendo there, and Clark Kendall's reputation in Washington had been ruined. Not only had Jake eliminated Clark's engagement to Laura, but he'd also eliminated a future political challenger. All there had been left to do was pick up the pieces.

He smiled slightly, his gaze never leaving Laura. When an aide handed him the phone, he brushed it off in annoyance, but the man whispered in his ear, "He says it's urgent."

MacKenzie jerked the receiver to his ear. When the caller identified himself, he said, "I hope the hell you made damned sure this line is clear."

"Don't worry, I'm an expert, remember?" the caller said. "I thought you might be interested to know the name of the man feeding information to the FBI."

He had Jake's full attention now. "Who is it?"

The caller paused for effect. "Lester."

A black rage descended over MacKenzie. Lester was one of his closest friends, a trusted adviser. He had betrayed him, sold him out to the damned Feds. Maybe in a day or two he could enjoy the irony. He'd bought one of the Bureau's finest, and now they'd retaliated by taking one of his. But right now revenge was the uppermost thought on Jake's mind.

"Take care of it," he said into the receiver. "Make sure he knows who sent you."

As Jake hung up the phone, Laura's companion got up and headed for the men's room. With a barely perceptible nod to the man behind the bar, Jake then got up and sauntered across the room to stake his claim.

Gentry located the pay phone in the lounge area outside the rest rooms, plugged in a quarter and dialed Greenwood's hotel room. When the younger agent finally picked up on the seventh ring, Gentry could hear the sound of the TV blaring in the background. "Turn that damned thing off for a minute, will you?"

The volume died away, then Greenwood came back to the phone. "Damn, Gentry, I'm impressed. Who's the girl?"

"Never mind that. Did you go by the gallery tonight?"

"Everything's in place, don't worry. The owner's co-operating without a hitch. Relax, Gentry. Enjoy yourself."

"That's not what I'm here for."

"Maybe you'd better tell that to the blonde," Greenwood said in amusement.

The door to the lounge swung open, drawing Gentry's gaze. "Damn."

"What's the matter?"

"Looks like trouble," he muttered.

Gentry eyed the two men who stood just inside the door glaring at him across the small space of the lounge. He recognized Tony, the bouncer, but the other man he'd never seen before. However, with his massive shoulders and thick neck, his blond crew cut and beady eyes, he looked every bit as intimidating as the bouncer. Together they looked like a wrestling tag team anxious for the bell. Trouble was, Gentry didn't have anyone to tag.

As if to confirm that thought, he glanced warily over his shoulder, then said into the receiver, "I'll talk to you later," and hung up.

He started across the room to the door, but the two men made no effort to step aside. Arms folded over chests, shoulders almost touching, they presented a barrier very nearly as impressive as the Great Wall of China.

Well, hell, Gentry thought, angling what he hoped was a steely look in their direction. It'd been years since he'd been caught in a barroom brawl, and he'd hoped it would be a good many more. Obviously the Bobbsey Twins here had other ideas.

"Shouldn't you be out front?" he asked Tony. "Wouldn't want any riffraff slipping in while you're not looking."

Tony sneered down at him. "Looks to me like one already has," he said in a raspy voice that was hardly more than a whisper. Slowly he removed his sunglasses, folded the frames and tucked them in his pocket. "We don't like your kind coming in here, mister. It's bad for our image."

"And that would be the image of bad taste, would it not?" Gentry asked, mentally bracing himself for the fight. His best chance would be speed and surprise, he decided. Hell, that was his *only* chance. If either of them ever landed a solid punch, there would be no need for the fat lady to sing.

"I've been feeling terribly neglected tonight."

The voice, like liquid silk, flowed into her ear. As she looked up to see Jake's blue, blue eyes, automatically Laura's hand moved to cover the quick sketch she'd made on the back of a cocktail napkin.

"You poor thing," she said with exaggerated sympathy. Her eyes flitted across the room to the crowded table he had vacated. "I can see just how lonely you've been."

The white teeth flashed against the perpetual bronze of his skin as he leaned over the table toward her. "You mean the Brainless Wonders? They have their moments, I must say," he conceded. "But I've missed you." He sat down in the chair opposite her and shoved aside Simon's empty glass with the tip of his finger. "So," he said, eyeing her with mild curiosity, "who's your friend?"

Laura recognized the look because she'd seen it in her mother's eyes a thousand times. An innocent question, a guileless smile that masked cold disapproval. "He's just an acquaintance. I'm thinking about using him in *Vicki Love*."

"With his permission, I hope. I'm not sure I could get you out of another lawsuit."

Laura frowned. "That was all a long time ago, Jake, and Mother never should have called you in the first place. I was perfectly capable of handling it on my own. But don't worry. I did learn my lesson. And since he's an attorney, I'm not likely to—"

"He's an attorney?" Jake broke in with quick interest.

The sharpness of his question startled her, made her wary for some reason she couldn't understand. "He's with a firm in New York. McConley and somebody, I think."

"Wyndam, Ford and McConley?"

Again, he surprised her. "That's it. You've heard of them?"

"It's a big firm, excellent reputation," he mused absently. He seemed to catch himself then, and threw her a disarming grin. "Tell you what. We're all about to leave and go out to the yacht for a midnight cruise. Come with us."

"Thanks, but no thanks." She declined the offer. "I'm really tired. When I leave here, I'm going straight back to the house."

"There's a full moon," he tempted. "The water's warm and calm. We could go for a swim—"

Laura shivered, remembering the last time she'd gone in for a swim. If Simon hadn't been there—she glanced at her watch and scowled. Come to think of it, he'd been gone an awfully long time. Certainly longer than it usually took to make a phone call—depending on who the recipient was, of course.

"Lunch tomorrow then," Jake was saying. "Just you and me on the *Valhalla*."

"What? Oh, sure...that'll be fine," she said distractedly, scanning the club.

"Your friend won't be coming back."

There was an edge to Jake's voice that brought her attention back to him. "How do you know?"

He shrugged, a lazy smile tugging at the corners of his sensuous lips. "I just have a feeling about him. He didn't

look . . . dependable.'' He reached for her hand and lifted it
to his lips. ''Trust me, my dear, you've seen the last of that
man.''

Laura headed toward the exit, weaving her way through
the gyrating bodies and flailing arms. She'd almost made it
to the entrance when someone plowed into her, dousing her
with whiskey.

''Sh—''

''*Perdonáme*. My apologies. Are you all right?'' He was
a short, heavyset man with oily black hair, a pencil thin
mustache and a thick, Spanish accent.

''My spirits are a little dampened at the moment,'' Laura
said dryly, swiping at the darkening stain on the white
leather sleeve.

''Your jacket is completely ruined! I insist that you allow
me to buy you a new one.''

She stopped fussing with her clothes and looked up in
annoyance. ''That really won't be necessary.''

He waved aside her argument with all the flurry of Latin
gallantry. ''Please. The fault was entirely mine. Let me at
least buy you a drink.''

''Thanks, but I'm just on my way out. Really,'' she said
in a rush as he made to protest again. ''Please don't give it
a second thought. It's too hot for leather anyway.''

She left him looking slightly dejected at the edge of the
dance floor as she made her way to the front and handed the
doorman her key. ''The white Vette.''

While she waited for her car to be brought around, she
headed for the ladies' room, wondering exactly what she
should do about the stain on her jacket. She pushed open
the door to the lounge area just as the door to the men's
room swung out directly opposite her.

Hands frozen on the doors, she and Simon stood staring

at each other for a full fifteen seconds before the full impact of the scene hit her.

And then she saw the blood.

At the moment, for a full thirty seconds before turning the page of the world's future.

And though nothing be proved

Chapter 3

Simon let the door swing closed behind him as he stepped into the lounge, clutching a wet paper towel to his right temple. Splashes of red dotted the collar of his white shirt.

"My God, what happened—" Laura's eyes, already round with shock, widened even more as her gaze took in the rest of the devastation around her. It looked as if a war had been waged in that room, and the casualties were still lying on the floor.

She recognized both men from the club. The dark-haired one, Tony, lay facedown on the floor, one arm sprawled at an odd angle beside him. The other one had worked behind the bar a couple of nights ago when she'd been at the club with Jake. Now he was sitting on the floor, slumped against the wall, his chin resting on his chest. Neither man moved a muscle.

Her hand flew to her mouth as her gaze lifted to meet Simon's steady, gray stare. "Are they—?"

"Just dazed. They'll come to in a little while." He lowered the paper towel from his head and stared at it for a moment. Obviously satisfied with what he saw, he casually tossed it in the trash can as though the red stains were nothing more than catsup from a messy meal.

"What happened?" she repeated breathlessly, taking a tentative step toward him.

Simon shrugged. "We had a slight disagreement."

"*You* did this?" she asked incredulously.

He grinned weakly. "I'm a bit surprised myself. I took a few self-defense classes a while back after I'd been mugged a couple of times. I guess I got more out of the classes than I'd realized."

"I guess you did." She looked around, still feeling dazed herself. "What did you disagree about anyway?"

Simon shrugged again. "They seemed to think I was out of my league in here."

"You mean they were trying to throw you out?" she asked in an outraged voice. "They can't do that," she muttered irrelevantly. It was quite obvious that they couldn't.

"Look," Simon said, stepping over Tony as he came to stand in front of her. "These guys'll wake up in a minute or two, and they won't be too happy. If you don't mind, I'd just as soon not be the first face they see."

He took her arm to guide her out, but she hung back. "Shouldn't we call the police or something? We can't just leave them here like this, can we?"

A groan from the blond brought both their gazes back to him. His hand had gone up to rub his neck as he tried to straighten his head. Following his cue, Tony groaned, too, and slid one knee along the floor as he tried to sit up.

"They wouldn't thank you for calling the police," Simon said, steering her toward the door. "Let's go."

The valet had parked Laura's car at the curb. He handed her the keys as they walked outside, and Laura watched as Simon pulled the other man aside and spoke to him briefly.

"What did you say to him?" she asked anxiously as they approached her car and Simon opened the door for her. The streets were practically deserted except for a dark Lincoln parked against the curb a few feet from hers.

Gentry smiled, his glance roaming over her shoulder toward the other car for a moment, then back again. "I told him someone had left quite a mess in the lounge, and that he might need to have it cleaned up."

She stood with one hand resting on top of the car door as she turned to face him. "Are you sure *you're* all right? Maybe I should give you a lift to the hospital or something."

"I'm fine. Never felt better."

She gave him a doubtful once-over. "At least let me give you a ride to your hotel."

"I wouldn't want to take you out of your way."

"Simon, the island's only about four miles long and two miles wide. How far out of my way can it be?"

"In that case, how can I say no?" he said with a grin.

He closed her door and went around to climb in on the passenger side. She reached forward to start the powerful engine, but her hand stilled on the key. She turned her head to face him as he settled in the seat, and a faintly sensuous look passed between them. "You're just full of surprises, aren't you?" she asked softly.

He laughed, a low, masculine rumble that made her completely aware of her own femininity. "So it would seem," he said obliquely.

She started the engine, shifted into first and they were off with only a mild protest from the rear tires. It took only a matter of minutes to arrive at his hotel, but rather than pulling up in front to let him out, she parked at the curb across the street and killed the engine.

An awkward silence fell between them, and Laura knew why. She wasn't ready to say goodbye to him yet. Apart from the fact that he was the most intriguing man she'd ever met, there was something about him that triggered a purely primal reaction in her. Secrets lurked in the depths of his gray eyes. Deep, dark, dangerous secrets that she longed to have whispered to her on hot, steamy nights.

"Thanks for the ride," Simon said, his left arm coming up to recline against the back of her seat.

Laura leaned her head against the leather upholstery and tilted her face toward him. "It was nothing. Call it partial payment of an old debt. I never did properly thank you for saving my life."

He shifted in the seat, leaning his body toward hers. She recognized the subtle glow in his gray eyes, and her stomach fluttered wildly.

"What would you call a proper thank-you?" he asked softly.

"I'm . . . not sure."

He merely smiled at her answer as he reached out and let a long strand of her hair slide between his fingers. "I knew it would feel like silk," he murmured, and there was something in his voice that sounded very much like regret.

His face was close to hers, so close, she could see the gray of his eyes deepening and intensifying as their gazes locked. So close, she could see the thin, white definition of the scar in his right brow. So close, she could see the faint shadow of stubble on the lower half of his face. So close, she could see the outline of his lips as they curved upward in an intriguing half smile. And then she could see no more because his lips were moving slowly toward hers and her eyes drifted closed.

He tasted faintly of bourbon and sea air, an alluring combination that wildly stirred Laura's senses. Her lips opened in response, and for one brief moment, she felt him withdraw in surprise at her submission. Then, as her tongue touched his, he captured her face in his hands, weaving his fingers through her hair as a slow, steady heat began to build between them. He deepened the kiss with a hunger that both surprised and thrilled her.

His tongue sought out every texture, every taste, every hidden secret of her mouth, conquering and plundering and ravishing her until she felt breathless with desire. It was as though, once he'd committed himself to the act, he meant to have it all.

Laura's fingers fluttered across the width of his shoulders, tentatively exploring the hard muscles beneath his clothing as his mouth continued the magic. The heavy scent of flowers and the silvery touch of moonlight added to the erotic flow of sensations spilling over her, making the night seem dreamlike, more fantasy than real.

Research, she reminded herself dizzily. *This is research.* But of all the things she'd done in the name of *Vicki Love,* the only thing that came remotely close to this kind of thrill was skydiving. She experienced that same sense now of rushing headlong toward some distant, but ultimate, destination.

For Gentry the kiss had been an impulse, a release for the adrenaline still pumping through his veins, a momentary weakening of his defenses. But the moment his mouth touched hers, everything else faded and the kiss became the sole focus of his attention. He'd half expected her to pull back, to push him away, but she responded in a way that had his own desire exploding.

Her mouth was open and knowing, and yet he could feel her lips trembling beneath his as though she'd never before experienced the passion of a kiss. There was something about her, a lost quality that didn't quite fit with the sophisticated veneer. And it was that hidden something, that tantalizing secret, that made her even more irresistible.

Gentry was no stranger to desire. He understood only too well the basic needs of the human body. He knew that, when deprived of one of those basic needs for any length of time, the body was apt to overreact. He understood, then, the almost uncontrollable passion raging through him. But what he couldn't understand was why he felt compelled to hold back, why his mind demanded restraint when his body urged him to push forward.

He wanted her, he realized. Desperately. Recklessly. He wanted to forget all the reasons why he shouldn't be here, all the reasons why he couldn't get involved with her and simply make love to her. He wanted no longer to think and to rationalize and to plan, but simply to feel.

And that would be a very serious mistake. There was no longer room in his life for emotions.

He broke the kiss hesitantly and his hands drifted from her hair. But he was still very close, and even in the dim light from the street, he could see the soft shimmer of her eyes as she stared up at him.

There was something so uniquely desirable about her, something so gloriously fulfilling about holding her against him, kissing her as though she belonged to him. Sex with her would be like paradise, he thought, like dying and going to heaven. Sex with her would be exploding stars and spinning worlds, soft skin and hot bodies and breathy promises in the dark.

Sex with her would be dangerously close to making love.

She sighed dreamily as her head rested against the back of the seat. "What was that for?" she asked softly.

He lifted a strand of her hair and brought it to his lips, closing his eyes for a brief moment as though drinking in the very essence of her. "Call it the grand finale to one hell of an evening," he tried to say lightly, but his smile held a bitter edge.

Laura let out a long, unsteady breath as she stared up at him. "In that case, your encore must be pretty spectacular."

Gentry let himself into his hotel room, switched on the light, threw his keys into an ashtray, then shrugged out of his jacket. A haunting remnant of Laura's perfume clung to the fabric. He lifted the jacket to his face and breathed deeply, his blood stirring at the seductive scent.

You must be out of your mind, Gentry.

"It was just a kiss," he muttered aloud, and then with a disgusted oath, he threw the jacket onto the bed. He scrubbed his hands across his face, as though trying to wipe away her image from his mind.

Who was he trying to kid? This was no longer a quest for information, a means to an end. In the space of one very short evening, Laura Valentine had gotten under his skin, had become a part of his dreams. He could still feel her skin beneath his hands, could still feel the tingling warmth where their bodies had touched. He could no more rid himself of that sensation than he could wipe away her scent from his clothing.

As if in denial, he began stripping, flinging clothes to the far corners of the room as he strode toward the bathroom and turned on the shower. He closed his eyes and let the cold water sluice over his skin.

Damn it, he could not let this happen. He would not let himself fall for a woman who could steer him from his course with just a kiss, a look, a touch. He would not let himself fall for a woman he had every intention of using, if she could help him snare Jake MacKenzie.

There was no way he would ever let himself fall in love with *any* woman again. Love gave a man a weakness, a vulnerability, a fatal flaw. Love gave a man's enemies the most powerful weapon of all. There was no way in hell he would ever allow himself to get that close to Laura Valentine, and for one good reason.

He didn't want her to end up like Caroline.

He hadn't thought about Caroline in ages, but suddenly, he couldn't get her off his mind. She'd been so young and so beautiful, with her whole life ahead of her, and because of him, she'd had to die.

With a sharp twist of his wrist, he snapped off the taps and stepped from the shower as he briskly dried himself with a white towel. He rummaged through his travel kit for toothpaste, toothbrush and the bottle of aspirin he always kept inside. His head was pounding, but whether from the blow to his temple or from pent-up tension, he didn't know.

He twisted off the cap and popped two tablets in his mouth, then for good measure, a third, rinsing them down with a glass of water from the faucet.

He stared for a moment at his reflection in the mirror as he leaned against the counter. *Damn.* Since when had he become so sensitive to pain? he wondered. He didn't remember it hurting this badly when he used to take an occasional punch. Of course, last time he'd been in a fight, he'd been considerably younger. His only consolation was that he'd left the two goons back in the club in a lot worse shape than he was in.

A cool head and a keen sense of survival. A combination that had served him well all these years. However, he wouldn't want to have to test his mettle too often.

He winced as his fingers touched the bruise on his cheekbone and he walked back out to the bedroom and collapsed on the bed. Lying on his back, head pillowed on his arms, he stared up at the ceiling, but he knew sleep would be elusive.

It was going to be another long night.

Laura Valentine wasn't the first woman he'd been attracted to since Caroline had been murdered, but she'd been the first one to lead him this far into temptation. Some of his relationships had dragged on for way too long, some had ended far sooner than he'd wanted. But all of them *had* ended. Sooner or later they all tired of the phone calls in the middle of the night, the unexplained trips out of town, the secrets that were always keeping them apart. Gentry could understand their distrust, their anger, but he'd never tried to ease the pressure. The trappings of his career provided him the perfect defense. His job always came first, always would. That was the way it had to be. He'd made the choice a long time ago.

But sometimes, sometimes on nights like these he had to wonder if the sacrifices had all been worth it, if the darkness inside him might somehow have gone away if he'd let himself get close to someone again.

Hell, you're not only getting old, you're getting sentimental, Gentry, and all because a woman like Laura Valentine decided to go slumming.

With practiced precision, he turned his mind back to the problem at hand, going over the events of the evening and trying to make sense of them. The attack in the club could mean one of two things, he decided grimly. Tony and his partner had been out for a bit of sport at Gentry's expense or... his cover had been blown, which would suggest that someone he knew, worked with, trusted, perhaps a friend, had sold him out.

There was, however, one other alternative, and possibly the most likely. Perhaps he had simply strayed too far into MacKenzie's personal territory. Laura Valentine was the kind of woman who would make any man feel territorial and possessive. She was the kind of woman who could make a man question his own judgment, the kind of woman a man might even kill for.

She was the kind of woman a man like him might never be able to get out of his system.

When she found out who and what he was, she would never want anything to do with him again, he thought with a bitter remorse that surprised him.

And maybe, just maybe, that was the best thing that could ever happen to both of them.

When the phone beside his bed rang, he jerked up the receiver, almost expecting to hear her soft, throaty voice on the other end.

"Oh, it's you," he said bluntly when the caller had spoken.

"At this hour, just who the hell were you expecting, Gentry?" asked Samuel Atwater, his immediate superior in the Bureau.

Gentry grinned, imagining Sam running his fingers through his thick tuft of white hair. If he was still at the office, he'd have a cup of coffee liberally laced with brandy sitting in front of him. If he was at home, he would have foregone the brandy and gone straight to the bourbon.

"Where are you, Sam? You sound like you're in the next room."

"Yeah, well, never mind where *I* am, Gentry." There was a strange edge of excitement in his voice. "Just tell me what's going on down there."

"Nothing much to report so far."

"I don't like the sound of that. You better make something happen, Gentry. You're sticking your neck out for this. We all are. If the powers-that-be get wind of your little operation, we're history and so are our pensions."

Sam didn't have to elaborate. Gentry knew exactly what he was talking about. Shortly after Gentry's investigation of MacKenzie had begun—when he knew he was on the right trail—he'd received orders from HQ in no uncertain terms to drop that particular line of the investigation or hand in his resignation. It was an eye-opening revelation that had shown him just how far MacKenzie's power reached. It had also been the ultimate challenge.

Gentry had neither resigned nor given up his investigation. Instead, he'd continued very quietly and very systematically, keeping the incoming information contained to a very small circle within the Bureau, a handful of men and women he had grown to trust, the closest thing to a family he'd had in years. Rogues of a sort just like him, they were agents who were willing to risk their jobs—and their lives—to help a friend who sought justice.

No, Sam didn't have to elaborate. Gentry knew exactly how high the stakes were.

"I'm keeping my eyes and ears open on this end," Sam continued soberly. "You've covered your tracks pretty well so far, but even if you get him, this won't go down pretty, Gentry. Senator Jake MacKenzie is a bloody hero in Washington."

"Hero?" Gentry asked sarcastically. "Try traitor. Try murderer. He killed one of our own, Sam. He ordered the crash that took Terry's life and ruined Cassandra Chandler's. I don't take too kindly to that. Do you?"

"I'm backing you, aren't I?" Sam said gruffly. "Just be careful, that's all I'm saying. Your whole operation down there is based on the credibility of your informant."

"I'd stake my life on the information Lester gave us this time."

"You may have to," came the terse reply.

Gentry ignored his boss's predilection for gloom and said, "I need you to do me a favor. I want you to run a background check on a woman named Laura Valentine. She's somehow connected to Jake MacKenzie. She says she's an artist, says they have a business relationship, something to do with the auction on Saturday. I want to know everything there is to know about her."

There was a pause, then Sam said, "You think she's involved?"

"I hope to hell not. But I'm not willing to take any chances."

Not even for her.

Laura walked into her room and stood braced against the door, eyes squeezed shut. "I think I'm in love." She sighed aloud.

Her eyes flew open at the sound of her own voice and she groaned. "No, you're not," she denied sharply, popping open the snaps of her ruined jacket and shrugging it down her arms. It dropped to the floor and she kicked it toward the closet. The shoes came next, followed by the skirt. She grabbed her pink silk robe from the hook on the bathroom door and belted it securely around her waist. Then she stood at the mirror and viciously brushed her hair.

"You are not in love with that man," she told her reflection sternly. "Six weeks ago you were about to marry someone else. That should tell you something. You're on the rebound. Your pride's hurt, your ego's bruised and he made you feel . . . well . . . like . . .''

Like a woman. A beautiful, desirable woman.

She closed her eyes as a wave of sensual awareness washed through her. Abstinence has done this to you, she told herself angrily. She'd been alone too long, even during her engagement. Now she was feeling too needy and susceptible to a man who was too dangerously sexy. Even now the memory of his mouth on hers made her feel warm and light-headed.

It was strange because when Clark had suggested they wait to sleep together until their wedding night, she hadn't felt in the least deprived. She'd gone along with what she thought were his old-fashioned morals because she hadn't particularly cared one way or the other. Of course, on the day of their wedding, she'd found out *why* celibacy had been so easy for him. She just wasn't quite sure why it had been so easy for her.

Laura slid open the balcony door and stepped outside, letting the soft, night wind sweep across her upturned face. She could hear the high-pitched squeal of the fruit bats as they circled and swooped over the thick canopy of coconut palms and eucalyptus trees.

With her fingernail, she clipped a spray of jasmine from the heavy vine trailing along the balcony and held it to her face. The scent was sweet and haunting, like a summer's night dream, and for some strange reason, it triggered an almost unbearable loneliness inside her.

Maybe she should have stayed on in the house on Big Pine Key for a few more days, she thought wearily, instead of coming to Key West early. But all of her work for the exhibit had been completed, and she'd suddenly gotten restless, bored with the solitude she usually welcomed.

Besides, she'd gone to her hideaway after that horrid scene with Clark to lick her wounds, but it had taken only a few days alone to realize that the hurt was superficial at best. Clark Kendall had been a rather desperate attempt to please

Crystal yet one more time. He was the kind of man her mother had always wanted for her—a handsome, dashing, upwardly mobile attorney with political aspirations of his own. He was the perfect man.

What bothered Laura the most, she realized, was not the fact that Clark hadn't loved her, but the fact that he'd betrayed her trust. He'd used her.

If she'd really loved him she wouldn't be thinking of him so calmly now, so coolly, so analytically. Admittedly her pride was hurt, her self-confidence battered, but as far as the relationship went, she felt no regrets, no remorse, no emotion at all except maybe relief.

But with the relief came loneliness, the old yearning—not for Clark, but for what she'd thought he represented. It was a need for the elusive something that had been missing from her life for as long as she could remember. She wanted someone who needed her as much as she needed him, but she wondered sometimes if what she searched for even existed. And that notion depressed her more than anything.

Maybe she'd lived in her own little fantasy world, Vicki's world, for so long that reality just couldn't live up to her expectations.

Except for Simon's kiss, she thought wistfully. In his arms, she'd been anything *but* disappointed.

The telephone rang, and Laura jumped, a sure indication of her edginess, she mused wryly. Simon Hunter had occupied so much of her thoughts that when she picked up the phone, she almost expected to hear his voice.

"Hello, darling."

Laura's heart sank. "Mother. Hello. I didn't expect to hear from you at this hour." *Or any other time, actually.*

"Oh, is it that late?" Her mother's soft, clear voice floated across the line, all feathery lightness and sugary innocence that gave no indication to the steel beneath. "I was calling Jake actually, but Maria said he was still out, so I decided to speak with you."

Gee, thanks. "Was there anything in particular you wanted to talk to me about?"

Crystal paused. "I just had to tell you who I ran into today. Clark! Can you believe it? He's really suffered a lot these past few weeks, Laura. All those awful rumors! But he's not bitter toward you, darling, and I really think if you'd only make the first move, apologize to him for that awful scene at the wedding, that he'd still take you back."

Laura pulled the receiver from her ear and stared at it in disbelief. Then she said, "Apologize to him! You can't be serious. He slept with my maid of honor the night before our wedding, for God's sake. Why should I apologize to him?"

"That's exactly the kind of attitude that's always gotten you into trouble," Crystal said scathingly, letting her steel shine through. "You never think anything is your fault, do you? Instead of blaming Clark, maybe you should be asking yourself *why* he did what he did."

Laura closed her eyes, feeling the old helplessness, the same old doubts creeping up on her. "It doesn't matter whose fault it was, Mother. The truth is that Clark doesn't love me, and I don't love him."

"What's love got to do with it?" Crystal asked in exasperation. "Honestly, Laura, you simply must learn to be a little more practical. After all, you're not getting any younger—"

"Mother, look, I have a big day tomorrow. I really need to get some sleep."

A hurt tone crept into Crystal's voice. "Well, of course, dear, I certainly don't mean to *bother* you."

For all Laura's education, for all her pretended sophistication, one phone call from her mother could instantly transform her into that same inadequate, unworthy little girl from her past.

Time to grow up, Laura, said a little voice in the back of her mind. A little voice that sounded very much like Vicki Love's. *Time to grow up and tell your mother to go to hell.*

Right.
And tomorrow, pigs just might fly.

Senator Jake MacKenzie arose from his bed and looked down in disgust at the sleeping woman sprawled on top of the covers. Her long, dark hair tumbled across her face, obscuring the lovely, perfect features beneath. The sight of her nude body, the heavy breasts, the lush hips and thighs, disgusted him now that his ardor had cooled. He didn't even remember her name, but it didn't matter. She was like all the rest of them, the clingers, the hangers-on, the groupies. They served one purpose and one purpose only.

He grimaced slightly, tossing a blanket over her naked-ness not out of kindness but because he could no longer stand the sight of her. He stepped into the black-and-gold bathroom, brushed his teeth vigorously, showered in water as hot as he could stand, then donned a robe and strode out of the luxurious stateroom.

A man stood guard just outside the door. "Get rid of her," MacKenzie ordered as he walked by, not even glanc-ing in the man's direction.

He strolled up on deck, letting the fresh night air dispel the lingering unpleasantness. His gaze roamed eagerly across the dark water, easily pinpointing the mansion. In spite of the hour, a light shone in one of the upstairs bed-rooms. *Her* room.

Outwardly Laura Valentine appeared to be just like all the rest. Cool, elegant, sophisticated. But it was all an act and he knew it. It was the layer of innocence, the vulnerability just beneath the surface that presented so many interesting possibilities.

The best part was that she had already proven to be so useful to him. She had unwittingly become such an integral part of his plan. It was *her* painting that would be used to smuggle out the microdots, and if anything went awry, *she* would have to take the fall. The machinery was already in place.

But that was if anything went wrong. And nothing would. Jake would see to that because he had other, more interesting plans for Laura. He had no qualms about using her, but he'd hate like hell to have to sacrifice her. At least so soon. She could prove to be an interesting challenge, and there was nothing he adored more than a challenge.

Particularly the challenge of smuggling government secrets out of the country in plain sight, while the American people hailed him a hero, while his party groomed him for the presidency. Not since the missions he'd flown in Vietnam had he gotten such a high, such a pure rush of excitement. It was a challenge, a risk, a thrilling, dangerous game.

That was the part most people were too simple and unimaginative to understand. He didn't particularly need the money, although the millions he was getting for the plans for the Pentagon's latest high-tech spy plane wasn't exactly pocket change. It would certainly come in useful at election time when there were always palms to grease, votes to buy, the occasional FBI agent to pay off, he thought with a sly grin. John Q. Public simply had no idea how many expenses a politician incurred on a day-to-day basis.

But it wasn't the money, or even the power, that drove him. It was the danger he craved, the thrill of the chase.

Even now the hounds were closing in, stupid and unsuspecting that the fox was now on *their* trail. He could feel their presence out there in the dark somewhere, could almost smell the titillating scent of spilled blood.

White teeth flashed in the dark. The anticipation was as heady as champagne.

Chapter 4

He would have to use her.

Gentry had always hated the idea of using innocent bystanders to get what he needed, but this time he could see no way around it. Laura Valentine was his only prayer of getting into MacKenzie's house without arousing suspicion.

Besides, who said she was so innocent? By all appearances, the femme fatale who'd sailed into the club last night knew the score pretty damned well.

That was just it, though. As Gentry well knew, appearances could be deceiving. When he'd kissed her, she'd been willing, eager even, but surprisingly lacking in experience—not at all what he'd expected.

Not that it had mattered, he thought dryly. The heat the two of them had generated had made up for her lack of experience and his lack of finesse. The chemical explosion between them had been a spontaneous, sexual attraction at its most basic.

That was what made his assignment this morning so dangerous. He was going to have to see her again, talk to her, listen to her, get to know her and maybe to like her. And if he liked her in addition to what he already felt for her, God help him, Gentry thought with uncharacteristic fatalism.

He drummed his fingers impatiently on the steering wheel of his rental car, a white Taurus SHO perfectly suited to his needs—a relatively unassuming exterior but an engine inside packed with pure, raw power. The portable phone lying on the console beside him rang, and Gentry grabbed it up.

"MacKenzie just left," Greenwood reported. "I've got him."

"Later," Gentry said, ending the transmission.

Time to go to work, he thought, his pulse revving in perfect synchronization with the engine.

"Good morning."

At the sound of his voice, Laura almost dropped the phone. "Simon! How in the world did you know I was here? And how did you get this number? It's unlisted."

"I'm a lawyer," he said lazily. "It's my business to be sneaky."

"Touché," she murmured, frowning. "How's the eye this morning?"

"Why don't you see for yourself?" he invited in a voice that suddenly made every vivid detail of the previous evening come rushing back to her.

Her grip on the phone tightened. "What did you have in mind?"

"Lunch? Maybe a drive?"

What to wear! she thought, her mind racing through her closet. Calmly she said, "I'd like that. Where shall I meet you?"

He paused, then said, "Why don't I pick you up? I'm almost there, in fact."

"Sounds like you were pretty sure of yourself," she accused.

"Let's just say, I believe in the power of positive thinking. I can be there in less than five minutes."

"Perfect... if you don't mind waiting."

He laughed softly. "Mind? Not at all...."

A dark-haired woman with a Cuban accent greeted Gentry at the door and led him into the spacious foyer. "The *señorita* will be down shortly. Would you like to wait in the sitting room?"

Gentry shoved his hands into his jeans and tried to look like a man on vacation. "That's okay. I'll just hang around here. She won't be long."

The maid eyed him with cool disapproval and then she turned and disappeared through an arched doorway. Gentry gazed around for a moment, getting his bearings. Straight ahead a wide, curving staircase with a carved oak banister led to the second floor landing, and to the right, the foyer opened into a huge, airy salon where a series of French doors stood open to the morning light. Suspended from the high ceiling, a Waterford chandelier stirred musically in the breeze, and the walls glowed with rich colors from paintings as priceless and unattainable to Gentry as the woman upstairs.

On the opposite end of the room a door stood slightly ajar. Quickly Gentry crossed the room, his footsteps muted by the thick, Persian rugs covering the hardwood floor. He pressed the door tentatively and it swung inward, revealing rows and rows of bookshelves, a massive stone fireplace and a gleaming, mahogany desk facing the door.

Glancing over his shoulder, Gentry stepped inside the library and headed for the desk. The drawers were locked as he suspected they would be, and he didn't have much time. He scanned the room, noting a set of French doors that opened to the terrace and pool area. At the far end he spotted a wooden door, almost concealed by the bookshelves and dark wood paneling. He tried that, too, but the knob turned uselessly in his hand.

He hurried back to the desk, extracted a tiny, plastic-wrapped object from his pocket and reached for the telephone.

Laura stepped into the library just as Simon hung up the phone. She felt the cold weight of suspicion settle over her as she glared at his back. She tried to squelch it, tried to tell herself that little warning voice in the back of her mind didn't know what it was talking about. But the evidence stood boldly before her.

"What are you doing in here, Simon?" she asked coldly, folding her arms across her chest as she leaned against the door frame.

He spun to face her, but his expression wasn't startled, just surprised. He gave her a wide, disarming smile. "Well, hello. I didn't hear you come in." His gaze dropped, traveling over her in a manner so warming, it was all she could do not to squirm.

She stood her ground, however, as she lifted one brow. "Obviously." She straightened and walked slowly toward him. "You didn't answer my question. What are you doing in here?"

He shrugged. "I'm sorry if I'm trespassing. The door was open, and I saw the phone. I thought it a good opportunity to take care of a little business while I waited."

A perfectly logical explanation. So why wouldn't that little gnawing worry go away? So why did he make her feel so vulnerable, so defenseless all of a sudden?

Maybe it was her own guilty conscience, Laura conceded. Maybe because she had her own ulterior motives concerning him she naturally suspected he did, too.

Or maybe it was because those gray eyes of his reminded her a little too much of still waters, so clear and light and calm on the surface, but with the deadly currents and riptides lurking just beneath, waiting to pull her under.

She let her gaze meet his again, and he smiled, a tiny, knowing smile that slammed into her like a bullet. Suddenly her suspicions faded as the memory of the kiss they shared last night sizzled between them like a live wire on a rain-slick highway. She knew, didn't know how she knew, but she *knew* that he was thinking exactly the same thing. Slowly, ever so slowly, he lifted his hand and smoothed back a strand of her hair.

"Am I forgiven?"

"For what?" she asked blankly.

"For making myself at home. For using the phone."

At that moment, and against her better judgment, Laura was afraid she just might be able to forgive him anything.

The pale drift of the trade winds in the noonday heat carried the haunting scent of frangipani, oleander and wild orchid from the land, mingling it with the sharper smell of the sea. As Laura and Gentry sped along the narrow streets, Key West glistened in the hot light, the white churches and gingerbread houses shimmering iridescently among the green haze of broad oaks, banyans and eucalyptus.

The crystalline waters of the Gulf danced with fire beneath a potent tropical sun, and the sky overhead was a clear, rinsed blue, as fragile as a robin's egg. Several fishing boats and pleasure cruisers headed toward the open water, their wakes sending gentle ripples of turbulence across the otherwise tranquil sea.

Gentry pulled into a space in the parking lot at the Dockside Bar and Grill, an open-air restaurant located near one of the marinas, and killed the engine. It was still early by Key West standards, so they were able to get a table near the water.

Actually, the way all the waiters were tripping over themselves to get a better look at Laura, they would probably have been given their choice of table anytime, Gentry thought dryly. But he could hardly blame them. She did look fantastic.

Today she wore pleated khaki shorts, white leather thongs and a well-worn cotton madras shirt that displayed the slender tapering of her waist and the barest hint of cleavage at the V neck. She'd tucked a red hibiscus blossom behind one ear, and her long, straight hair hung down her back, almost to her waist, in translucent shades of flaxen and gold. It was the type of casual outfit she'd probably donned without a second's thought, but her extraordinary beauty gave it a distinction that would be impossible to duplicate.

She caught his look and smiled, almost hesitantly, as she reached up and lightly touched her fingertip to the bruise on his cheekbone. "That's quite a shiner you've got there."

He winced, but more from his body's reaction to her touch than from pain. He'd managed to convince himself during the middle of the night that his response to her had been brought on by the excitement of the evening, but staring at her now, noticing everything about her in one detailed sweep, he knew, with a quickening of his pulse, nothing about her had been his imagination.

His gaze strayed reluctantly from her to the open expanse of sea. The *Valhalla* was a gleaming, white dot on the horizon. Gentry knew Jake MacKenzie's life history as well as he knew his own. But as the volumes and volumes of files flashed across his mind, he mentally added a new footnote, perhaps the most important one. Laura Valentine.

Logic told him there was no reason to suspect that she knew anything about MacKenzie's dark side, or that she could in any way be involved. But the fact remained that she was staying with him, obviously knew him a little better than she tried to let on, and if Gentry could learn anything useful from her, then that's what he would have to do.

"So, how did you find me, Simon?" Her eyes narrowed suspiciously, but there was a spice of mischief sparkling in the mossy depths.

He took a sip from the icy beer the waiter had set before him, then traced his finger down the streaming side of the bottle. "You wouldn't want to know all my secrets, now would you?"

"Have a lot, do you?"

Was that suspicion in her eyes or amusement? Suddenly Gentry felt as unsure of himself as a rookie. "A few." He took a stab at looking innocent and hoped to hell he'd succeeded. "No more than the next guy, I imagine."

She looked almost as though she wanted to challenge him for a moment, then changed her mind. She folded her arms on the table and gazed out at the sea. "This is nice," she murmured. "I've never been here before."

The sun glinted on a tiny heart charm that lay nestled in the center of the V of her blouse. The flash of light drew Gentry's gaze like metal to a magnet.

"It's not exactly Club Kenya," he remarked dryly.

She shrugged without replying, then asked a question of her own. "Do you come to Key West often on vacation?"

"I don't often take vacations."

She eyed him narrowly. "I would have guessed as much. That's why you look so tense most of the time, I'll bet."

He looked at her in surprise. "Do I look tense? I could have sworn I was completely relaxed."

"For you, maybe." She laughed. "It takes a workaholic to know one, you know. I get a little caught up in my own work sometimes. I find it's a good way to forget."

"Forget what?"

She looked slightly disconcerted for a moment, as though she'd spoken before she'd thought. Then she lifted her eyes and met Gentry's gaze. Something had changed in those green depths, but it was an elusive alteration, an emotion that defied definition. Confusion, embarrassment, even a touch of sadness—he wasn't quite sure—but for a moment, he could have sworn he'd witnessed the same vulnerability he'd glimpsed the first time he'd seen her.

She shrugged and laughed, and the moment faded, leaving Gentry feeling oddly disappointed.

She took a sip of her own beer, and Gentry watched in fascination as her tongue flicked out to lick away the tiny specks of foam that clung to her lips. He had the almost unbearable urge to do it himself.

"So, were you all alone in that big house today?" he asked casually.

"Are you kidding? Jake—Senator MacKenzie—always has tons of people around. I sometimes wonder if he's not a little paranoid..." she murmured, trailing off.

"What do you mean?" Gentry hoped she didn't notice the quickness of his question. He added, a little more casually, "From all I've read about him, he'd not just a powerful man in the Senate, he's also one of the wealthiest men in the country. I'm sure that could make him even more of a target. You could hardly blame him for taking precautions."

She looked up at him, a sort of vague uneasiness in her eyes. "I suppose you're right. It's just that lately..."

"Lately?"

Press her, Gentry urged himself. With a little manipulation, she could probably be convinced to tell him a lot more than she was even aware of knowing.

But after all his questions last night, pressure from him today might only succeed in arousing her suspicions once again. He already felt as though he were walking a tightrope with her. A part of him believed—probably because he wanted to rather badly—that she was nothing more than an innocent bystander in this nasty business. But another part of him—the part who knew how easy deception could be—demanded caution with her.

"It's really starting to warm up, isn't it?" she replied vaguely, lifting the silky strands of her hair and touching the cold beer bottle to her neck.

Gentry thought he had never seen a more provocative gesture in his life, and his body responded in kind. He was grateful when the waiter placed their sandwiches before them, and he could turn his attention momentarily to something less pressing.

They ate in silence as a salt-scented breeze drifted through the restaurant, swaying the hanging baskets of ivy and fern. Laura used the time to covertly study Simon. For some reason, she found herself filled with a curiosity about him that went far beyond her initial interest in him. He wasn't like any man she'd ever known before. He was confident without being arrogant, aggressive but not overbearing. She couldn't help speculating what kind of woman usually attracted him. Beautiful, glamorous, exciting women? If he knew exactly how ordinary Laura was, would he still be interested in her? she wondered.

This morning he wore faded jeans and a cotton shirt rolled up at the sleeves, displaying tanned muscular forearms dusted with light brown hair. He *looked* the part of a man on vacation, Laura decided. Except for his eyes. Those eyes that she couldn't seem to get out of her mind.

After he'd kissed her last night, she'd decided—in the long, sleepless hours that followed—to abandon her plan in using him for Vicki's hero. Her own reaction to him had scared her. She wasn't ready for an involvement. It was too soon, her confidence too shaky. But in spite of her resolve, when he'd called this morning, she couldn't resist another encounter—if only to see whether last night had been her imagination.

Now she knew it hadn't been. Her stomach still fluttered at his nearness. Her knees trembled, her pulse quickened and Laura knew she could no longer deny or ignore her reaction.

With a start, she realized he was returning her appraisal. His stare was vivid and penetrating, bolder and warmer even than the Florida sun. She felt her face grow warmer still as she continued to look into eyes that were as keen as silver lightning.

He was the first to break the contact this time. He idly studied the horizon as he said, "Listen, I've been thinking about something. You mentioned last night some of your work is on exhibit in one of the local galleries. I have a few hours to kill this afternoon. I thought I might go by and check it out. Which gallery is it?"

She looked at him in surprise. "You'd really do that?"

"Why not?"

Because no one else has ever really been interested in what I do. "You just don't strike me as the art connoisseur type," she said lamely.

"You'd be surprised where my interests lie."

"In that case, maybe I'd better make a confession."

He cocked one brow. "This sounds intriguing."

She frowned as she twirled the bottle of beer in her fingers. "Not really. The exhibit premieres tonight at the Kramer Gallery, but it's...well...the collection may not be what you're expecting. It's...different."

"The Kramer Gallery has quite a reputation down here. I'm sure they wouldn't be exhibiting your work if you weren't very, very good."

"Well, let's just say, they were convinced to display mine," she said bitterly.

Gentry couldn't believe the change that came over Laura Valentine. Her voice tightened around a bitter little smile, and she folded her hands in her lap, as though not quite knowing what else to do with them.

"You see, this showing wasn't exactly my idea," she said with a sudden frown.

"What do you mean?"

"I was sort of coerced into it."

Gentry's hand tightened on his beer bottle. "By whom?"

"By Jake, but ultimately by my mother, I think. I can't prove it, of course."

It was Gentry's turn to frown. "You've lost me, I'm afraid."

She paused, shoving away the remainder of her sandwich. "Have you ever heard of *Vicki Love,* Simon?"

"It's a comic book, isn't it?"

She nodded. "Well, I'm her. I mean, I'm her creator. I'm a cartoonist."

He looked at her in astonishment. "You mean, like Bob Kane?"

She gave a short laugh. "Not exactly. I'm hardly in his league. I write and illustrate a monthly comic book called *Vicki Love.* She's sort of a female James Bond."

His smile held a trace of irony. "A comic book, huh? I'm a big *X-Men* fan myself."

"You don't read comic books," she said in an accusing voice.

"Not anymore. But I did when I was a kid, avidly. *The Dark Knight, Superman, Silver Surfer.* It used to drive my mother nuts."

"It still drives my mother nuts," Laura said dryly.

"Why?"

Because nothing I do pleases her. She shrugged. "It's a long, boring story. Let's just say, my mother doesn't exactly approve of *Vicki Love.* A cartoonist is a little too frivolous an image to suit her. That's why I'm having a showing, you see. The paintings are my 'serious' side."

"I can appreciate having a serious side," Simon said smoothly. "But what does Senator MacKenzie have to do with all this?"

"He arranged it all," Laura said simply.

"How so?"

For some reason, Laura found it remarkably easy to talk to Simon, possibly because he seemed so far removed from the type of men she'd always known. He seemed perfectly content to sit back, sipping his beer and asking an occasional question. He was a good listener—maybe too good. Laura thought suddenly how natural it seemed, their being here together, sharing a simple lunch, enjoying the breeze and the sun and the sea.

He made her want to drop her defenses even more than she already had. But she wasn't quite ready for that. Men wanted women like Vicki Love. Strong, capable, beautiful women who weren't consumed in the middle of the night with self-doubt, weren't stricken in the middle of a cocktail party with uncertainty. Insecurities were distinctly unattractive, and she'd already let Simon see a little too deeply past her facade.

They left the restaurant and climbed back into the car. Simon left the marina area and circled around on North Roosevelt Boulevard, heading across the bridge on U.S. Highway One. Laura sat back against the leather upholstery and let the breeze from the sunroof whip her hair into frenzied streaks of gold.

"How did you start writing a comic book?" Simon asked quietly as they traversed Stock Island and headed for the open sea.

"Vicki Love was a character I created years and years ago," she told him. "We sort of grew up together, but the character really came to be *Vicki Love* when I was in boarding school in Switzerland. I had a lot of time to myself, especially on holidays when all the other girls had gone home."

He threw her a sharp glance. "You didn't go home on holidays?"

"Not very often. At Christmas Mother was usually off on one of her honeymoons or a quickie divorce excursion. Summers she spent abroad with friends, looking for a new husband. She bounced around quite a lot. There wasn't really a home to come back to." She shrugged carelessly. "It was no big deal."

But it was a big deal. For just an instant, gone was that air of glamour and sophistication, that perfect creature who had awed Gentry last night. He had the disturbing feeling that the vulnerable, almost painfully honest woman who sat beside him now could easily be more dangerous to him.

She didn't seem to notice the grimness of his own expression when he asked, "How did you meet Senator Mac-Kenzie?"

She peeled a strand of hair from her face as she gave him an apologetic glance. "I have another confession to make. You've probably figured out by now that Jake and I have more than a business relationship."

His insides suddenly felt raw. "How much more?"

"His father was married to my mother when I was seven years old. They were divorced shortly afterward, but even though Jake was a lot older than me, he kept wavering in and out of my life. We'd go for long periods of time without keeping in touch, and then, out of the blue—or probably more likely when Mother called him—he'd be there, quietly pulling strings in the background."

She paused, knitting her fingers together in her lap. "Actually, he's the one who got me admitted to art school. I always felt horribly guilty because space was so very limited, and I took someone's place who probably deserved it a lot more than I did. Jake was just trying to do me a favor, though. I guess that's why, when he approached me about doing an exhibit for the Kramer Gallery, I felt I couldn't turn him down. But the pressure for the last few months has been tremendous, what with trying to get enough decent paintings together, deadlines for *Vicki,* planning my wedding—"

Gentry's breath stopped in his throat as his gaze flew to her ringless fingers. "What do you mean planning your wedding? You're not—?"

She smiled grimly. "Jilted? Afraid so."

"He must have been a real jerk to let you go."

Gentry wasn't sure whom he'd startled more by his statement—Laura or himself. Her eyes misted slightly, and then she smiled. "You really are nice, aren't you? I don't even know why I've told you all this. I hardly know you, and I'm giving you my whole life's history." She hesitated for a moment, then let her gaze drift back to his. "You're easy to talk to, Simon. There's something about you. Something about your face." Her eyes peered into his, searching for some elusive answer. "I don't understand why—maybe because you saved my life—but I feel I can trust you."

Don't, Gentry wanted to warn her. *Don't trust me.* Caroline had trusted him, too, and he'd failed her. In spite of

her trust, he hadn't been able to save her. He didn't want
Laura Valentine trusting him.

Because he didn't want to fail her.

His foot stepped heavily on the accelerator and the car
shot forward. They both fell silent as the breathtaking
scenery absorbed their attention. On either side of the
highway, the gilded water shimmered like yards and yards of
undulating turquoise satin. The vast emptiness of the sea
was broken now and again by dots of land, each a unique
gem in the necklace of islands that made up the Lower Keys.

For Laura it was an afternoon suspended in time. Everything about Simon Hunter intrigued her. Now and then,
if she turned her head suddenly, she would catch him
watching her, studying her with an almost wistful expression in his eyes. It made her heart ache a little just to see
him, to be with him when she knew their relationship would
probably never develop beyond what they already had.

She caught his gaze again, and spontaneously, almost reluctantly it seemed, they shared a knowing smile.

Stopping from time to time at various points of interest,
they drove as far as Sunshine Key and the magnificent Seven
Mile Bridge before Simon turned the car and headed back,
into the most breathtaking sunset Laura had ever seen.

As they neared the end of their destination, Key West
sparkled before them like a jewel, all golden and emerald
and aquamarine. This time Simon followed South Roosevelt Boulevard around the island to the ocean end of
Whitehead Street. Several tourists were milling around by
the mile marker "0" that designated the southernmost point
of the United States. Laura read the sign as they drove by:
The End of the Rainbow.

For some reason she couldn't fathom, it felt more like the
beginning of something to her.

The car idled to a stop across the street from the mansion. Instead of turning off the engine, Simon put the car in

neutral, set the parking brake and turned to face her, propping his arm across the back of the seat.

"I'm sorry I kept you out so long," he said softly. "Time got away from me, I'm afraid."

His mood had altered, so subtly, Laura wondered if she'd imagined the change. But he no longer seemed relaxed and unhurried. There was a new tenseness about him, ever since they'd crossed the bridge into Key West. He wore an air of restless impatience, and she realized with a keen stab of disappointment that he had grown tired of her company. She had shown him too much of the real her, and he'd lost interest.

She fumbled with the door handle. "You're right. I have to get going," she said in a rush. "Thanks for lunch and for the drive . . . and for listening."

"Wait a minute." His hand reached out and closed over her arm. His eyes were oddly intense as she met his gaze. "Would you have dinner with me tonight?"

"I can't. I mean, I'd love to, but I really can't. I have this business thing tonight."

"With him?"

There was no mistaking whom he meant. "Yes," she admitted reluctantly. "But it *is* business."

"Forget it," he said abruptly. "I had no right asking that. It's just that— Damn it, he's too old for you."

She gazed at him in surprise. "I don't think he's much older than you are," Laura pointed out bluntly, then smiled at his deepening scowl. "Besides, I've never thought age mattered much anyway. I like older men."

"In that case, would you consider changing your plans tonight? For me?"

At that moment, Gentry had never despised himself more. It was one thing to question her, find out what she knew, but to continually lead her on when he was by now absolutely sure that she was in no way involved made him feel a little sick to his stomach.

He cursed himself soundly for the loss of perspective. *This is not a frigging personality contest, Gentry,* he warned himself in disgust. This was a dangerous game he had to win at any cost. He'd accepted the fact that he would use Laura—or anyone else—to achieve that victory. What he hadn't accepted was the fact that he was beginning to want her as the prize.

"I really can't," she was saying. "Actually, my premiere at the gallery is tonight."

"Oh, yes, I forgot. And I suppose it's by invitation only," he said with just the right amount of regret in his voice. *The end justifies the means, Gentry.*

Right.

But he wondered why, lately, he had to keep reminding himself of that fact.

"If you're really serious about seeing the exhibit," she began doubtfully, as though she didn't quite believe he was, "you could come tonight. I'll have an invitation delivered to your hotel for you. If you really want to come, that is."

"I wouldn't miss it," he said seriously. "What time?"

"Eight o'clock." She glanced at her watch and gasped. "That gives me less than an hour. Holy—" She squelched an expletive as she jumped out of the car and slammed the door.

"It's black-tie," she called over her shoulder as she crossed the street toward the mansion. "But I don't mind a man with an imagination!" She waved one last time and opened the wrought-iron gate, disappearing inside.

Gentry watched the house for a moment longer, then shook his head, as though clearing away the remnants of a dream.

"You're a damned fool," he muttered to himself as he pulled away from the curb.

"Mr. Hunter! You have a message, sir!"

Gentry checked his stride as he hurried through the lobby toward the bank of elevators. He glanced over his shoul-

der. The desk clerk, dressed in a safari jacket and pith hel-
met, rushed forward, weaving an erratic trail through the
potted palms and the hanging ferns. When he had Gentry's
attention, he waved a white envelope in the air like a flag of
surrender.

Gentry grinned at the image as he waited for the shorter
man to catch up to him. "This was left for you a little while
ago," the clerk said breathlessly as he presented the envelope to Gentry with a flourish.

Gentry accepted the envelope and flipped it over in his
hand. It was blank on both sides. "Man or woman?" he
asked without looking up.

"I beg your pardon?"

"The person who left this. Was it a man or a woman?"

"I really couldn't say, sir. I just came on duty a few minutes ago. The message was already in your slot."

Gentry shrugged. "Okay. Thanks."

He turned back to the elevators as he pried loose the
sealed flap with his thumbnail and extracted the contents.
He'd expected to see the invitation to Laura's premiere inside, but the single sheet of paper contained only one hast-
ily scrawled line. *Meet me at the Hemingway House. ASAP.*

There was no signature, but Gentry recognized the hand-
writing. The note was from Samuel Atwater. He had flown
down from Washington, and that could mean only one
thing. Something had gone wrong.

Casually Gentry glanced at his watch, then refolded the
note and slipped it in his pocket. When the elevator doors
slid open, he was already on his way back outside.

The old coral-stone house on Whitehead Street was listed
in the travel brochures as a "must-see." Sleek, double-toed
cats, rumored to be descendants of Papa Hemingway's own,
roamed the luxurious grounds and perched on top of the
brick wall, eyeing the few remaining tourists with lazy in-
solence.

Gentry reclined against the wall as he unwrapped a piece of gum and folded it into his mouth. The laconic movement of his hand belied the alertness of his gaze as he observed the light pedestrian traffic along the street. A group of young people headed toward Mallory Square stopped to mill about outside the wrought-iron gate, talking and laughing and posing for pictures.

No one paid Gentry the slightest attention.

He had never entertained any delusions about his appearance, nor any regrets. He had what he'd always considered a very forgettable face, and that ordinariness had stood him in good stead many times. He could easily blend into a crowd.

So what was there about him that would attract a woman like Laura Valentine? he wondered uneasily. Apart from the fact that he had saved her life, of course. Gratitude could go a long way, but the kiss they'd shared last night had been a hell of a lot more than that. The sexual attraction between them had been hot enough to ignite a fire, so hot, in fact, that he had awakened this morning still warm from the heat. Seeing her again today had only confirmed the chemistry.

He lifted the guidebook he'd purchased at the door and pretended to study the pages. A shadow of annoyance moved in his eyes, but he kept them fixed on the book. Why couldn't he get her out of his mind? She was a beautiful woman, but he'd known beautiful women before. What made her so different, so special? The quietly simmering sensuality in the depths of her eyes had left him breathless and shaken and scared, he had to admit. Scared, because wanting could easily change to need.

He knew she was attracted to him, as well, and that should have made his job easier. But it didn't. The occasional glimpses of vulnerability he'd seen had left him wondering, in fact, whether he still had the stomach for deception.

A movement beside him caught his attention but he didn't react. His eyes were steady on the book in front of him.

Samuel Atwater stopped beside him, fiddled with the lens of his camera, then snapped a picture of one of the cats that reclined on the brick wall in the fading light. He straightened the aviator sunglasses perched on his broad nose and adjusted the bill of his Houston Astros cap. In his golf shirt and plaid pants, he looked more like a good ole boy from Texas than a seasoned FBI man.

He turned and motioned for someone—Gentry had no idea who—before turning back around to study the house.

"I had your friend checked out as you asked me to," he said, smiling pleasantly at Gentry.

Gentry lowered the guidebook and returned the smile, nodding toward the house. "That was fast."

"She has a rather distant family connection to Mac-Kenzie, but I presume you already know that."

"She told me. What else did you find out?"

"Not a lot. It was a very superficial check, school and college records—she was a straight A student, by the way—tax returns, police reports."

"Police reports!"

Atwater moved closer to the sleek, gray cat and snapped another picture. The animal slit its green eyes, yawned, then lowered the lids again. Casually Gentry followed Atwater. The cat suddenly sprang to life and leapt from the wall in alarm.

"She was arrested for inciting a campus riot during her junior year at Georgetown. She and the rest of the staff of the campus paper took exception to a ruling by the administration that they deemed an obstruction to freedom of the press. The demonstration got out of hand, and the campus security called in the local police to help break it up." Atwater shrugged. "Pretty innocent stuff, for the most part, but it seems your Miss Valentine has some fairly radical political views. She dropped out of college over that incident, then later enrolled in the American Academy of Arts and Sciences. A pretty tough school to get into, unless you know someone."

The implication wasn't lost on Gentry. "She isn't in this," he said, his eyes scanning the area, abstractly noting that the lighthouse directly across the street was perfectly situated for a sniper.

"I doubt very seriously that she is," Atwater agreed. "But as you well know, the most effective foreign agents and traitors are usually people we least suspect. You can't afford to lose your perspective, Gentry."

"I'm not losing anything. I'm checking her out, just as I would anyone associated with MacKenzie."

Atwater's brow rose fractionally as he looked at Gentry. "Good. Can you use her?"

Gentry's jaw clenched. "Maybe," he said tightly. "But I don't want to do anything that might put her in MacKenzie's cross fire. If he thought she was involved with us in any way, she could end up dead."

"You're right about that," Atwater agreed. "In fact, that's why I'm here. Your informant was found dead early this morning."

"Lester?" Gentry's head jerked around in shock, then he caught himself and steadied his movements, forcing another smile to his lips. "What happened?"

"Bullet through his head. His arms were bound behind his back. There was no mistaking—it was an execution."

"MacKenzie somehow found out he talked," Gentry said. "I've maintained all along that we have a leak on this case. He's been one step ahead of us for too long."

"There's no way of knowing what Lester told his killer before he bought it," Atwater remarked calmly.

"About the operation down here? He didn't know much."

"If he admitted giving us the information about the alleged exchange here in Key West, then MacKenzie would be a fool not to suspect some sort of undercover operation."

"That bastard is just arrogant enough to think he can pull it off right under our noses. In fact, I'm sure that's icing on the cake for him. I say we proceed with the plan. Greenwood's already in place, and I've made arrangements to attend the party tonight at the gallery.'' He glanced again at his watch. ''I'm late in fact.''

''You still want to move even though your cover may be blown?'' It was an offhanded question, in no way an indication of how Atwater felt about the situation.

A soft, scented breeze played through the leaves of the banyan and palm trees, but there was something in the wind, a heaviness, that might have been the harbinger of a storm. Somewhere in the distance a church bell tolled the hour, a curiously melancholy sound in the hushed silence of twilight.

Gentry lifted his gaze to meet Atwater's. ''We go,'' was all he said, but both men knew the portent of his words. The hunt would continue, but whether Gentry was now the hunter or the hunted, neither of them knew.

Atwater turned, adjusted his cap, then shoved his hands deep into his pockets as he strolled away. Without looking back, he said, ''Watch your back, Gentry.''

Chapter 5

He wasn't coming.

For the umpteenth time, Laura glanced at the elegant Bertolucci gracing her slim wrist. The diamonds sparkled brilliantly under the gallery's track lighting, but all Laura noticed was the fact that it was half past eight, and Simon hadn't shown.

And no wonder, she thought scornfully. When she considered the way she'd unburdened her soul to him this afternoon, she could hardly blame him for keeping his distance. A man like that couldn't possibly care about her petty little problems, her rather sordid family life. What she had mistaken as his quiet interest had probably been in reality well-disguised boredom. Small wonder he couldn't wait to get away from her.

And she'd done so well last night, keeping up the pretense. Even when she'd seen him after the fight, she hadn't lost her cool. She had played the role of Vicki Love almost to perfection, but today...

Today she had found him too easy to talk to, and for some reason, she'd wanted him to see the *real* Laura. In some perverse way, she had wanted to know if she could compete, in his eyes, with Vicki Love.

Well, now she had her answer. He wasn't coming.

She wandered through the crowded gallery, smiling graciously and accepting congratulations as she stopped before the pièce de résistance of her meager collection. A frown of disapproval creased her brow.

The painting was a fantasy creation in soft, dreamy pastels, pleasant enough to look at on first glance, but if one studied it long enough, the crudeness of the brush strokes, the innocence of detail were painfully evident. And yet some people insisted that was the charm of the painting, a young girl's idealistic vision of her knight in shining armor. But not Laura.

The Knight was the first major painting she had ever attempted. She'd wanted it to be a triumph, but the image that had been in her mind and the reality that was on the canvas were widely divergent, an all-too-painful reminder of her limitations.

"Well, congratulations. It seems you're quite a success." She whirled at the sound of Jake's deep voice. His white teeth gleamed in the brilliant lighting as he bent toward her and kissed her cheek.

"Who would have thought," he asked softly, "when you first presented me with this painting all those years ago that it would have come so far?"

"I'm surprised you wanted to make it part of the exhibit," Laura admitted. "It's not one of my better works. At least I hope not."

"I've always thought it held a certain amount of charm," Jake replied gallantly. "And, of course, I've always been gratified to be the subject of one of your fantasies. It makes me feel a little sad to part with it."

Laura grimaced. "You may not have to. Of all the paintings here, it seems a strange choice to donate to the auction. I'm not so sure anyone will bid on it, Jake."

"Oh, I am," he replied with every confidence. "Trust me, it'll bring more money than you could ever imagine."

"Now, who's living in a fantasy world?" Laura asked wryly.

"I've never denied I had my little...idiosyncrasies." Smiling, he lifted two glasses of champagne from a passing waiter's tray. "Come with me. The press will be clamoring for a statement in a moment, and I want to have a little private conversation with you first."

Puzzled, Laura let him lead her out of the room and through a set of French doors that opened into a courtyard. He set both glasses down on a nearby table and turned to her with a smile.

"And now for this," he said, and then bent suddenly to kiss her lips, tracing their outline with his tongue.

Stunned by his action, it took Laura a moment to react. Then she stepped back in shock. "What do you think you're doing?" she whispered furiously.

Jake's arms fell away from her as he laughed softly. "Don't look so outraged. It was just a kiss."

"But...why?"

He shrugged expressively. "Why not? I've kissed you before."

"Not like that!"

"Maybe I've never noticed you in quite the same light before. You look positively radiant. So soft and pure..." His voice trailed off suggestively as he traced a finger along her jaw.

Laura jerked back. "Stop that! You're acting as though..." She trailed off helplessly, shoving her bangs back with a nervous hand.

Jake's brow arched upward. "Like what? Like I want to make love to you? Would that surprise you?"

"Yes! We're friends, practically family! If this is your idea of a joke, I'm afraid I don't find it amusing, Jake," she said coolly.

He straightened his tie as he stared down at her. "Oh, come, Laura. You had to have seen it coming for weeks now. Why do you think I invited you to stay with me?"

Laura turned away from him, her heart thudding in agitation. "I thought it was because we're friends. Jake, you're shocking me. I've never thought of you, of us, in that way."

He cocked an arrogant brow. "Never? What about that painting inside? You portrayed me as your knight in shining armor. I'd say that's very romantic."

"I was just a kid when I painted that," Laura protested. "I had a crush on you because you were always so nice to me. I've always had special feelings for you," she added softly. "Let's don't ruin it."

"I don't think what I have in mind would ruin anything." He paused, staring down at her with an indefinable glimmer in his eyes. "I'm asking you to marry me," he said softly. "Just think how shocked—and pleased—Crystal would be if we announced our engagement tonight at your premiere."

"I can't marry someone just to please my mother, Jake," she said solemnly. Maybe at one time she could have. But not anymore. Not since she'd met a man who pleased her so much.

The blue eyes glittered in the moonlight. "You should know by now that I don't take no for an answer," he said, bending quickly to drop another kiss on her lips. He laughed softly when she tried to push him away.

"You don't have to give me your answer tonight," he said magnanimously. "But I know when you've had time to consider my proposal, you'll see, as I do, that it's inevitable."

He reached for her again, but Laura moved away; and when she did, she saw a shadow move at the windows.

Someone was standing in the open French doors, watching them.

"Simon." The name whispered through her lips on a suspended breath. Their gazes clung for a moment, and from the distance across the courtyard, she could feel the chill of his stare. "I have to go, Jake," she said urgently.

He murmured something in response, but she didn't hear it. She started across the flagstones toward the open doors, but just as she approached them, Simon turned away, an expression of disgust clearly etched on his features. The look stopped Laura for a moment as she realized what he must have witnessed. He would have seen Jake kissing her, but he wouldn't have heard her response.

She rushed inside, scanning the crowd. When she finally spotted him, she hurried to catch up to him.

"Simon, wait!" But her voice was drowned in the buzzing conversations around her. Shouldering her way through the tightly knit group who was milling around *The Knight,* Laura saw Simon's back disappear around a corner just as someone grabbed her arm.

"I'm very anxious to hear more about your work, Miss Valentine." A man with a Spanish accent beamed up at her as his hand grasped her forearm. "Perhaps I could commission you to do a portrait of me. You could come stay with me in my villa in Caracas—"

"That sounds very nice," she said impatiently, pulling her arm from his grasp. "If you'll excuse me, I have to find someone now."

She didn't wait for a protest, but pushed her way through the crowd, ignoring the congratulations and well-wishers as she made her way toward the entrance where the throng suddenly cleared.

"Looking for someone?"

Even before he spoke, Laura sensed his presence behind her. His hand touched her bare shoulder, and beneath his fingers, her skin burned with awareness. Butterflies went wild in her stomach as she turned to meet his smoky gaze.

But the look he gave her was oddly daunting. There was something different about him tonight. He looked taller and tougher. His eyes were cool, his voice remote, and his long study left her shaken, almost frightened.

"I thought you weren't coming," she said breathlessly.

"Obviously. But now that I'm here, I think you and I need to have a little talk."

She stared at him, mesmerized by the grave, intense look deep in those gray eyes. "I want to talk to you, too, Simon," she said, almost urgently. "Could we get out of here for a little while. Go someplace private?"

Almost coldly, he said, "You don't waste time, do you? What would the good senator say about this?"

"Look, it's not what you think—"

"If I had a dime for every time I've heard that," he said quietly.

The penetrating regard of his slate eyes confused her. He seemed to be watching her, waiting for...she couldn't imagine. Nervously, she moistened her lips with the tip of her tongue.

The action drew Gentry's gaze like an insect to light. She wore lipstick tonight, a dark rose that accentuated the lushness of her lips. It didn't take much effort to remember the way those lips had felt beneath his. Just looking at her now made his insides tighten with desire, with need.

She wore a royal blue minidress that flashed and sparkled in the lighting as she moved. A matching silk chiffon scarf was draped artfully around her neck, and the ends flowed seductively down her back. Diamonds winked from her lobes and around her wrist, rivaling the brilliance of her dress but dim in comparison to the lights in her emerald eyes. She looked sensational, sexy, and suddenly very, very lethal.

He took a quick swallow of bourbon, draining the glass he'd been holding mainly for show, but the burning liquid only added to the sickening roll of his stomach. He tried to equate the woman he'd kissed last night with the woman he'd seen kissing Jake MacKenzie a few minutes ago, but no matter how he added it up, the answer left a bad taste in his mouth.

He'd thought he could detect a phony by now, but Laura Valentine was one cool number—the way she'd looked at him last night, the way she'd talked to him today—all that had led him to believe one thing, but the reality of the scene he'd just witnessed told him something very different.

But could she really have feigned that touch of hurt and vulnerability he'd glimpsed today?

Probably, he admitted bleakly. It had been his experience that women could fake just about anything if the motivation was sufficient. But what was Laura Valentine's motivation? That was what he had to find out. Or die trying, he added bitterly.

"Would you just please listen to what I have to say before you jump to conclusions?" she asked, and he saw a spark of righteous anger in her eyes.

Oh, she was good all right. Even now, he found himself wanting to hear what she had to say. He wanted to hear her denials and excuses and rebuttals. He wanted to hear her say Jake MacKenzie meant absolutely nothing to her.

And at that moment, the sense of danger within him had never been stronger.

Across the room Greenwood, who had successfully—and discreetly—finagled his way into the gallery, was watching them from his place beside the bar. With an almost imperceptible nod of his head, Gentry sent him a silent message: *Keep your eyes and ears open.* Then he turned, and with his hand at her elbow, guided Laura toward the entrance.

Behind them Senator Jake MacKenzie's baby blue eyes followed their retreating backs out of sight. He lifted his glass to his lips and killed the remainder of the champagne, his hard gaze still on the door.

"It's got to be tonight," he said to the man at his shoulder.

"Tonight it is," his companion said cheerfully.

"Finish the job this time, and make sure you don't hit the girl." His voice was even and controlled, but the crystal stem of his glass snapped between his fingers. A white-coated waiter scurried forward to pick up the gleaming shards as the senator turned and walked away without a word.

The night was beautiful, with a full moon pale behind a thin veil of clouds. The music followed them, floating along on the wind that breezed through the palms as Simon led Laura across the street toward the public dock. Her shoulder brushed a spray of jasmine, loosening a shower of fragrant stars on the balmy night air.

Several motorboats bobbed and swayed in the dark waters at the dock as the sea lapped against the hulls with tiny, sloshing sounds. Farther out the green-and-red running lights of a fishing vessel cast a furtive light against the black water, and farther out still, a cruise ship passed silently into the night. Outlined in lights, it looked as gay and magical as a carnival midway.

Simon bent and leaned his forearms against the railing of the dock, his gaze lost somewhere at sea. Several seconds ticked by before he spoke, and when he did, the cold, accusatory tone of his voice sent new shivers up Laura's spine, reminding her that here was a man she knew very little about.

"What exactly is your relationship with Jake MacKenzie?"

She sighed deeply as she leaned back against the railing. "I thought I explained it to you this afternoon."

"Explain it to me again. And this time, don't leave anything out."

He turned his head suddenly, trapping her with the intensity of his gaze. In the sterling light of the moon, she could see the grim set of his jaw and mouth, the hard glitter in his eyes, and she realized her first impression of him had been correct. He was a dangerous man.

"You saw him kiss me, didn't you?" she asked softly. When he didn't answer, she said angrily, "You must have also seen how I responded, how I pulled away—"

He straightened and glared down at her. "What I saw was you and he alone and cozy in that courtyard. What I saw was you on his yacht, you meeting him at that nightclub. What I saw was you in his house today. There's a hell of a lot more to this relationship than you've led me to believe, isn't there?"

She straightened and their eyes were almost level, their chins and jaws set in almost the exact same challenge. "I'm not exactly sure why you care, Simon," she said coolly. "You ask a lot of questions when this is really none of your business."

His tone was grim, resolved. "Maybe I'm making it my business. Maybe I want to know just where I stand in all this. Maybe I want to know exactly what the hell you want from me."

The slanting moonlight highlighted the starkness of his face. Laura studied his silent features for a moment. "What do you mean?" she finally asked.

"I mean, are you using me to make him jealous? Is that the game?"

"I'm not using you, Simon," she said softly, her tongue tripping slightly on the lie. It was only a half lie, she consoled herself. She wasn't using him in the way he thought.

A lie is a lie, Laura, she thought, grimacing inwardly.

"Are you in love with him?"

She thought for a moment he was joking, that his sense of humor had returned, but when she looked at him, there was no amusement, no warmth of any kind in the cold, bleak depths of his eyes.

"There's never been anything between us except friendship... at least on my part." Her gaze dropped to the glittering jeweled toe of her shoe.

"But not on his." When she failed to respond, he said grimly, "I thought as much."

She sighed again, lifting her face to the breeze. "I don't know when things changed between us. Lately, *he's* changed. There's something so restless and moody about him. He's always tense, like a tightly wound spring." She gave him a skeptical glance. "He's not unlike you in that respect."

She saw him frown in the moonlight. "What do you mean?"

"I don't think you ever completely relax, either, at least not with me. Even this afternoon, when we were driving, I got the impression afterward that you'd just been biding your time, waiting for something to happen. I've never known anyone quite like you."

"Maybe you've just been lucky up until this point."

"Don't do that," she said with a soft note of urgency in her voice. "Why do you always try to make me see the worst in you? It's almost as though you're trying to warn me away from you, and yet I know . . . at least it seems that . . . you're attracted to me," she said tentatively.

His smile had a cutting edge. "I'm definitely attracted to you." His eyes dropped and his warm gaze skimmed over her. "What fool wouldn't be?" he added softly with deep regret. "But I don't want you to have any delusions about me. For one thing, I'm a lot older than you, Laura."

"You seem to be the only one who has a problem with that," she pointed out in annoyance. "Maybe you just want me to go away, Simon. Leave you alone. Is that it?"

She started to move away, but he put a hand out and drew her back. Her heart began to pound as he reached out to trace the tiny heart pendant she wore. Then his hand moved upward to touch her hair, slipping his fingers through the golden mist. Her own hand lifted to circle his wrist, bringing the back of his hand against her cheek.

He recoiled slightly as her fingers found the callused ridge of a scar. She pulled his hand away from her face and held it in front of her, gazing down.

"Looks like a knife cut to me," she murmured, running her finger lightly across the ridged surface.

For the first time that night, she saw the hint of a smile. "Now, what would a nice girl like you know about knife cuts?"

She lifted her eyes. "I know a lot of things that might surprise you."

His breath sucked in sharply at the look. "I don't doubt it," he murmured, not sounding pleased.

"What about this one?" She raised his hand and traced the crescent-shaped scar over his eye with her fingertip. He caught her hand and brought the palm to his mouth, skimming the warm skin with his lips. Laura felt her whole body react to that slight touch. Then he entwined his fingers with hers and brought their linked hands downward.

"That was my prize for coming in second in a rock-throwing contest with my sister. I might have done better except she happened to be the only one with a rock at the time."

Laura smiled, shaking her head slightly. "I'll bet there's more to it than that. What did you do to her?"

Even in the moonlight, she could see the amusement dancing in his eyes. "I told her boyfriend she stuffed her bra with toilet paper."

Laura gave a startled shriek of laughter. "No wonder you have so many scars. I'm surprised you're alive to tell the tale."

"A lot of people feel that way, I'm afraid." His voice altered slightly. "I guess my body has taken quite a beating over the years."

He was still smiling, but the look he gave her was purely sexual, full of compelling male heat that left her utterly breathless. She felt her heart quicken, a sensation very like one she'd experienced as a child on a roller coaster.

"I have a feeling you still have a few miles left," she said on a whisper.

"Well," he said, almost casually, "I suppose there's one way to find out."

The wind shifted, gusting across the dock as it snatched the chiffon scarf from her throat. The gossamer fabric floated on air for a moment, like a shimmering ghost, before it dived downward toward the water. Laughing, Laura leaned over the rail to grab it, snatching the end just before it dipped into the water. When she turned to face Simon, he was waiting to cover her lips with his.

His mouth was hot and incredibly erotic. Her heart raced like a powerboat at full throttle. The fiery flow of desire pulsing through her left her too stunned to struggle, too hungry to reason.

No one had ever kissed her as Simon did. It was as though, by touching his lips to hers, he could draw from her her every guarded fantasy, her most precious secrets. Her soul would reveal all to him until he knew exactly what she wanted, what she needed. And then he would give them to her.

She moaned softly, letting her mouth open beneath his like a flower to the sun. Had this passion always been inside her? she wondered. Had it been there all along, waiting and simmering and building until someone came along who could release it?

The daring cut of her dress exposed her back, and Simon's hands moved over her skin, pressing her closer to the hard warmth of his body. Where their bodies touched, she could feel the rhythm of his heart, steady and strong as it beat against her own.

Her tongue met his, and he deepened the kiss with a fierceness that had her swaying against him. Her hands gripped his shoulders, but not to push him away. Instead, she threaded the silken scarf around his neck and pulled him closer, moving her mouth against his in a sensuous, purely instinctive rhythm that had both their hearts pounding.

He took his hand on a slow journey down her back, tracing the outline of the deep V of her dress, slipping his fingers inside to trail up and down her bare skin.

Dear God, how he wanted her, he thought with a rush of consuming heat. The delicious scent of her perfume assailed his senses, acting like gasoline on flames. The warmth of her skin, the power of her response, had his own passion raging for release. His body burned with need, and for one long, agonizing moment, he held her against him, let himself glimpse an image that was both heaven and hell. Then slowly, very slowly, he released her, and took a step away.

Her beautiful eyes stared up at him, misty with passion, dark with confusion. She didn't have to say a word because he knew exactly what she was thinking. It was written all over her face. *Why? Why did you stop? Why did you pull away from me? Is it me? Did I do something to turn you off?*

He took an unsteady breath, wondering how he could possibly make her understand. He knew she was confused, but how could he tell her—without telling her too much—just how much he did want her? He wanted to hold her, kiss her, make love to her and then keep on holding her until her body and her life and her soul would be aching and lonely and lost without him.

But all the wanting and the needing and the wishing in the world wouldn't change the fact of who he was, and what he had to do. If he took her now, he could end up losing his heart, maybe even his soul. But she could end up losing her life.

And there was no way he could ever risk that. Not with her.

Laura wanted him to say something, do something, but he just stood there, his eyes as bleak and cold as a winter's night.

"Simon—"

Looking back later, Laura was never quite sure what she had intended to say. As it was, her tentative beginning was cut short by the *swoosh* of a silenced bullet whizzing past her ear. She was looking at Simon and saw the surprise register on his face the moment the bullet slammed into his left arm. Then he reeled backward, catching himself against the railing.

Chapter 6

"Simon!" Laura jumped forward as she screamed his name. Another bullet fractured the wood railing between them.

"Get down!" he growled as his body collided into hers, flinging them both to the floor of the dock. He shoved her head down as a third bullet whizzed over them, followed by another.

Laura's heart pounded with terror as she lay crushed beneath Simon's body. She couldn't think, could barely breathe as one tiny prayer repeated itself in her head. *Oh, God, oh, God, oh, God.*

With lightning speed Simon rolled off her, propelling himself toward the edge of the dock and dragging her with him. In the next instant she landed, bottom upward, in one of the sleek boats bobbing alongside the dock.

"See if you can get her started," Simon shouted, already working at the moorings.

A bullet shattered the windshield, mobilizing her into action. Laura scrambled toward the front of the boat, plopping herself into the the driver's seat. She felt under the dash, searching for the familiar, magnetic box she knew most boat owners had that contained the spare key. Within seconds, her quest was rewarded, and she not only had box in hand, but the key in the ignition, as well. The powerful Mercury engine roared to life.

Another bullet plowed into the fiberglass hull as she jerked the throttle into reverse, and the boat literally jumped away from the dock, sending Simon flying. He scrambled for a handhold as Laura veered the boat around, and then slammed home the throttle. The bow careened upward, then gradually planed off as the powerful boat quickly picked up speed.

Gentry positioned himself toward the back, gun drawn to return fire, but within seconds they were out of range. He stowed the gun back in his pocket as he staggered toward Laura and collapsed on the front seat, groaning as he clutched his arm.

Now that the adrenaline rush had subsided, his arm was hurting like a son of a bitch, and the wind tearing through the boat was like a slap in the face. Every bounce on the waves sent jagged streaks of pain up his arm. But Laura showed no indication of slowing down.

With one hand on the steering wheel, the other clasping the throttle, she manipulated the powerful boat like a well-trained lover. The huge outboard motor alternately roared and purred to her finesse as they skimmed across the dark water like a hydroplane.

Gentry knew he was dangerously close to blacking out. Stars exploded inside his head. Colors streamed past his eyes. He blinked several times, trying to clear his vision, but everything seemed as inconsistent as mist and shadow. A warning flashed in his brain, however, as brilliant as a strobe. *She could have been killed. Because of me, she could have been killed.*

He was shivering, he realized, but not from the chill of pain nor from the cold. For the first time in a long time, he felt the sting of real fear. He was afraid of dying, he realized, but he was more afraid of Laura's death, of losing her in the same brutal, violent way he had lost Caroline.

He'd lived through Caroline's death, lived through the pain, the anguish, the obsession to find her killer. If Laura were to die, he might live through that, too. But he didn't think he'd be able to survive.

He grimaced from the images his mind had conjured. All the more reason he had to get away from her as fast as he could and never, ever look back.

He turned his head against the thick padded seat to look at her. He thought it strange that he could be so nearly gone, and still have startlingly vivid impressions of her. She handled the powerful boat with a competence that terrified him. Her long, flaxen hair streamed behind her like a silken scarf, and the sparkly blue dress, plastered against her body like a second skin, rode up her thighs. God, she was so beautiful, so brave, and there was no way he could ever have her. Pain ripped up his arm, almost as keen as the ache deep inside his soul.

With a low groan, he fought the black haze and maneuvered in the seat, gripping his left arm as he turned to look over his shoulder.

"We're not being followed if that's what you're worried about," she shouted over the roar of the engine.

Staring straight ahead, she seemed oblivious to everything but the flying darkness in front of them. She had headed them straight out to sea, but now she turned northeast, following the coast. Key West blazed against the black horizon, and the soft glow of the Overseas Highway trailed outward from it like the tail of a brilliant comet.

Pulling back on the throttle, Laura brought the boat to an abrupt halt, killing the engine as they rocked and swayed with the motion of the waves. They weren't being followed and Gentry supposed she needed to get her bearings. He sure as hell did.

She sat for a moment, silent as stone, staring out the shattered windshield. When she lifted a hand to swipe back the damp bangs, Gentry saw how badly her hand was shaking.

"Laura?"

He called her name softly, but she whipped her head around as though he'd screamed it. Her eyes were wide with shock and fright, and the moisture on her face looked suspiciously like tears.

Tenderness welled inside him. "Are you all right?" he asked quietly.

She held out her trembling hands and stared down at them, as though wondering whom they belonged to. "I guess so," she said in a voice that sounded strangely calm. "Those were real bullets," she said inanely.

He laughed without humor. "No kidding."

Her gaze lifted to his. "Why was someone shooting at us, Simon? With real bullets."

"I don't know, Laura." His insides tightened at the lie. It was one thing to use her to gain information, it was another to put her life in jeopardy.

For the first time, she noticed the blood on his sleeve and she gasped. "My God, you were hit. I forgot... I'm so sorry." She put a hand to her forehead, as though that action could make her think clearer. "Simon, are you all right? Is it bad?"

Bad enough, he wanted to moan, but he knew they were not out of the woods yet. He couldn't afford to have her panic. Not that she was, he thought, amazement overriding his pain momentarily. "It's not as bad as it feels."

"How do you know?"

"Because I'd be dead if it were." He did moan then as a wave of nausea washed over him. He hoped to hell he wouldn't disgrace himself right here and now, but the only other alternative seemed to be unconsciousness. He deliberately let his mind slide toward oblivion. But her next statement jerked him back with a vengeance.

"What should I do?" she asked desperately. She bit her lip in urgent contemplation. "Maybe I should radio the Coast Guard for help. They can escort us to the police. We can get you a doctor, and I can call Jake—"

His hand shot out and grabbed her arm, causing her to cry out in shock. He immediately relaxed his hold, but he didn't release her. "Don't do that."

"Why, for God's sake? Simon, we need help. For all we know, that madman's still back there, shooting at someone else. We have to warn them—"

His grip tightened again as their gazes slowly collided in the moonlight. "Don't."

Her eyes challenged his for a long, tense moment. "My God," she breathed shakily. "What have you done?"

The disillusionment and disappointment in her eyes was hard to stomach, but seeing the fear that followed on its heels was the worst of all.

Well, so what? he thought with bitter defensiveness. He'd deceived before and would undoubtedly do so again, because that was what he was paid to do, all in the name of truth, justice and the American way. He'd always told himself the end justified the means. He dealt in terms of life and death, national security, issues that went beyond the scope of an individual's tender feelings. Laura Valentine was a means to that end. So why was he having so much trouble remembering that?

"I didn't do anything wrong, Laura. I give you my word."

"But people don't get shot for no reason," she insisted desperately. "Please tell me—"

He knelt beside her seat, ignoring the searing pain in his arm. He took both of her hands in his. "I know this looks bad, but please try to believe me. I'm not involved in anything illegal. Apart from that, I can't tell you much else. But I do need your help. I know it's a lot to ask, but please... trust me," he said, his voice intense and shadowed with a hint of self-loathing.

She hesitated for a moment. "What do you want me to do?"

His voice was low and urgent. "We can't go back to Key West tonight. I'll explain everything to you as soon as I can, but just get us out of here for now. Take us to one of the other islands. We'll get a room somewhere and figure things out in the morning." He lifted one of her hands and brought it to his lips. "I'm sorry you're in this," he said, realizing with a sick jolt that it was the sincerest thing he'd said to her since their first meeting.

Laura could sense the power of his gaze in the darkness, could feel her susceptibility to his appeal. She didn't want to look at him, to see in his face what had almost happened to him. But her eyes were drawn to him as a moth to flame. She bit her lip, trying to control the tremble.

"You need a doctor—"

He cut her off short. "No. No police. No hospital. Just . . . get us out of here," he rasped.

His breathing was getting more labored, she thought in panic. He looked as though he might pass out any minute. He struggled back into the seat, then slumped against the upholstery as he clutched his left arm. His eyes fluttered closed again.

She had to be a complete imbecile, Laura berated herself, flashing him another worried look. If she had any sense at all, she'd radio the authorities and let them take over. Whatever kind of trouble Simon Hunter had landed himself in was none of her concern. She couldn't afford to get involved.

She could just imagine what Jake would say. She could hear his exact words: *Grow up, Laura. This is the real world. What the hell is the matter with you?*

What the hell *was* the matter with her? Laura wondered as she shifted her gaze to the dark waters ahead of them. Maybe Vicki Love could handle this sort of thing, but Laura Valentine couldn't. She should be worrying about getting as far away from him as fast as she could, because obviously he wasn't giving her the whole story. You didn't get shot for no reason at all—well, maybe you did, she reflected. She'd lived in the city long enough to know that. But if you *did* get attacked, you reported it— Unless...

Her gaze raked him once more. He sagged against the seat, head back, eyes closed. In the dim light from the moon, she could see his face, blanched and drawn with pain.

She made herself finish the sentence. *Unless you had something to hide.*

And the hell of it was, she had trusted him. In spite of his questions, in spite of her intuition, in spite of her bad experiences with men in the past, she had trusted him...and now this. Was she doomed to always fall for the wrong man? she asked herself in despair.

Simon Hunter was definitely the wrong man. So why wasn't she heading toward the police station? Why wasn't she distancing herself from him, calling the police and dropping the problem in their laps?

The answer was simple. Because he'd saved her life. Because she owed him. And if there was one thing that could be said for Laura Valentine, it was that she always paid her debts, no matter what the cost.

Shivering violently against the heavy night chill, she turned the key and the engine roared to life.

By the time they reached their destination, her rented hideaway on the island of Big Pine Key about thirty miles from Key West, Simon was no longer responding to her. As she pulled into the boathouse, Laura tried to tamp down her panic. She killed the engine and turned toward him.

"Simon? We're here." She touched his arm, feeling the warmth of his skin beneath her fingers. "Simon?"

He stirred when she gave his leg a firm nudge. "Come on," she begged, giving his face a couple of mild slaps. "I can't get you out of here unless you help me."

"Where...?" The question trailed off on a groan.

"We're at a friend's house. It's okay. I have the key. Come on, Simon," she said a trifle desperately as she climbed out of the boat and knelt beside it on the wooden floorboards. "Time to wake up."

His answer was a louder groan this time as she put her hands beneath his arms and tried to lift him upward. He resisted the movement, and Laura relaxed her hold, blowing the damp bangs from her forehead. "Simon, please try to help me, okay? I'm strong, but I'm not strong enough to carry you all the way up to the house. So come on. On the count of three. One. Two. Thrree."

"All right, all right," he mumbled, managing to propel himself upward as she pulled and tugged. The momentum sent them both sprawling onto the wooden floor of the boathouse.

"That's it," she encouraged through gritted teeth, trying to breathe beneath the solid weight of his body.

He shifted off her, lying flat on his back and flinging an arm over his face. "I don't feel so good," he said on a groan.

She knelt beside him, smoothing back the damp hair from his forehead with her fingertips. "I know you don't, Simon. But we have to get you inside so we can see how badly you're hurt. Come on. You're scaring me."

"I'll...be all right in a...minute," he mumbled, his eyes still closed. "Just need to...catch my...breath."

With her hands beneath his shoulders, she managed to lift him so that he was half sitting, half leaning against her. He nestled his head against her breasts, uttering a faintly sensuous groan. He put his right arm around her waist, holding her so tightly, she wondered whether he might be faking. But the ugly red stain down the front of her dress where his wounded arm had been against her assured her he was not. The sight of so much blood generated her into action once more.

"Let's go," she urged softly, struggling to her feet as she draped his uninjured arm over her shoulder. "Let's get inside, and then you can rest."

"I have to leave," he muttered as he heaved himself upward and was at last standing. "I have to get away from you."

"You'd last about two seconds on your own," Laura scolded as she slid her arm across his back, guiding them out of the boathouse and across the few feet of yard to the back door of the house. She paused, shifting her weight to accommodate his while she groped over the door frame for the house key. Simon leaned heavily against her as she opened the door and helped him—half dragged him—inside. They stumbled through the kitchen, down a hallway and into a small bedroom at the end.

"At last," she gasped, wriggling from beneath his arm as he collapsed on the bed. She stared at him for a moment, panic bubbling inside her.

"Simon?" She bent over the bed. "Can you hear me? How bad are you hurt? Should I call a doctor?"

Just a faint moan, but it sounded like a negative one.

Laura bit her lip, stifling her own moan. "My God," she whispered, wringing her hands helplessly. "Now what? I'm not equipped to deal with anything like this!" Emotionally or physically, she thought. But fast on the heels of a brief moment of terror came the resurgence of common sense. *Think, Laura. What would Vicki do?* "The first-aid kit," she answered promptly.

She stood over him, touching his forehead with the back of her hand. His skin was warm. Too warm, maybe. "Simon, I'll be right back, okay? I'll have a look at your arm," she said with a lot more enthusiasm than she felt. With one last worried glance, she hurried from the room, closing the door behind her.

Ironically, it was the soft click of the door latch which brought Gentry fully conscious. He'd been drifting for some time in his own comfortable numbness, but he made the effort now to galvanize himself. His eyes flew open as the thick fog surrounding his brain began to clear. His gaze darted around the unfamiliar room basked in moonlight. *Where the hell am I?*

Dead, was his immediate thought, but where was the long tunnel, the brilliant light, the overwhelming sense of well-being he'd read about lately?

All he felt was hot driving pain in his arm as he raised himself on his elbow. Cursing darkly, he fell back against the pillows, perspiration beading across his brow. With the back of his hand, he swiped away a trickle of sweat that coursed down his temple. But when he brought his hand away, he saw in the pale light of the moon that it was blood.

Just his luck, he grimaced irreverently. He'd gone to the other place. An image from another lifetime floated to the surface of his mind. He could hear his grandmother's firm voice admonishing him.

You know where little boys go who don't tell the truth?

I'm sorry, Gram. I took the pie from the window. I don't want to go to hell.

Then promise never to lie to me again.

I promise, Gram.

An easy careless vow from a ten-year-old, and one he'd broken many times over. He felt a peculiar sense of regret that he couldn't go to his grandmother now and confess his sins. She'd be shocked at the extent of his deceit, no matter how noble he'd once believed the cause. With an unaccustomed pang of sadness, it hit him suddenly just how disappointed his grandmother would be in him as a man.

But the end justifies the means, Gram.

Horsefeathers!

"Horsefeathers," he mumbled as he swung his legs over the side of the bed and sat for a moment, trying to get his bearings. He had to get out of here, had to get away from her . . . before she got hurt. Or worse . . .

"Think, Gentry," he commanded himself as he glanced at his watch. She'd headed northeast and it hadn't taken that long to get here. They were on one of the other islands, probably Sugarloaf Key or maybe a little farther north than that. But whose house was this? Where the hell had she brought him?

He heard voices. It took him a minute to realize they weren't coming from inside his head but from somewhere outside the bedroom door. He rose on unsteady legs and walked soundlessly across the room, patting the comforting weight of the gun in his jacket pocket. Pausing at the door, he opened it a crack and peered out.

For a moment he thought he might really have died, because here was the long tunnel with the light at the end. And the soft voice he heard did instill in him a sense of comfort and well-being. He stepped into the hallway and followed the sound.

"Yes, I'm sure I know what I'm doing."

Her back was to him as he approached the living room, but he could tell by the one-sided conversation that she was talking on the phone.

"Jake, would you please just trust me this once? I'll take care of it. I won't let you down, I promise."

Gentry froze as he flattened himself against the wall in the darkened hallway. She was talking to MacKenzie on the phone! Distorted visions from the evening came racing back to him, crowding together in his mind.

A setup. Pure and simple, and he'd been a sucker all the way. Even with all his suspicions, betrayal from this quarter still hurt whether he wanted to admit it or not. He rested his head weakly against the wall, his eyes closing briefly.

If something seems too good to be true, it more than likely is, boy.

I know, Gram. I know.

His hand went automatically to his pocket as he stepped into the room. He could smell her perfume, an intoxicating fragrance mixed with the scent of blood and danger. She hung up the phone and turned, her beautiful eyes going wide with shock and fear when she saw the semiautomatic leveled at her chest.

Chapter 7

The metal box in her hands slipped soundlessly to the floor, the impact muted by the thick, white carpet. Laura took a step toward the box, but a slight movement of the gun stopped her. She lifted her frightened gaze to Simon's.

"Who the hell are you?" he asked in a low, menacing tone.

He stood leaning against the wall, his face still drained of color. But the gun he held in his hand was steady, the glint in his gray eyes sharp as a dagger. And just as deadly, she thought.

But what worried her most was the fact that he seemed to have developed amnesia since she'd left him a few minutes ago. For some reason, he didn't seem to remember her.

"I'm Laura," she said in a soft, soothing voice. "Laura Valentine. Don't you remember?"

"I'm remembering a lot of things just now and most of them make my blood run cold. Like that cozy scene I walked into at the gallery tonight," he said, sneering. Then, "You set me up back there."

"I helped save your life 'back there'!" she cried incredulously. "You could be dead right now if it wasn't for me."

"That's what I thought at first," Simon agreed. "But then, I wasn't exactly in the right frame of mind to be rational. A slug in the arm can sure undermine your powers of deduction. But I'm thinking a little more clearly now. And what I'm thinking is that this has *all* been a setup—that nifty little trick on the yacht, your showing up at the bar the next night, the premiere tonight—what I want to know is why. *Why?*"

His accusation seemed to take the last of his strength. He slumped heavily against the door frame, the hand holding the pistol going up to clutch his left arm. His eyes closed briefly.

"Simon, this is crazy—" She started across the room to him, but his eyes opened and the gun came back around. She halted, shaking her head in confusion. "Why are you doing this?" she asked, her hands spreading wide in appeal. "I don't understand why you're treating me as though I'm some sort of…threat to you. What's going on, Simon? I have a right to know—"

His eyes were narrow slits of steel as he glared at her. "Spare me the act. I want some answers, and I want them now. Why did you bring me here?"

"You asked me to!"

"Exactly where the hell are we? Whose house is this? Is anyone else here?"

"Why is an attorney carrying a gun?" she shot back, anger suddenly overtaking her fear. "Who shot you tonight? And why? What happened, Simon? A drug deal go sour? No honor among thieves?"

"My questions first," Simon said coldly, swiping the back of his hand across his brow.

"Why should I answer any of your questions if this is the way you repay me for my help?"

He smiled grimly. "That's simple. Because I'm the one with the gun."

A circumstance with which she could hardly argue. Simon must have sensed her hesitation, for he prompted, "Why don't you start with that phone call I just overheard. What did you tell MacKenzie?"

"Nothing! Damn it, Simon, this has gone far enough. I'm calling the police." She spun around and reached for the phone, but he was across the room in two strides, his quickness belying his obvious pain. He jerked the phone from the outlet and hurled it across the room. Laura saw her chance and grabbed for the gun, but Simon flung her away. Still clutching his arm, she tumbled backward, pulling him with her.

Arms and legs sprawling awkwardly in several directions, they landed on the white leather sofa, grappling for position. Straddling her, Simon pinned her between his thighs, but Laura twisted and turned beneath his weight, writhed and struggled until they both slid off the leather couch. Simon's head banged against the coffee table as he landed on his backside, and the gun was knocked free.

Ignoring his groan, Laura crawled over him and scrambled for the pistol. When he opened his eyes, she was standing over him, the barrel leveled at his chest.

"Ooh...damn!" He groaned again and felt his head gingerly. "I'm getting too old for this sh—"

"Stay where you are!" Laura commanded as he made to sit up. "I'm warning you, Simon. I know how to use this." She tossed her hair over her shoulder, and her earrings swung violently, shooting prisms of light in every direction.

She looked like an avenging angel standing over him. Her long, blond hair was in wild disarray, her stockings were torn and the tight, blue dress was wrinkled and hiked up well above mid-thigh. One shoulder strap slipped down her arm, and absently she used the gun barrel to shove it back up.

God, she looked great!

And he was a damned idiot, Gentry swore to himself. After everything he'd learned about her tonight, after everything he'd been through, he could still feel that rush of

warmth through his body from just looking at her. Maybe
he wasn't as old as he thought, he decided disparagingly. Or
maybe he was just a lot dumber.

"What now?" he asked cautiously.

"You can start by getting up," she commanded, "but nice
and slow. No sudden moves."

Her vocabulary read like a bad script for a gangster
movie, Gentry decided as he struggled to his feet, stagger-
ing slightly. He let the room stop spinning before he ad-
dressed her again. "Why don't you put that thing down
before you hurt yourself?"

She laughed dangerously, her voice altering dramatically
as if she'd suddenly donned a whole new persona. "Don't
be ridiculous. I'll ask the questions now, if you don't mind.
Who are you? Who attacked you tonight? And why are you
carrying a gun? I want to know everything, Simon. I risked
my neck for you."

"Yes, yes, you did," he agreed quickly. Perhaps a little
too quickly, he worried. Laura's eyes narrowed on him.
"And believe me, I'd like to tell you everything, but there
are reasons, *important* reasons why I can't." He spread his
hands helplessly. "Let's just say I was shot and leave it at
that."

"Then let's just say, we call the police. I mean it, Simon."

"All right, you win. I know when I'm licked," he said in
a conciliatory tone. "Why don't you just put down the gun
and we'll—"

Laura aimed a little to the right of his head and fired. A
brass plate on the wall behind his head clanged to the floor.
Gentry's head whipped around, first to the neat hole
through the center of the plate, then back to her.

"Jesus H. Christ! Are you crazy? You could have killed
me!"

"I could have," Laura agreed blandly. "If I'd wanted to.
I advise you, Simon, to start talking or I get on the phone
and call the local authorities, who in turn will alert the Key
West police. Maybe even the FBI."

"Oh, God, this is rich," he mumbled, then noting her aim, rushed his words. "All right, all right. But do you mind if I lie down while you conduct your little investigation? I suddenly feel sick."

Her eyes dropped to his blood-stained clothes, and something twisted inside her. Something like fear, except she knew she was no longer in danger. With her eyes still on him, she motioned toward the hallway.

He walked out of the room as Laura stood for a moment, staring after him in consideration. Then, retrieving the first-aid kit she'd dropped earlier, she hurried to follow him down the hall.

He was already stretched out on the bed when she walked into the bedroom, his long legs crossed at the ankles, his right hand gripping his left arm. Laura drew the curtains at the window, then flipped on the light and laid the gun on the bureau—within her reach.

Meanwhile, Simon's face, if possible, had grown even whiter. Dark lashes shadowed his cheeks, and his chiseled lips were drained of color. His hair was mussed and his clothing all askew, stained with blood and dirt. Laura was hard-pressed to stifle the nurturing instinct that kept creeping up on her.

"Simon?"

One eye opened to a slit.

"I want to remove your clothes."

Both eyes popped open at that.

She ignored his pointed stare. "I need to have a look at your arm," she clarified. "Sit up for a minute."

When he complied, she shoved the tux jacket over his shoulders and slipped it down his arm, then gasped as she saw the bloody sleeve of his white shirt. He sat with shoulders slumped as she unbuttoned his shirt and slid it away. The fabric stuck to the blood on his arm; she tugged gently but firmly to free it, and Simon's face turned at least three shades paler.

Cursing soundly, he fell back against the pillows, his legs still hanging over the side of the bed. "What are you trying to do to me?" he groaned.

"I'm sorry, but I have to get this shirt off."

"Why didn't you just shoot me?" he asked, his voice muffled by the pillow.

"I'm sorry," Laura said again. She grimaced as she peeled the shirt down his arm, then stared in shock. "My God, your arm. Simon, your poor arm . . ."

"It's all right," he said as he gritted his teeth. At her look, he confessed, "It hurts like hell, but the bullet just nicked me. I'll be fine."

She put her trembling hands to her face, appalled by the thought of touching the raw, open wound. "I'm not qualified to treat a gunshot wound," she said in panic. "Simon, we *have* to get you to a doctor."

"Gunshot wounds have to be reported to the police, and I can't afford to get tied up in red tape right now. Just clean it up a little and slap a bandage on it. By morning, it'll be fine."

With increasing trepidation, Laura discarded the soiled shirt, then knelt and untied his shoelaces. Within seconds, shoes and socks joined the growing pile beside the bed. She swung his legs onto the mattress, then sat down beside him, contemplating her next move.

Her fingers moved to probe the broken skin on his temple where he'd hit the coffee table. He winced slightly and she drew back her hand, her gaze dropping reluctantly to his arm. She'd never in her life had to deal with anything remotely resembling the bloody mess that was his arm. She hadn't the faintest idea where to start. But once, when Vicki's ex-partner had been shot, the secret agent had cleaned the wound with river water from her canteen and bandaged it with her underwear. At least Laura had a little more to work with than that, she reminded herself grimly.

"Simon, I'm going to get some warm water and a washcloth from the bathroom to clean your arm."

Simon merely closed his eyes, whether affirmatively or in resignation she had no idea. Laura opened the first-aid kit and removed a bottle of antiseptic, along with cotton balls, Q-Tips, gauze bandages, tape, scissors and aspirin. Then she fetched the warm water and washcloth from the bathroom, along with a glass of water to wash down the painkillers, and sat back down beside him.

"All right, you better start talking," she ordered as she handed him the water and two aspirin. He held up three fingers indicating he needed another. Laura obliged, then wet the cloth and wrung it out. "It'll help take your mind off what I'm doing."

"Not bloody likely," he muttered darkly, his eyes squeezed shut against the pain.

"Tell me anyway," Laura instructed, tentatively touching the cloth to his arm. "And you better make it good. Because if I don't buy it, I have every intention of calling the police, the FBI and maybe even Jake."

His eyes flew open again. He stared at her for a moment, apparently undergoing some rapid mental adjustments. She wet the cloth again and resumed her task, ignoring the recoil of her stomach.

"Whether you believe it or not, you can trust me, Simon. I'm no threat to you," she said softly.

He looked on the verge of protesting, but changed his mind. His expression softened. "I know that I overreacted, and I'm sorry. You didn't deserve that scene."

"Then you'll tell me what's going on?"

Simon sighed wearily. "As much as I can. But don't waste your time calling the FBI, Laura. That's who I work for."

Her hand paused in midair. "You mean...you're an agent or something?" Her interest quickened, then died. "Wait a minute," she said skeptically. "Where's your identification?"

"I'm not carrying any," he said impatiently. "I'm undercover."

"You mean your real name isn't Simon Hunter? Who are you then?"

"I can't answer that—the less you know the better. I can only tell you enough to keep you from calling the police. I can't have the local authorities blundering into something they know nothing about. This is a very important operation, Laura. A matter of national security—not to mention life and death. I can't stress that enough."

"You also 'can't' prove you're telling me the truth."

"That's right. You have only my word."

"In light of the lies you've already told me," she said coolly, "I'm not sure how much that's worth."

His gray eyes, shadowed with pain, stared straight into her own. She knew without a doubt that she had suddenly become involved in a very dangerous game, and she was very possibly getting in way over her head. She had no reason in the world to trust this man. Her instincts had steered her wrong too many times in the past, and yet there was something about him, something that spoke to the emptiness inside her and told her he'd been lonely, too. In spite of the differences in their ages, their backgrounds, their occupations, Laura knew, without knowing why or how, that they were kindred spirits, and she wanted to believe him. She wanted to help him.

"I need more than that, Simon," she pleaded softly as she cleaned his arm with the wet cloth. He flinched as her fingers probed too firmly. "What kind of operation are you talking about? And what does it have to do with Jake?"

"What makes you think it has anything to do with Jake?"

"I'm not stupid," she said angrily, pausing in her ministrations to glare down at him. "He's a very important man, Simon, and you were shot outside the gallery tonight. Is he in danger?"

Only a minute hesitation. "Not at the moment."

"What does that mean?"

"It means the gunman was after me, not MacKenzie."

"But why?" Laura persisted.

"I suspect my cover was blown. That's why I can't call in reinforcements at the moment. There's a leak somewhere down the line. The wrong word to the wrong person could jeopardize the whole operation. Other agents' lives could be endangered. I've got to think this thing through before I make a move."

"Exactly what are you doing down here?"

He hesitated again, and then shrugged in resignation. "I have reason to believe that there is a man—a South American—in Key West who is looking to buy sensitive military information."

What he neglected to tell her was that the man he really wanted was the one *selling* the secrets. Sometime during the day he'd spent with her, Gentry had become convinced of Laura's complete innocence. Call it instinct. Call it hormones, he thought dryly. Whatever it was, he trusted his own intuition. But he still wasn't sure he could trust her with the information about MacKenzie, or if he even had a right to. He'd involved her enough as it was. Making her choose where her loyalties lay wasn't a prospect he particularly relished.

"What does that have to do with you getting shot at the gallery tonight?" she continued.

"It means I'm on the right track."

Laura gasped. "You mean he was there tonight?"

"Looks that way."

"Was that why you came tonight?"

His gray eyes sought hers. "Partly."

"Well, at least you didn't lie," she said, feeling unaccountably hurt by his admission.

"I'd like to tell you more," Simon said softly, drawing her gaze again. "But the less you know—"

"The better off I'll be," she finished in exasperation. "Right now, that doesn't give me a good deal of comfort."

"All right," he agreed. "I'll tell you as much of the background as I can."

While she dealt with his arm, he told her briefly the history of the case, of the agent who had been killed, of the witness who had lost her memory. But of all the things he told her, it was what he *didn't* say that most interested Laura. Something in the way his face changed when he spoke about the witness made Laura pause and take note. His color was gradually returning to normal, but the lines around his mouth and eyes were still deeply etched. She could tell by the raggedness of his breathing that he was still in pain and trying to control it.

But none of that had anything to do with why he'd suddenly dropped his gaze, as though fearful she might read something in his eyes that he wanted to keep hidden.

He'd been hurt, she thought suddenly. The woman he spoke about, whoever she was, had somehow hurt him. Laura felt an unexpected—and highly unreasonable—anger toward that unknown woman, and was surprised to recognize that the anger stemmed from jealousy.

With the wet cloth, she tentatively blotted the bloodied skin around the wound. Simon grunted, and she looked up quickly, her hand pausing. "Are you all right?"

"Just get on with it," he ground out, squeezing his eyes tightly closed.

Laura bent to her task, hurrying as much as she dared. Once the dried blood had been cleaned away, the arm didn't look nearly as bad. Simon, however, looked a good deal worse. A fine bead of sweat lined his brow and upper lip.

He sucked in his breath as she touched the saturated cotton ball to the wound. "God...bless...America," he gasped, when he finally caught his breath. "What is that stuff?"

"Call it truth serum," Laura said with a grim little smile. "Almost as effective as bamboo shoots under the fingernails, wouldn't you say?"

"Hell, yes!"

"Then tell me this," she said as the cotton ball hung poised over the wound. "Why did you think I'd set you up?

Did you think I was somehow working with this man? Is that why you pulled a gun on me earlier?''

The gray eyes were devoid of expression. "It occurred to me that you might have an ulterior motive for your apparent interest in me."

She looked at him in astonishment, then said coolly, "Well, you're right. I did have an ulterior motive." She touched the cotton ball to his arm again, and this time Simon didn't flinch, didn't move, didn't show any reaction whatsoever. But Laura could sense the sheer force of will he used to remain so still. She threw the soiled cotton in the wastebasket and stood up, staring down at him from the advantage of her height. "And to think I felt guilty for using you when all along you were using me."

"How were you using me?"

There was nothing in his voice that betrayed anything of what he might be feeling. He was every inch the consummate professional, cool, unruffled, emotionless. Ice, Laura thought.

He raised up in bed, propping himself against the headboard, the gray eyes continuing to stare at her. Laura's own gaze slipped downward, reluctant to survey the expanse of bare chest and shoulders, the ripple of long, smooth muscles beneath the tanned skin.

"How were you using me?" he repeated heavily.

She lifted her eyes to meet his. "I thought you were a hero," she said softly. "I thought you would be perfect for Vicki..." She trailed off, daunted by the incredulous look dawning on his face. She stiffened her shoulders in defiance as her voice rose defensively. "I model my characters on real people. I always have. That's the only way I can do it. That day on the yacht, when you rescued me, I was getting desperate. I'd already decided to take the first man I saw and turn him into a hero, no matter what he looked like."

The gray eyes darkened to the color of a thundercloud just before the storm hit. "Thanks a lot."

"I didn't mean it the way it sounded." She rushed to amend herself. "You *did* save me. It seemed almost like fate. I'd been looking for a hero for so long, and there you were...."

He shot her a glance that made her thankful looks couldn't kill. "I told you I'm no hero," he said bitterly. "What I did was no more than what any other decent human being would have done."

"Yes, well, in case you haven't noticed, decent human beings are a little hard to come by these days. Besides, you're hardly in a position to cast stones at me. I may not have leveled with you, but I didn't out-and-out lie to you. And I'm not the one who almost got us both killed tonight."

She could tell she'd hit a nerve. She knew the moment the storm hit his eyes, but it was a very brief impression because suddenly he was on his feet, and his hand shot out to grip her wrist.

"Let me ask you a question, and I'd certainly like to know the truth for a change," he said coldly. "Just what was the purpose of those kisses? Research?"

She tried to back away, but his arms held her. Their heads were close together, and the fan of her breath warmed his cheeks and lips. Gentry searched her face, his gaze landing on her mouth. Her lipstick had long since faded, but her lips still looked incredibly tempting, soft and full, and it took very little effort to recall the way they felt beneath his. He glanced down and saw the swell of her breasts teasing the low-cut neckline of her dress, remembering, too, the way he'd touched her earlier, the way she'd immediately responded.

His eyes rose to meet hers, and he saw that they were soft and misty and he knew that she was remembering, too. Then the warmth chilled as her chin came up in defiance.

"I could ask you the same thing," Laura whispered, her lips trembling beneath the power of his devastating gaze. "What were you after when *you* kissed *me?* Information about your alleged spy? Just how far were you willing to go, Simon?"

"I don't know, Laura," he said roughly, his hand coming up to caress the line of her jaw. "How far were *you* willing to go?"

Her palm itched to slap him, but something in his eyes—a flicker of something she couldn't define—stopped her. Instead, she jerked away from his touch, and executed a sharp turn on stockinged feet, storming out of the room without another word.

The door slammed behind her, and Gentry winced, putting a weak hand to his throbbing temple.

Congratulations, Gentry, he inwardly berated himself. *You certainly handled that with your usual finesse.*

Hardly realizing what he was doing, he followed her across the hall and rapped on the bedroom door she'd slammed closed behind her. "Look, I'm sorry about that crack I made. I was totally out of line. Come back out so we can talk about this."

"Go to hell."

The command sounded strangely muffled, as though she had a pillow to her face. Gentry's hand on the door froze and he stood listening for a moment.

"You're not crying, are you?" he asked a trifle desperately. If there was anything he couldn't stand, it was a woman's tears. His sisters had learned that at an early age and had used it against him mercilessly. They still did.

He ran a hand through his hair, standing it on end as he stared morosely at the door. "Look, there's no reason for you to be so upset. We both used each other, but now it's all out in the open and we can talk about it rationally, like two adults."

Something bounced off the door of her bedroom, and Gentry jumped back as though he'd been shot. Again.

He took a deep breath, considering his options. In hindsight, he realized that had been the wrong tactic. Women were sort of touchy about their emotions. Maybe he should try to lighten things up a bit.

"Hey, it's just like you said. This whole thing is rather ironic—amusing even—when you think about it. You were looking for a secret agent and, well, you found him."

Something big—like a lamp—shattered against the door.

"Strike two," he muttered. There was only one thing left to do. He hated to pull it, but he had to admit it usually worked. If his sisters had used tears against him, he'd learned that sympathy worked against them. His grandmother had been the only woman he'd ever met who had never fallen for that ploy.

"Laura," he called, trying to make his voice sound weak and pitiful, which wasn't that much of a stretch. He felt pretty pathetic at the moment. "Honey, what about my arm?"

Her voice came back loud and strong this time, as though she'd tossed away the pillow. He had no trouble at all hearing her when she shouted, "I hope it falls in the dirt!" A slight pause. "That goes for your stupid arm, as well!"

With a long, suffering sigh, he went back to the other room and sat down on the edge of the bed. He picked up the gauze bandage Laura had removed from the first-aid kit and opened the package with his teeth. Applying the bandage to his arm, he reached for the tape. The gauze slid down his arm and onto the floor.

With a muttered "Damn," he bent to retrieve it. This time he had the presence of mind to cut a section of adhesive first. Then he carefully placed the bandage over the wound. But by the time he'd accomplished that, the tape had gotten stuck between his thumb and forefinger. He tried to shake it loose, but it wouldn't budge.

As soon as he let go of the bandage, it slipped to the floor once more. He pulled the tape loose with his left hand, where it immediately stuck to his left fingers.

"Damn it!" He shook his hand viciously, sending tremors of pain shooting down his arm. For a good sixty seconds, he wrestled with tape and bandages until finally he had both hands free. He wadded the whole mess up and threw it against the wall.

With a heavy groan, he fell back against the pillows and lifted his legs onto the bed. Closing his eyes, he clutched his arm, trying to ease the pain. In less than two minutes, he was out like a bad light bulb.

"Simon?" Laura hovered just inside the doorway, studying his silent form. Her heart jumped to her throat. He was so still!

Panic replaced her anger as she padded barefoot across the room and touched her fingers to the pulse point at his throat. The strong and steady cadence filled her with heady relief, but the warmth of his skin worried her.

She tried to rationalize her concern. He might have used her to get information he thought she had, but she didn't relish having an unconscious man on her hands—a liar or otherwise. Besides, the sooner he was up and around, the sooner he could get out of here, out of her life and out of her system.

Removing a fresh bandage from the kit, she cut two strips of adhesive and secured the gauze into place. Simon never moved a muscle.

She wet a fresh cloth in cool water and sat on the bed, bathing his face with soft, steady strokes. The wide span of his chest rose and fell in even rhythm. She could see the ripple of muscle beneath his tanned skin. She had thought him too lean for such powerful muscle formation, but he obviously kept himself in marvelous shape. *Marvelous,* she thought absently as she splayed her fingers across his skin and let his heart beat against her hand.

There was little else she could do for him now except perhaps make him as comfortable as possible. Her gaze slipped downward, to where the sprinkling of brown hair arrowed toward the waist of his trousers. Without giving herself time to reconsider, her fingers unbuttoned his pants, then low-

ered the zipper. He moved restlessly against her hand, forcing an intimacy she hadn't counted on.

Her gaze flew to his face, but he was still asleep, still
breathing deeply. Her fingers curled around the waistband
of his pants as she awkwardly tugged them downward, past
his lean hips, over his muscled thighs and down his legs until they fell to the floor at the end of the bed.

The sight of him—in all his masculine glory—sent hot
color surging to her face. She stared at him for a moment,
her scrutiny taking in little else but his rather disturbing vi-
rility.

What are you doing? she scolded herself as she jumped up
to turn off the light. The man was entitled to privacy, even
if he had lied to her.

Keeping her gaze averted, Laura fetched a light blanket
from the hall closet and spread it over him. Going back to
her own room long enough to shower and change clothes,
she came back and stretched out on top of the cover beside
him.

Just to make sure he doesn't get worse during the night,
she assured herself firmly.

Lying on her side, her face pillowed against her hands, she
watched his shadowy profile until she finally fell into a deep,
dreamless sleep.

Chapter 8

Gentry slowly raised his head, supporting himself on one forearm as he squinted and tried to focus on his surroundings. The blinds at the window had been slatted so that, mercifully, only streaks of sunlight filtered through. He gazed around, taking in his surroundings with quick appraisal. The furniture was bleached pine, as light and airy as the ocean breeze that blew in through the open window, stirring the hanging basket of feathery fern. A corner etagère housed a seashell collection, and seascapes adorned the walls. The walls themselves were painted a cooling hue of green, just a shade or two lighter than his own complexion, he judged.

He swung his legs over the side of the bed and sat for a moment, holding his head between his hands before he realized that—except for his briefs—he was naked as a jaybird.

"What the hell—" He jerked the covers back on the bed as though expecting to find his clothes underneath. He looked on the floor, under the bed, around the room, but his clothes were gone and so was his memory of what had happened to them.

Easing himself to his feet, he gingerly stretched, feeling the resistance in the muscles of his left arm. Absently he massaged the soreness, pausing when he felt the thick bandage encasing the wound. He realized that Laura must have come in after he'd fallen asleep and finished wrapping his arm.

He had dim recollections, vague images, of being roused several times during the night, of a soft voice calling his name. He'd thought at first that he was back home in Tennessee, with his grandmother taking care of him, but the hand that had soothed his forehead had not been the dry and callused skin of an old woman. It had been velvety smooth, with the warm blood of youth surging through it.

He stumbled to the bathroom adjoining the bedroom, vaguely noting as he started the shower that the shelves were well stocked with all the amenities, from fresh towels to an expensive brand of shampoo claiming to work miracles on thin hair.

Gentry read the label skeptically as he stepped into the shower, then with a shrug, poured a generous amount into his palm and lathered his hair as vigorously as he could with his right hand while maneuvering to keep his left arm dry.

Draping a towel around his lean waist once he was all clean, he stood peering into the mirror. "You look like hell, Gentry," he muttered, squirting a dollop of shaving cream into his palm, then smearing it on his face.

The razor was the first thing that gave him pause. It wasn't one of those flimsy pink plastic jobs women used on their legs and underarms, but a real razor, a man's razor, metal with a double blade. Now that he noticed, the signs were everywhere. This was definitely a man's bathroom, but—what man?

Uncomfortable with the discovery, Gentry finished the job in a hurry, nicking himself several times in the process. He stepped out of the bathroom, dismayed to find clean clothes laid out on the bed—jeans, a faded blue shirt and a very skimpy pair of purple underwear—but no sign of Laura.

Gingerly he lifted the purple briefs with one finger as he glared at them. He swore under his breath. What the hell kind of man wore *purple* underwear? If he'd felt uncomfortable with the notion of using another man's razor, he sure as hell didn't relish the idea of wearing another man's underwear.

But as he stood there staring at those briefs, a very disturbing vision began stirring in his head. Long, silky blond hair falling across a naked, masculine chest. Luscious, full lips trailing a hot path down that same bare skin, and soft, lovely hands curling around the waist of those purple underwear and tugging. He shook his head slightly and the image shattered. He dressed quickly, foregoing the bikinis in spite of the fantasy, and stepped from the bedroom into the hallway.

The house was quiet and cool. The kitchen and living areas were wide open spaces of white—white walls, white carpet and tiles, white leather furniture. The result could have been stark and blinding except for the views. In the living room, floor to ceiling windows framed a breathtaking scene of sea and sky, and atrium doors in the dining room opened onto a lushly landscaped terrace and a sparkling aquamarine pool.

After a quick appraisal of the house, including outside exits and ground-level windows, he went in search of Laura. He spotted her from the living room windows. She was sitting on a tiny square of beach, her back bent to some project he couldn't quite discern. He opened the front door and stepped outside, his gaze darting around the landscape, taking in every minute detail.

Sunlight flashed brilliantly off the blue-green water as sea gulls soared and swooped, searching for their morning meal. The smell of the sea carried on the breeze, and across the water, he could see the shimmering green haze of another island.

He let his gaze drift to Laura's silent form. She wore denim shorts rolled up just above the knees and a white cotton blouse tied at the waist. A wide band of golden skin peeked between the two garments. Her long, sleek legs were bent in front of her as she leaned forward and scribbled in the sand with a stick.

He approached her with a fair amount of caution. "Morning."

The long lashes lifted, revealing the green eyes that seemed to have the power to make his heart stop. His eyes lingered on her face, drinking in each perfect feature. Their gazes mingled for a long, tense moment before she looked away.

"You should still be in bed," she said with a coolness in her tone that belied the concern of her words.

He shrugged. "I feel much better today. I want to thank you for everything you did for me last night. I know some of it wasn't pleasant."

She glanced at him then. "I could hardly let you bleed to death."

"Thanks," he said with a twisted, little smile. "Look, as soon as I have a little time to think, make a plan, decide what to do, I'll get out of here. I don't want to bring you any more trouble than I already have."

"I'm not kicking you out, Simon," she said softly. "You could hardly stand on your feet last night. I don't think you're in any position to go rushing off to defend the world right now."

"I'm okay," he said, but the dull throb had started up in his arm again, contradicting his good intentions. Time was when a good, stiff drink was all he needed for a painkiller. *Time was,* he thought grimly. Not anymore. He felt his age this morning and a good ten years besides. Laura's unlined face, her perfect body made him only too aware of the miles—hard miles—between his age and hers.

For the first time, he dropped his gaze from her face and glanced at her handiwork in the sand. She'd traced a huge heart with an arrow sticking through the middle. Inside, she'd written in big block letters: I HATE MEN.

He cleared his throat self-consciously as he sat down beside her. "I'd really like to clear up that little misunderstanding we had last night. I don't blame you for being ticked," he said quickly, noting the warning glint in her eyes. "But you have to understand my position. I'm down here working an assignment, and my first instinct is to distrust everyone. I've been working on this case for three years. I can't let it get away from me now. But you have to know, I didn't fake my feelings when I kissed you. I wanted you."

"But for what reason?" she asked, her tone heavily laced with sarcasm. "The fact still remains that you tried to use me, Simon. You used what I felt for you, to get information—information I didn't even have—and that hurts. It's also very degrading."

"I'm sorry," he said lamely, at a loss for what to say. There was a look in her eyes that made him feel about as low as an earthworm. "I never meant to hurt you."

"Men never do," she said quietly. "Even though my ex-fiancé slept with my maid of honor the night before our wedding, he never meant to hurt me, either."

Gentry gaped at her in astonishment. "What?"

"Oh, yes. Clark has some pretty lofty political ambitions, you see, and he saw a way to ingratiate himself with Senator Jake MacKenzie through me. He never really loved me. So you see, I'm quite accustomed to users."

She threw down her stick and hugged her arms around her knees, looking for all the world like a lost little girl in a great big department store.

"How did you get hooked up with him in the first place?" Gentry asked bluntly.

"My mother met him at a political fund-raiser last winter, and she introduced us. He was young and handsome and ambitious—he seemed to represent everything I thought I was supposed to want." She lifted one shoulder without looking up, seemingly absorbed with the tiny pockets of sand she'd dislodged with the stick. "I thought marriage was the right thing to do, the right thing to want. I thought... I thought I wouldn't be lonely anymore..." Her voice trailed off to a whisper.

Something twisted inside Gentry's gut at the bewildered look in her eyes, the sad wistfulness.

He took a long breath. "Were you in love with him?"

"I guess I thought I was, but now..."

"Now?"

Her gaze lifted, and Gentry found himself lost in the shimmering green depths of her eyes. "I don't know. I guess some part of me saw Clark as a substitute for this image I had of the perfect man. And he saw me as some sort of... possession, someone who served his purpose."

"What about Jake MacKenzie?" Gentry asked quietly. "Is he your idea of the perfect man?"

"If you'd asked me that before last night, I might have said yes."

"What happened last night?"

She glanced away. "He asked me to marry him."

Jesus. "And what did you say?"

"I said no. When I took a longer look, I discovered he wasn't so perfect after all. At least, not the way I always thought he was." She sighed deeply. "So now you know my secret. I'm a total failure when it comes to relationships. I'm starting to wonder," she mused softly, almost abstractly, "if I don't subconsciously set myself up for failure."

Something echoed inside Gentry, deep down, in a place he'd forgotten existed. A place that might well have been his heart, or maybe even his soul—if he thought he still had one. "I can't say I've done too well in the relationship department myself."

"Are you talking about the woman you told me about last night? The witness in the relocation program?"

Her eyes probed his face with keen perception, making him realize she saw a good deal more than he would have liked. His gaze faltered, then swept toward the ocean.

He sat quietly for a moment, staring at the liquid horizon. Laura found, quite to her own amazement, that she was actually holding her breath, waiting for his response. It mattered rather a lot, she discovered, what he still might feel—or not feel—for that woman.

"I don't know," he finally said, his voice tense, strong fingers plowing restlessly through his hair. "I guess I might have thought I was in love with her at one time. At least...I cared for her a great deal."

Laura's own gaze drifted toward the ocean. Her arms tightened around her knees. "What happened?"

"She was married. Still is. But even when she had no recall of her husband, she was never interested in me. She relied on me, trusted me—" He broke off for a moment, shrugging his shoulders. "When he showed up, she still didn't remember him, but she left with him and didn't look back twice. He was a very important man with an impressive career. He gave it all up—everything—for her."

Absently Laura picked up the stick and resumed scribbling in the sand. "I've often wondered if love like that really exists."

"For some people, I guess it does."

Their eyes met briefly, and he shrugged again, but not before Laura had seen the longing—like a sharp, stab of lightning—flash through his eyes.

"I think I've always tried to play it too safe," she admitted. "I've always deliberately sought out men who I knew would appeal to my mother, but who I knew I could never really fall in love with. When you're not in love with someone, you don't care as much what they think of you. You don't worry about disappointing." She paused, biting her lip in embarrassment.

"I can't imagine you'd ever disappoint anyone." He shouldn't have said it. The moment the words were uttered,

he wished he could take them back. Not because he didn't
mean them. God knows he did—she was everything a man
could want—but the little flicker of gratitude in her eyes
made him realize that she could easily come to expect too
much from him.

She was hurt, she was lonely and he was available. That
was the only possible explanation for her attraction to him.
He'd been around the bend more times than he cared to remember, and she was young and fresh, with her whole life
ahead of her. The last thing she needed to do was get tangled up with a man who could never give her what she
wanted, what she needed.

No matter how much he wanted to take away that lost
look in her eyes, the best thing he could do for the both of
them was to keep his big mouth shut.

Her eyes were shimmering as she looked up at him. "Why
is it I always feel the compulsion to bare my soul to you,
Simon?"

"I don't know," he said, his smile tense. "Maybe it's because you're not in love with me."

The silence hung heavy between them. Each of them had
shared something with the other that might have best been
left private. But last night had forced an intimacy between
them, an intimacy Laura wasn't sure either of them wanted.
She was still hurting from Clark's betrayal, regardless of
whether she'd loved him or not.

That relationship was one more failure chalked up on her
slate, and she certainly wasn't ready to risk another. Rushing into a relationship on the rebound was doomed to begin
with, especially with a man who, by his very profession,
could never be completely honest with her.

But Simon Hunter, whoever he was, had shown her exactly what it was she had been searching for all these years.
Laura had been alone most of her life, but solitude had
never bothered her. She had been lonelier in crowds, with
friends, then she ever was by herself. But sitting here with
Simon, she could already feel the ache of a loneliness far

greater than any she had ever known because it was loneliness not for something, but for *someone.* To think about the time when he would walk out of her life left her feeling empty and lost, as if losing her best friend.

"What are you going to do?" she asked softly.

He shrugged as he continued to regard the water. "At some point, I'll need to contact the other agents involved in this case, let them know what happened. If my cover was blown, the whole operation could be in jeopardy."

"I thought you said you couldn't trust any of them now."

"I can't. But I can't sit around and take a chance that they may walk blindly into a trap, either. I'll have to warn them."

"Even though *you* may be walking into a trap?" she asked perceptively.

"I'll be careful." He added hesitantly, "There's one more thing I need to ask you. What exactly did you tell Mac-Kenzie last night?"

She frowned as she turned to stare at him. "I told him I'd decided to leave early because I was upset over our... conversation. I told him I had to get away to think."

"You told him to trust you, you wouldn't let him down."

"I was referring to the auction Saturday night. I reassured him I'd be back for it." She paused, giving him a piercing stare. "What did you think I meant?" When he didn't answer, she said slowly, "Why are you asking me all these questions about Jake? You can't suspect he's involved in any of this?"

"My job is to suspect everyone."

His evasiveness was maddening. Laura gave him a frustrated glare. "How can you live like that?"

"It isn't difficult," he said, and she knew there was something deeper being conveyed in those three simple little words. For some reason, Simon didn't *want* to trust.

"You told me once that maybe I trusted too easily," she said softly. "But I think not being able to trust at all is worse, because if you can't trust, how can you ever love?"

"I gave up thinking about love a long time ago."

"Why?" she asked with a ragged edge to her voice. "You have so much to give."

His eyes glittered like chips of ice. "I have nothing to give. I think we both better remember that."

"I don't think you'll let either of us forget it," she said, her smile bitter.

"Laura—"

"Don't," she said wearily. "Don't try to explain. It seems when you and I talk, we merely go around in circles. Let's just forget it, and go have some breakfast."

He smiled, and in so doing, erased at least ten years from his face. "At least we can finally agree on something this morning."

"Whose house is this?" Simon asked as he cut into his omelet with gusto. "And whose clothes am I wearing?" His fork paused in midair. "Not Clark's, I hope."

He made the idea sound so distasteful, Laura couldn't help laughing. "No, I assure you, if I had anything of Clark's—which I don't—it would have long since met the incinerator."

She poured herself a glass of orange juice as she sat across from Simon at the patio table. A soft breeze rippled through the banana trees, the heavy fronds rustling like taffeta. The same breeze gently lifted the bangs across her forehead.

"The house belongs to an old friend of mine," she told him, blotting her mouth with her napkin. "My roommate from college, actually. She and her husband are in Europe for several months, and they agreed to lease the house to me." She paused, sipping her juice as she eyed Simon over the rim of the glass. "I called them the day my wedding was canceled, and I came down that same night. Until a few days ago, I hadn't seen any of my family or friends in over six weeks. I talked to both my mother and Jake on the phone several times, but neither of them know about this place."

She hoped the significance of her statement was not lost on Simon. She was letting him know that, for the moment at least, they were safe. He looked up with a speculative gleam in his gray eyes. "Are you planning on telling anyone about it anytime soon?"

She bit her lip, studying him. "I don't know," she said slowly. "I've only known you a few days, Simon. What you're asking me to believe now is totally inconceivable. I don't even know who you are. Why in the world should I believe you?"

He tossed his napkin aside and rested his forearms on the table, leaning toward her as he returned her study with unwavering regard. The gray eyes intensified as he held her gaze. "Because I have no reason to lie to you. Because I think you have a very fine sense of justice, and you wouldn't want crimes of this magnitude, no matter who the perpetrator, to go unpunished."

"You don't know anything about me."

Simon slid his hand across the table to grasp hers. "I know you better than you think I do, Laura. If there wasn't some small part of you that believed me, you wouldn't still be here."

"I don't know what to believe anymore," she admitted bleakly. "Someone tried to kill you last night. If you know who it was, I think I have a right to know."

He shook his head regretfully. "I can't tell you that now."

"I don't see why not. If it was someone at the gallery, then I could help you find him. I might be able to—"

"Get yourself killed," he cut in harshly. "Don't you understand? This isn't some fantasy you've dreamed up for *Vicki Love.* This is for real, Laura. And these people play rough. People die all the time—innocent people who happen to be at the wrong place at the wrong time with the wrong person. I won't be responsible for your getting hurt . . . killed. I *can't.*"

"You don't have to be responsible for me. I thought I'd proven to you last night that I can take care of myself," she said in a wounded voice. "I got the better of you, leastways."

"Congratulations," he said derisively, offering her a mock salute. "I wouldn't hold my breath until someone pins a medal on you for that."

She stared at him for a long, angry moment before she shrugged, seemingly accepting what he'd said. She rose and began stacking the dishes onto a bamboo tray. She could feel his measuring gaze on her as she bent over the table to retrieve his plate.

His hand reached out and stilled her movements. His voice softened. "I don't want to drag you into this any more than I already have. Your life could be in danger now. It's imperative you tell no one, I mean *no one,* that I've been here. Not even after I'm gone."

"Gone?" Her fingers, enclosed in his hand, trembled.

"I still have a job to do."

"But you were almost killed," she argued desperately. "You said yourself, someone in your own ranks betrayed you. You can't go back there."

"Did you think I could stay here indefinitely?" he asked softly.

"I thought—" She bit her lip, trying to stop the quivering.

Their gazes met and held as Simon slowly brought her fingers to his lips, as if sensing her need. There was a look in his eyes, a darkness that seemed to be whispering, *I know this is wrong, I know I shouldn't be doing this, but I can't help myself.* And Laura knew her own gaze was answering him, pleading with him, *It's not wrong. I've never felt anything so right.*

"Simon—" Her voice was ragged, needy, almost desperate with intensity.

She closed her eyes as a wave of heat—which had very little to do with the Florida sun—washed over her. Simon's hand swept up her arm, caressing the inside of her elbow. His arm went around her waist, and he pulled her down until she was lying across his lap, her head cradled against his shoulder.

"What are you doing?" she asked breathlessly.

"I haven't thanked you properly for saving my life last night."

She tried to get up, but he held her.

"I don't want to hurt your arm," she protested, pulling away so that she could see his face.

The moment their gazes locked again, all her struggles ceased. It was as if the world had come to a complete standstill for that one split second that she looked deep into his eyes, and their souls finally touched. He lowered his head, and his mouth took hers.

She didn't even pretend resistance. Driven by the urgency of the moment, she let herself go, putting the very essence that was her—not Vicki this time—into that kiss. Her hand slid along his face, tracing his jawline, then plunged into his hair as she pulled him closer.

And Simon responded to her every move. Oh, how he responded! His tongue penetrated with bold insistence as his hand deftly untied the tail of her blouse, then slipped inside, feathering across her skin until she shivered deliciously.

Her skin was like warm satin, Gentry thought in amazement, his hand riding the tiny contours of her waist, then upward, his thumb barely grazing the underside of her breast. His fingers probed higher, closing over her lace-covered fullness, and Laura gasped, breaking the long kiss to bury her face in his neck. Her body tensed as he continued to stroke her, but she made no attempt to stop him. He wasn't sure he *could* stop—until he felt the warm moisture of her tears against his neck.

The movement of his hand instantly halted. He sat for a moment, holding her, before he tentatively touched her face. "What is it?" he whispered, his lips moving in her hair. "Did I hurt you?"

She shook her head, pulling away from him as she sat up and wiped the back of her hand across first one cheek then the other. "Oh, Simon, this is terrible. Your arm's hurt and you're leaving and your life's in danger and I'll probably never see you again and... Oh, God...I think I'm really falling in love with you and I don't even know your name."

There was a stunned silence, then his words came out in a rush. "You're not in love with me." He stood abruptly, almost dumping her onto the patio. "You can't be in love with me."

"That's what I keep telling myself," she said miserably, struggling to regain her balance. "But my heart seems to have a mind of its own. I'm sorry."

He ran his fingers through his hair, looked at her incredulously, then glanced away. Finally his gaze met hers again as he took both of her hands in his and drew her down until they were sitting face-to-face. "Look...I'll admit there's a rather...extraordinary chemistry between us. You're the most beautiful woman I've ever known, and I do want you. I mean, I *really* want you. And for some strange reason, you seem to be attracted to me, as well. What I think this is— what we're both feeling—is a very deep lust."

Laura shook her head slightly as her eyes probed his. "I've been attracted to other men before, Simon. That's not it."

"Well, it can't be love," he insisted. "It's the situation you're reacting to. Danger and deception are very powerful aphrodisiacs."

She jerked her hands from his and jumped to her feet, glaring down at him. "Damn you. How dare you make it sound so casual, so...ordinary. You don't know what I'm feeling. I *do*. I tried to be honest with you, but obviously that's a concept *you* can't understand."

"For God's sake, Laura, be reasonable about this," he said in exasperation, spreading his hands in appeal. "Look at you—you're young and beautiful and talented—you have your whole life ahead of you. In case you haven't noticed, honey, I'm starting on the downhill slide."

"Oh, for pity's sake, give me a break," she said disparagingly. "You're the most vital, virile man I've ever known.

You use your age as an excuse like you use everything else so you never have to get involved, never have to get close, never have to take the chance of falling in love.''

"It's not an excuse, it's reality," he said through gritted teeth. "And that's a concept *you* seem to have difficulty accepting. You treat all this as some big romantic adventure, but that's not the way it is, Laura. You could have been killed last night, *because of me.* Can't you understand how that makes me feel?''

He tried to take her hand again, but she flung his aside. "I understand only too well. Tell me the real reason you're rejecting me, Simon. It's because of her, isn't it?''

"Her?" The accusation caught him off guard. He stared at her blankly, wondering how she knew, how she'd found out—

"Don't pretend you don't know who I'm talking about," she said coldly. "The woman you told me about last night. Your witness who lost her memory. She's the real reason you don't want to have anything to do with me, isn't she?''

He hesitated only a moment before answering her, but it was a moment too long. Laura whirled away from him and started toward the door. He caught her arm, and swung her back around. Their gazes met and clashed for a long, heated moment.

Gentry sighed wearily. "She's part of it," he admitted reluctantly. *But there's more,* he thought, so much more that he wasn't telling her, that he *couldn't* tell her, because then he'd have to think about it, see the images in his mind once again, relive the pain and anguish and guilt he'd buried a long time ago. He couldn't do that. Not even for her would he do that. Instead, he repeated lamely, "She's part of it, but not the way you think. I can't let anything interfere with this case. I'm so close, I can almost taste it. I don't want to hurt you, but right now, I have a job to do—and I won't let anything, or anyone, stop me from doing it.''

"Or anyone," she repeated bitterly. "Not even me." It wasn't a question, because she already knew the answer. "It sounds to me like you've already let something get in your way. Your own stupid pride. This sounds like some sort of vendetta to me."

"You're wrong," he said coldly, his eyes frosting over. "This isn't personal. This is justice."

"It's that simple for you. Black and white, no in-between, just right and wrong."

A muscle in his jaw tightened. "Yes."

It was his drive, his single-minded devotion that probably made him a good agent. And he was a good agent. Her instincts told her that. But if he was that pledged to his career, to "always getting his man," then she would be a fool to think there could ever be room in his life for her.

"Well, I wish you and your sense of *justice* the best," she said calmly as she turned once more and walked into the house.

She always fell in love with her heroes.

That was the only possible explanation for this obsession she seemed to have for Simon Hunter. She'd let herself feel what Vicki would feel, let herself think what Vicki would think. And in the process, Laura had somehow fallen in love.

As she stared down at her cartoon heroine on the half finished storyboard, Laura was reminded only too vividly of how much they looked alike, but how little they *were* alike.

Was that why Simon had been attracted to her? she wondered. Because she'd pretended to be Vicki? Men liked bold, confident, beautiful women, and Laura Valentine wasn't any of those things. Oh, outwardly she knew she was physically attractive, but that wasn't enough, not nearly enough for a man like Simon.

Even now the memory of the way he'd held her, kissed her, filled her with a shivery anticipation and a tingling excitement of what it could be like if he made love to her. The fluttering in her stomach, the thumping of her heart made her feel like a kid with her first big crush . . . only, this was more than a crush, and she knew it.

The way he looked at her at times, the way he touched her, made her burn in a way she'd never even imagined. She cursed her limited experience because her imagination couldn't supply her with all the details she wanted, all the things she needed to know.

If they made love, would he be disappointed with her in-experience, her lack of expertise?

She shook her head slightly, realizing the full impact of what she was thinking. Just six weeks ago, when she'd called off her wedding, she'd sworn she would never get involved with another man. Reason told her it was too soon and she was too vulnerable. And she could easily buy that, except for one thing—she hadn't been in love with Clark. Deep down, she'd always known marriage to him would be a mistake. What she was feeling now for Simon had absolutely nothing to do with her breakup with Clark.

She'd never met anyone like him, never been with anyone who made her feel so whole, so wanted. It was as if she'd been waiting all her life for him, but now that he'd finally come along, was she supposed to ignore her feelings because the timing wasn't perfect?

That's what *he* wanted her to do. He wanted them both to ignore the attraction between them. And maybe that was the smart thing to do, the right thing to do. Maybe that's exactly what Vicki would do.

But it wasn't what Laura would do.

He knew he'd hurt her feelings.

Gentry stood looking out the living room window, his expression bleak. But what else could he do? There was no future for them, no chance they could ever be together. The danger and excitement of the previous evening had stirred her senses, made her think she was falling in love with him. Under the circumstances, it wasn't unusual to let one's emotions get out of hand.

It wasn't unusual, but it would be damned foolish.

He let his gaze travel down the hall, stopping at the closed door to her bedroom. She'd been in there all afternoon, avoiding him, and he could hardly blame her. He hadn't handled the situation at all well this morning, but, *damn,* she'd taken him completely by surprise.

I think I'm really falling in love with you. In spite of himself, he couldn't help feeling a tiny little thrill of pride, of wonder that a woman like her could fall—or think she had—for him. Sure, it was more than her outer beauty that attracted him, but a man, especially one who'd hit forty with a vengeance, couldn't help being flattered by the interest of someone as beautiful as Laura Valentine.

But when he held her, when he kissed her, it was more than just the physical attraction he felt. Oh, the sexual desire was there all right. No question about that. But with her in his arms, he felt an almost overwhelming sense of completeness, of fulfillment, as though something had been missing from his life he hadn't even been aware of.

And she could be his. At least for a little while. He knew that instinctively. All he had to do was walk down the hall, walk in that door and take her in his arms.

But what then? What price would they both pay when he walked back out again? Because sooner or later, that's exactly what he would have to do.

Walk out of her life and never look back.

"Are you sure the girl's not involved? It sounds mighty suspicious to me."

"She's not involved, Sam. Take my word for it." Gentry shifted the receiver to his other ear as he reclined against the kitchen counter, casting an uneasy glance toward the hallway. He couldn't see Laura's bedroom door, but he knew it was closed. She'd been sequestered inside for hours, ever since their argument that morning. He shrugged, as though trying to dismiss the image of her disillusionment as he said,

"We've got a hell of a lot more to worry about than Laura Valentine. Have you heard from Greenwood?"

"He's made contact. He wants to see you. The message said it was urgent."

Gentry took a sip of the reheated coffee, then grimaced at the bitterness. "When and where?"

"There's a vacant house at the end of Whitehead Street across from the park. We've used it before. I'll get word for him to be there at midnight tomorrow. Meanwhile, I want you to lay low, let me assess the damage in Key West. I want you to call back tomorrow and check in. And, Gentry—"

"Yeah, Sam, I'll watch my back."

Gentry hung up the phone, then turned, suddenly aware that he was no longer alone in the room. Laura stood in the hallway entrance, arms folded across her chest as she stood staring at him.

"Where have you been all day?" he asked carefully, watching her with wary regard as she crossed the room toward him.

"I've been working," she said, still unsmiling. "Apparently so have you."

He poured the remainder of the coffee down the sink and rinsed his cup. He'd been relieved to discover the cabinets and refrigerator were well-stocked, eliminating the necessity for an immediate trip to the store. Also, his little recon mission that afternoon had assured him that they were fairly isolated. The house was at the end of a road, and the nearest neighbor was a quarter of a mile away. They could hole up here for days, Gentry thought, annoyed at how very appealing he found that idea. He forced his movements to remain calm and controlled as he said over his shoulder, "I've talked to my superior. I'll be making contact tomorrow night with another agent. Until then, I think it would be best if I found another place to stay."

She shrugged, as though it didn't matter to her one way or the other. "Where would you go, Simon? You shouldn't even be on your feet. You lost quite a bit of blood last night.'' Her eyes lit on the bottle of aspirin on the counter behind him. With a tiny catch in her voice, she asked, ''Does your arm hurt?''

''Not much.'' But it was a lie and they both knew it. His arm hurt, his head throbbed and his eye was still bruised. He looked like hell, and felt it, but he shrugged anyway. ''Look, I've had worse than this. You don't need to feel sorry for me.''

Her gaze flew to meet his. ''I don't feel sorry for you. I'm sorry you got hurt, but I don't feel sorry for you. Is that what you think?''

''I think we've both been thrown into a situation in which we have to be very careful how we react to it. And to one another,'' he added slowly, his gaze shifting away from hers. ''I meant what I said this morning, Laura. I still have a job to do, and I intend to do it.''

''At any cost.''

''Yes.'' But the price was far higher than he would ever have imagined. Dear God, what would she say when she found out the truth about the man he sought? What would she do when she learned the extent to which he'd used her and why? Would she still want him then?

Staring at her now, so beautiful and proud and strong, the urge to forget about the days ahead of him had never been stronger. He needed her, he thought, with an ache that grew stronger and more urgent by the second. And knowing he couldn't have her, didn't dare have her, his soul had never felt more bleak, his life never more barren.

Not since Caroline's death had his arms felt so empty.

Chapter 9

Sometime around midnight Gentry abandoned all hope of sleep. His arm throbbed, his head pounded, and to make matters worse, there was an ache, an almost physical pain, in the lower part of his body that no amount of aspirin or bourbon would make go away.

As if to undermine his resolve, earlier he'd found a half empty cigarette pack in the nightstand that someone had left behind. The red-and-white package sat on top of the bureau now, just out of reach but drawing his gaze time and again. Swearing under his breath, he got up and pulled on his borrowed jeans, tucking his gun into the waistband as he grabbed the cigarettes, opened the bedroom door and slipped out.

The hallway was dark and shadowy. As he passed Laura's closed door, Gentry paused for a moment, listening for signs of her own restlessness, but all was quiet.

He walked on, resisting the almost overwhelming urge to open her door, to watch her while she slept, to drink in every last detail about her so that he could store it away and have it for the long, lonely nights ahead of him. But somehow he knew that memories of her would never be enough.

He turned on the light in the kitchen just long enough to locate a book of matches and pour himself a stiff drink from the bottle of Ezra Brooks he found in the cabinet. Then he turned off the light and slipped quietly outside.

Moonlight on the pool shimmered like liquid silver. The breeze had died with the twilight, and the night was still and warm, with a kind of waiting tenseness that mirrored his own restlessness. He sat down in one of the lounge chairs facing the pool, lit his cigarette and blew a perfect smoke ring toward the glittering stars in the night sky.

"I didn't know you smoked."

The soft voice, so unexpected, startled him. His gun whipped out before her presence registered with him. She laughed softly in the darkness. "Your reflexes are impressive, Simon."

She got up from her place in the shadows and drifted toward him, a golden-haired mist in the darkness. She sat down in the chair next to his, and Gentry's heart tripped back into place as he laid his gun on the table next to his drink. "Didn't anyone ever warn you about sneaking up on a man with a gun?" he asked grimly.

"I didn't know you were carrying your gun."

"I always carry my gun. Except when someone relieves me of it," he said pointedly, but his tone held the faintest trace of amusement.

She laughed again. "How many times has that ever happened before?"

"None. You should be proud."

"Why? Because you're the best?"

Their eyes met in the moonlight. "No. Because I'm always careful."

"So I've noticed," she said with a tiny sigh as she lifted her face to the sky. "Look, there's Orion, the Hunter. I'll bet you feel a certain kinship with him, don't you?"

"Sounds a little too poetic for me. I just do my job."

"I understand," she said very quietly.

"Do you?"

Her teeth tugged on her bottom lip for just a split second of indecision. "Yes," she whispered. "I believe I do."

Though he made no move to touch her, there was still the physical awareness, the deep wanting that was almost a tangible presence, between them. Gentry smoked his cigarette, sipped his drink and wondered how in the hell he'd ever gotten so involved with a woman so quickly, a woman he'd lied to, used and might very well have to use again, if it meant protecting the nation's security.

She was just about the age Caroline had been when she'd died, he reflected. Just about the age *he'd* been, when he stopped living. He could look in her face and see the lost years of his youth, almost believe that through her he could recapture them.

But there was no going back, no way of finding what he'd lost. The years had marched relentlessly onward. He'd lived his life, day by day, trying to forget the past, trying not to think about the future, only of the present.

But with Laura, it was almost as though he were being handed those years again. As though he were being given a second chance. And if he were being given a second chance at love, there might also be a chance it could all be taken away again.

And this time, he might not be able to save himself.

"When I was a little girl," she said very quietly, "I used to study the stars. I knew every constellation by heart. I fancied I could find my way home from anywhere in the world, just by following the stars. Except that I knew when I got there, there was a good chance it wouldn't be my home anymore." She laughed softly, but there was a tinge of sadness to her laughter. That sadness in her tugged at Gentry's resolve, threatened him in a way his physical desire for her could not.

He ground out his cigarette in a green metal ashtray on the table and shoved it aside. "How many times was your mother married?"

"Six or seven, I think. I lost count."

"Did you mind?"

One slender shoulder lifted. "When I was little I did because she was always too busy trying to impress her new husband or future husband to spend time with me. Later, when I was older, I was glad for her to have the diversions. Mother could be very wearing on one's self-esteem."

"She criticized you?"

Laura grimaced. "Endlessly. She wanted me to be perfect, and I could never measure up, no matter how hard I tried. I was too fat, too thin, too tall, too short. She was...relentless."

Gentry listened silently, his gaze trained on the stars. He heard the slight tremor in her voice, and knew that, deep down, she still hurt from her mother's rejections. He ached to comfort the lonely little girl she had been, wanted to hold the woman she'd become.

In a voice that was harsh with suppressed anger, he said, "Maybe she was jealous of you, threatened by you. Some women are like that, even mothers."

"Oh, I doubt that," she said softly. "Mother is a beautiful woman. She just can't stand imperfection. I remember once, when I was about sixteen or seventeen, my swim coach put me on a weight-training program to build up my arms and shoulders. When Mother saw me after a few weeks, she told me in no uncertain terms that I was getting fat and ugly, and if I wasn't careful, I'd end up looking exactly like my father's mother, whom I knew she couldn't stand.

"Even though I loved it, excelled at it, I quit swimming the very next day because she wanted me to. For about two years after that, I suffered from an eating disorder I developed, trying to get as thin as I thought she wanted me to be." Her voice faltered, then she said, "I've always been so ashamed of that time in my life, ashamed of having that weakness. I've never told anyone about it before."

"It's not a weakness to want your mother to love and support you," Gentry said softly. "And it's not your fault she didn't. Some people are incapable of love."

"Rationally, I know that. But it's still hard to accept even after all these years. From the time I was old enough to consciously be aware of feelings and emotions, I knew she didn't love me, didn't want me. I've often wondered what might have happened in her life to make her so cold, so loveless. I don't think a person is born that way."

"No. Usually there's a catalyst," Gentry agreed grimly.

He found himself wanting to tell her about his own past, about his own life, to explain to her why *he* could no longer love.

Maybe he was making too much of this, he decided. Maybe a night spent together was all either of them really wanted. Maybe they didn't need a happily ever after.

He smiled bitterly. Maybe he didn't, but she did. She wanted and needed what he'd once had but was no longer capable of giving. All the rationalizations in the world wouldn't change that fact. He had absolutely no justification for taking her to bed, for making love to her simply because his control seemed to be slipping away. In the end, all he could do was hurt her.

Abruptly he stood, and picked up his gun from the table. "It's late. We'd better try to get some sleep."

"You go ahead, Simon," she said absently. "I want to stay out here and watch the stars for a while."

"Are you okay?"

She smiled up at him, her features misty in the moonlight. "I'm fine. I'm sorry I unburdened myself to you again. It's becoming a habit, I'm afraid."

A habit he could all too easily get used to. "For whatever it's worth, I hope you find it someday," he said softly.

She looked up in surprise. "What?"

"Home. I hope you find your way home."

She must have dozed off shortly after Simon went inside. When she woke up, the wind had picked up. It blew across the terrace in moist gusts, swinging the hanging baskets of fern and bougainvillea and tinkling through a set of wind chimes made from seashells. The aquamarine surface of the pool rippled with silver.

She was cold, Laura discovered, as she lay huddled on the lounge. Cold and stiff. She got up and stretched, trying to relieve the kinks in her neck and shoulders.

A bank of low-lying clouds obscured the stars, and the moon looked hazy and indistinct. A storm was coming, she thought, feeling a slight thrill of exhilaration at the prospect. She loved the wind, loved the feel of it through her hair, on her face, across her skin. It made her feel free, unencumbered, as though it could blow away all her fears and insecurities.

She wished Simon hadn't gone in. She wished he were here with her now, so they could experience the storm together. With a sigh of regret, she turned and went inside, closing the door to the coming rain.

The house was dark except for a thin sliver of light coming from Simon's door, which stood slightly ajar. Laura paused, wondering if the light meant he was still up, if something was wrong. She knocked softly and pushed open the door. "Simon?"

The rumpled bed was empty. Laura stepped inside the doorway, her eyes going immediately to the open bathroom door. The light blazed from inside. "Simon?"

"In here."

His voice was low and edged with pain. Laura's breath caught in her throat. Quickly she stepped to the bathroom door, and then gasped.

Clad only in jeans that were unfastened at the waist, Simon was sitting on the edge of the tub, his face as white as the porcelain. Blood dripped from his arm and splattered against the pristine surface, like red paint carelessly splashed onto canvas. Laura gasped again, then crossed the room and sank to her knees beside him.

"My God, what happened?"

"It was stupid," he said with a disgusted grimace. "I got up to get a drink of water and didn't turn on the light. I ran into the door and opened my arm up again."

"How long have you been in here?"

"It just happened. It was a stupid thing to do," he muttered again.

"Here, let me help you," she said briskly. Where last night she had been hesitant, this time Laura took charge without a second thought. She got to her feet and grabbed a clean, white towel from the rack by the sink, folded it and pressed it firmly against Simon's arm.

While she knelt beside him, applying pressure, she glanced up, meeting his gaze. His lips were thin and drawn with pain, but his eyes watched her steadily with a brooding intensity that took her breath away. Suddenly the bathroom seemed unbearably small.

This close, she could smell the lingering scent of soap from his shower and bourbon from his drink, a strangely masculine mixture that made Laura feel slightly lightheaded. Or maybe it was just the sight of blood, she told herself firmly.

Whatever the reason, for the first time that night, she became overly conscious of the white silk nightshirt she wore. Outside the shadows had hidden her, but in the glare of light in the bathroom, every curve, every tiny crevice was revealed for Simon's inspection. Warmth stole through her as her breasts tightened beneath his gaze. The paper-thin silk erotically defined her taut nipples, clearly proclaimed her awareness.

This is ridiculous, she scolded herself. *He's bleeding, he's in pain, and you're sitting here thinking about how wonderful he looks without a shirt on!*

He did look wonderful, though. Her gaze greedily traveled over the naked skin of his shoulders and arms, his chest and stomach, following the thin sprinkling of light brown hair as it arrowed toward the open waistband of his jeans. Her heart skipped a beat as her memory supplied her with more details.

She must have tightened the pressure on Simon's arm because he winced, drawing her gaze back to his.

"I'm sorry," she said stiffly, her face blushing bright red. "I . . . lost my concentration for a moment."

"That's okay." His gray eyes were slightly reproachful. "I'm hardly in a position to complain right now. Look, I think the bleeding's almost stopped. I can finish up in here. You go on back to bed."

His words were slightly rushed, as though he were trying to get rid of her, as though he were feeling the same rampaging emotions she was feeling. A tense silence filled the room as she continued kneeling beside him. She moved slightly, grazing the side of his muscular thigh, and he gasped slightly, a sound that seemed to startle them both. Their glances locked, and something flashed in the gray depths of his eyes, a flicker of heat he quickly tried to conceal.

Laura tried to pretend she didn't see the sudden blossoming beneath the opening of his jeans, tried to ignore the loud thumping of her pulse in her ears.

"Go back to bed, Laura," he said hoarsely.

"I haven't been to bed yet," she whispered. Then, as if being freed from an imprisoning spell, she said, "Let me at least finish what I started. Here, hold the towel while I get a fresh bandage." When his hand pressed against hers, she slipped hers out. Then, she stood, retrieving the first-aid kit from under the sink, ever aware of Simon's hooded gaze following her every move. She sat beside him on the edge of the tub as she cleaned away the last of the blood. The muscles in his arm tensed slightly as she stroked around the wound.

"Looks pretty clean," she commented, giving the wound a thorough examination before she began to bandage it. If she concentrated on the task at hand, Laura decided, she could ignore the fact that they were sitting together half-naked. If she concentrated hard enough, she could ignore the fact that her knees were brushing against the side of Simon's thigh, the fact that the pulse in his throat seemed to be beating as erratically as her own, the fact that her fingers were trembling so badly, she could hardly hold the bandage in place. If she concentrated hard enough, she could ignore Simon altogether.

A trickle of sweat coursed down her spine as she bent back to her task, biting her lip in an attempt to let the pain drive away the other sensations. Her fingers busy with the bandage, she tried to blow back a lock of hair that fell across her face. Instantly Simon's hand reached up and smoothed it back with surprising gentleness. His fingertips traced along her brow, downward, following the line of her jaw and chin as though memorizing every soft curve.

Laura's stomach quivered with a strange fluttery sensation. She couldn't speak, couldn't breathe, didn't dare look at Simon as she finished pressing the adhesive into place. Only when his hand moved away did she lift her gaze to his. Her breath caught in her throat.

He stared at her with eyes that weren't just hungry, but ravenous, starving, the eyes of a man who paid dearly for his stoicism. But when he bent and touched his lips to hers, it was a kiss as tender and light as an ocean breeze.

He drew back as if to assess her reaction, but Laura's hands reached up and cradled his face. "Again," she whispered desperately.

Gentry closed his eyes, trying to gather his willpower, but found he had none left. Slowly he lowered his head. His lips moved like a whisper over hers, then drew back for a heart-pounding second as he once again found himself fighting a losing battle. With a muttered, "Oh, hell," his mouth crushed hers as his control blew into a million pieces that scattered into the night.

Their arms found each other at the same time, and almost as though their minds had also fused, they slipped from the edge of the tub and knelt facing one another on the thick, white rug. The throb in Gentry's arm was ignored for a lower, more urgent throb elsewhere. He kissed her with a reckless abandon that was astounding, frightening, but he didn't pull away. Instead, he pressed closer, harder, letting the intense sensations drive away the remnants of his resolve.

Laura's own response was far from astonishing because she'd known, somehow, it would be like this, that her ultimate surrender wouldn't be a conscious choice but an all-consuming need for him. With one hand behind his head, she drew him closer, opening her lips for a deeper, more demanding kiss.

They tumbled sideways, letting the thick bathroom rug absorb the shock of their fall. Arms and legs entwined, they lay facing each other, indulging in long, soul-shattering kisses.

His hands raced over her, following a seductive course from the back of her neck, down her spine, over her hips and then back up again, leaving Laura tingling in every place he touched. He stroked her hair while his lips touched her eyelids, her nose, her chin, planting tiny pinpoints of heat all over her face. Her pulse hammered in her ears, her heart thrashed against her chest as he whispered her name against the sensitive skin of her neck.

Dizzied, drowning with sensation, she tilted her head, allowing his lips the freedom to wander at will. He shifted his weight so that all of a sudden she was on her back and he was lying over her. Her body trembled with anticipation as his fingers sought the tiny, silk-covered buttons of her shirt. He groaned, a low, masculine sound against her lips as his fingers parted the silk and slipped inside. His mouth took hers with a savage intensity that stormed through her like a cyclone.

Her restless hands glided over his shoulders, his uninjured arm, the column of his back. She couldn't touch him
enough, couldn't seem to satisfy her need to feel every part
of him. She kissed him back with a need that reflected the
very deepest, emptiest part of her soul.

"I want you," she said with a sigh. "You make me feel so
wanted, so needed, so perfect."

Her hushed voice rippled through him, driving the heat
deeper and lower until he could think of nothing but how
badly he wanted her. "God, you are perfect," he whispered back. Or at least the closest thing to perfection he'd
ever known.

"Kiss me, Simon." Her breathy demand sent shivers of
delight tripping along his bare skin. "Kiss me like you mean
it."

With a dark murmur of surrender, he lowered his head
and complied. Her lips were parted and waiting, and her
tongue met his in a frenzied dance of desire. She was a
thousand times better than any painkiller, he thought in a
daze. His arm could have fallen off and he would never have
known it because every feeling, every sensation, every single nerve ending in his body seemed to be concentrated in
one crucial spot. He tore his mouth from hers, letting his
lips skim downward, finding the hollow of her neck where
her pulse pounded and raced. He drew back, stunned by the
extent of her excitement.

God, she was so soft and she smelled so delicious and she
looked so beautiful and *you can't do this, Gentry. You can't
do this to her.*

The lies, the deceit, the days ahead of him were like a sly
whisper, an insidious voice warning him to stop before it was
too late. He closed his eyes, trying to will away the conflict-
ing emotions, but he couldn't. Deep down, he knew he
didn't have the right to be with her like this.

Taking an unsteady breath, he pulled away. Laura's eyes
opened, all heavy-lidded and misty as her hand reached to

draw him back. He pulled away even farther, and died a little at the hurt, confused look that crept into her eyes.

"Laura—honey—" He stumbled over the words he knew he had to say because he could see the realization already dawning across her lovely face. "This isn't a good idea."

He sat up and pulled her along with him. Her lips were bruised and swollen from his kisses, her cheeks—already reddened from the stubble of his beard—flamed now with embarrassment. She pulled the nightshirt together in front, then drew her knees up and wrapped her arms around them. She looked utterly forlorn and dejected, and Gentry felt as though someone had just given him a knockout punch in the stomach.

"I don't believe this," she said weakly.

"You don't know anything about me, about who I am and what I've done, Laura. I can't use you like this. It's not right—"

Her head jerked up as a flash of anger blazed in her eyes. "*Use* me? That's all this was to you? A physical release, nothing more?"

He winced. "I'm sorry. That was the wrong choice of words." He paused, struggling to find the right words, but he knew instinctively nothing he could say would make her feel better. To her this had to seem like one more rejection, and it killed him to think he was the one who had made her feel that way.

"Honey—"

"Please don't call me that."

His fingers shoveled through his hair. "Laura, you don't understand. I've . . . done things . . ."

She looked at him with wide, soulful eyes. "You've killed people," she said with a tremulous note in her voice.

His jaw hardened. "Yes, when I had to."

"You've lied. You've used people."

"When I had to."

Her eyes compelled his to meet her gaze. "You're wrong, Simon. I know a lot about you. And it doesn't matter."

His eyes darkened with regret. "Maybe not now. But it will. Believe me, it will matter, a great deal."

Outwardly she didn't react to his words, didn't move a muscle, but he could feel her withdrawal just the same. She took a deep, trembling breath. "You don't want me."

Oh, God, this was too much. He could ignore the passion, could deny his own raging need, but what he could not resist was *her* need. He pulled her to him, cradling her cheek against his shoulder as he held her.

"It's not you," he whispered raggedly. "It's me."

"I don't understand," she said in a small voice that tore at his heart.

"I know you don't. And I can't explain it."

Dear God, not want her! Even now, holding her in his arms, he could feel his body stirring to life again. If she only knew how intensely he wanted her at that moment. He wanted her, God help him he wanted her—but he knew he couldn't have her, didn't dare have her because her safety, her very life, depended on his ability to stay away from her.

Tonight he had weakened. He'd allowed her to get to him in a way no woman had in a long, long time. Maybe ever. With just a kiss, she'd slipped inside his heart, found her way to the places he kept secret, defended. He'd lost control, let down his guard, and he had no one to blame but himself. Her pain and humiliation—not to mention his own aching state of arousal—were all his fault. But it would stop here and now with this one sobering experience. He would do everything in his power to protect her, keep her safe— even from himself.

He held her for a moment longer, but he could feel her resistance, her own inner battle, even though she didn't push him away. It was as if she needed the comfort of his touch, the warmth of his nearness, and for Gentry, that was the most dangerous need of all.

"I'm sorry," he said, touching his lips to her hair one last time.

The sound of his voice seemed to be the catalyst Laura needed to pull herself together. She drew away from him and scrambled to her feet, ignoring the hand he offered to help her up. She couldn't look at him, couldn't stand for him to see how badly he'd hurt her, humiliated her.

"One last thing," she said, her spine stiff as she headed for the door. "Don't you ever, *ever* try to use me like that again. Is that clear?"

"Yes," he said, and his voiced sounded as empty as her heart.

The storm didn't break until morning. Laura stood at the window in the living room, watching the rain buffet the beach as waves pounded the shoreline. Palm trees bent precariously in the wind, and the morning sky deepened to slate with only an eerie yellowish glow on the horizon for relief.

She glanced at her watch, checking the time against the Art Deco clock on the marble mantel. They each showed that a minute and a half had passed since the last time she'd looked. Pushing back a strand of unkempt hair, she gazed back out the window as a streak of lightning cracked the sky over the ocean.

Where the hell was he? It had been hours—just after dawn—when she'd heard the Kellys' Jeep start up in the garage. By the time she'd gotten up, thrown on some clothes and rushed outside, the garage door was closing and the Jeep was already backing onto the road. For just a second the headlights had captured her in their beam as she stood in the rain, watching him drive away with no explanation and no goodbye.

Her first thought was that he'd gone to make contact with another agent, and she'd been glad at first not to have to face him after the humiliating episode earlier. But then, when she'd gone back inside, cold and shivering and drenched to the bone, the house had seemed so quiet, so empty.

She'd ignored the loneliness, though, and let her anger fire her thoughts as she'd showered and dressed. He hadn't even bothered to say goodbye! Well, *good riddance,* her mind railed against him. He'd brought her nothing but trouble from the first moment she'd looked into those stormy gray eyes.

Then, as she'd fixed herself coffee and toast, listening with one ear for the Jeep, her anger had turned more toward revenge. She'd her first plan into motion, she'd decided. She'd use him as the role model for Vicki's hero whether he wanted her to or not, and at least something good, something productive could come of the whole traumatic mess.

But after she'd finished breakfast, rinsed the dishes and made the beds, a little niggling worry began to itch in the back of her mind that maybe he really *wasn't* coming back.

She sat down at the drawing table in the living room, tried to concentrate on the half finished storyboards in front of her, but all she could see was Vicki's perfect features smirking up at her. *Why do you always fall for the wrong man?* her smug smile seemed to suggest.

"Oh, shut up, before I decide to give you fat thighs," Laura threatened, her gaze straying back to the storm outside as she watched lightning dart from cloud to cloud.

The wind was dying away and the rumble of thunder was more distant, but the sky was still bleak and gray. Rain spattered against the windows with annoying repetition, grating on Laura's already jagged patience.

What if he'd had an accident? she thought. What if he'd been hurt again, or set up by the agent he'd gone to meet?

As the minutes crept by the treacherous little images marched across her mind. Visions of Simon lying in a ditch somewhere, unconscious, bleeding, needing her.

He didn't need you this morning, a nagging little voice reminded her.

Don't think about that now, she argued, but she couldn't leave it alone. Why had he turned away from her? Was there someone else in his life? A wife, maybe? Or was it the woman he'd told her about, the witness who had lost her memory?

He'd admitted that he cared for her, but Laura sensed there was something more, something deeper that drove him, made him so obsessed with his job. But what?

The lead in her pencil snapped from the unconscious pressure she applied, and Laura flung it aside, her nerves ragged. Damn him, where was he? He had no right to leave her like this without a word of explanation. He had no right to make her sit here wondering and worrying and waiting. He had no right to make her feel so helpless and useless and unwanted.

And she had no right to expect anything else, she thought bleakly.

Gentry sat in the Jeep in the parking lot of a convenience store right off the Overseas Highway. He watched the rain pound against the windshield as his fingers beat an impatient rhythm against the steering wheel.

Damn, what to do. His first impulse this morning had been to leave and not go back. But somehow he'd been unable to rid himself of the image of Laura standing out in the rain as his headlights touched her for a brief instant. In spite of her height, she'd seemed so small and fragile and vulnerable. That image pecked at his resolve, made him feel low and mean for slinking out the way he had. He at least owed her a proper goodbye after all she'd done for him.

He owed her a lot more than that, he thought grimly. He owed her a full explanation, but that was something he wasn't able to give, not yet anyway.

With a heavy sigh, he opened the door and got out, hunching his shoulders against the downpour as he hurried around the Jeep to the pay phone at the curb. He dialed the familiar number, then listened for the series of clicks and beeps that told him he was being put straight through.

"Atwater," the familiar voice growled into his ear.

Gentry grinned in spite of himself. It was good to hear his boss's voice. "It's Gentry."

"What's that noise?"

"It's raining cats and dogs down here," Gentry said, casting an eye skyward. "I'm standing outside at a pay phone."

There was a pause, then Sam said, "Always careful, aren't you, Gentry? Less chance of a trace. I've talked to Greenwood. The meeting's set for tonight. Can you make it?"

"I'll be there. Listen, Sam, what's the situation in Key West?"

"I'd rather let Greenwood fill you in tonight. There're a lot of ears around here, Gentry."

Gentry scowled into the rain. "That bad?"

"Worse. There's an internal investigation going on concerning our activities in Key West."

"*Our* activities. Jesus, what does it take to get through to these clowns anyway?"

"Proof, Gentry. Solid, concrete proof. Don't make a move until you have it, understood? This is my carcass on the line, right alongside yours."

"That's never bothered you before," Gentry said carefully, sensing an unaccustomed wariness in his old friend. "Just what the hell's going on?"

"Greenwood will fill you in tonight. I've already said too much."

"You haven't said—"

The line clicked in Gentry's ear, leaving him with a dead receiver and a nagging suspicion that Sam had said a helluva lot more than he'd picked up on.

Laura was in the kitchen when she heard the sound of the Jeep pulling into the garage. She set the coffeepot down with a thud and flew across the room, settling down at her drawing board just as the back door opened. When he came into

the room, her head was bent studiously over her storyboard.

"Good morning." There was a tentative note in his voice,
as though he wasn't quite sure of his welcome.

Laura glanced up casually. "Good morning. Have a nice
drive?"

His clothes and hair were soaking wet and he stood across
the room staring at her as though he'd entered the wrong
house. Warily he glanced around, then fastened his gaze
back on hers. "I had to make a phone call."

"The phones are working here," she assured him. "I've
made a few calls myself."

He lifted one brow, but made no comment. "Well, I guess
I'd better get out of these wet things."

"You'll find some dry clothes in the closet in my room.
Take whatever you need."

When he left the room, Laura glanced down at her hands.
They were shaking despite her outward composure. The
moment she saw him, her anger had dissipated like mist in
the morning sun. All she could feel was relief that he was
unhurt, and a sort of shivery excitement in the pit of her
stomach.

In the quiet after the storm, she could hear the muffled
sound of the shower running, was even more aware when it
was turned off. She could imagine him stepping from the
stall, briskly toweling off with quick, masculine efficiency.
Lost to her daydream, she was startled when the object of
her fantasy materialized in the doorway.

Embarrassed, she turned back to her work. Simon crossed
the room to the kitchen, poured himself a cup of coffee and
carried it with him to the window, where he stared with a
brooding frown out into the rain. She wondered what he was
thinking, what had brought on such a fierce scowl. Was it
her?

He looked up, caught her staring and smiled hesitantly.
"What are you working on?"

Was he interested or only being polite? she worried. She shrugged. "It's a new story line for Vicki."

His smile deepened, curving his lips upward in a sexy, enticing way. "You talk about her like she's a real person," he said softly as he walked to the drawing table and glanced over her shoulder.

"Sometimes it almost seems she is," Laura admitted.

"You don't sound too happy about it."

"She's a pretty hard act to follow."

"Oh, I don't know," he said lightly, but when she glanced up, his gaze was dark and pensive. "I think there's a lot of Vicki in you. You're a lot tougher than you think you are. Look how you've handled all this." He made a vague gesture with his hand.

Laura shrugged. "I'm not sure I've handled it very well at all. Vicki would never have—" She broke off, realizing what she'd been about to say. *Vicki would never have fallen in love with a man who wasn't in love with her.* But then Vicki Love was the type of woman men *would* fall in love with. Laura said, almost wistfully, "I've created the perfect woman. Brilliant, beautiful, brave, sexy—"

"Like I said, I think there's a lot of Vicki in you."

But not enough, Laura thought helplessly. *Not nearly enough.*

Almost as though against his will, Simon lifted his hand and touched her hair, smoothed it back from her face.

"You underestimate yourself so needlessly," he whispered, his fingers feathering across her cheek. "Your mother really did a number on you, but you're old enough to know better now. Don't you see what I see when you look in the mirror? Don't you know how beautiful you are? How desirable? How incredibly sexy? Vicki Love is a product of your imagination. You're a real, flesh-and-blood woman, honey. I think it's time you made that distinction. Give yourself a break."

Laura said hesitantly, "For what it's worth, Simon, I think you were right to stop…things this morning. I've been doing a lot of thinking while you were gone, and I'm not sure I'm ready for..." She faltered, groping for the right word.

"For what?"

"An encounter. An interlude. A one-night stand. I don't have much experience with that sort of thing," she admitted. "In spite of what you might think, I'm not anything like Vicki Love."

Simon grinned suddenly, and Laura's heart thudded against her chest. "In case you haven't noticed," he said ironically, "I'm not exactly James Bond."

"You don't understand what I'm trying to say," she said seriously. "I could tell you in about five seconds the name of every lover I've ever had and the times and places and positions in which we did it."

His brows drew together like a thundercloud. "That won't be necessary."

"Don't you see?" she asked a trifle desperately. "I'm not *experienced* in this sort of thing. You did me a favor by pushing me away this morning, by making me see that our being together would be a big mistake. Because what would I do afterward, when you walked away?" Her voice trailed off to a whisper. "Because you'd still walk away, wouldn't you, Simon?"

Comprehension flickered in his dark gaze, followed by regret, and something that looked very much like sadness. But at least he was man enough not to lie to her. She had to give him that.

"Yes," he said in a low, tense voice. "I'd still walk away."

The rain finally stopped in the late afternoon, and the sun broke through in a glorious burst that sent the clouds scurrying. Laura went outside for a walk on the beach, and Gentry prowled the house, restless and impatient for the coming meeting with Greenwood.

Something was wrong. His instincts supplied the details Atwater had left out. Maybe because of Gentry himself, the operation was somehow in danger. MacKenzie could very well be slipping through his fingers again, and there was no way in hell Gentry would allow that to happen. If he had to take the bastard out himself, he'd do it, proof or no proof.

Glancing at his watch in disgust, he realized it was still hours until rendezvous time with Greenwood. The house seemed to be getting smaller, claustrophobic. With a muttered oath, he opened the front door and stepped outside.

He spotted Laura on the deserted beach. Standing on the porch, he watched as she bent and picked something from the sand and rinsed it off in the swirling waters around her ankles. She examined it for a long moment, then stuck it in the pocket of her white shorts before continuing on.

Gentry clambered down the wooden stairs and followed her, calling himself a damn fool with every step he took. *Leave her alone,* his mind ordered, but without hesitation, his legs carried him closer and closer to her silent form.

"What did you find?"

She whirled around, startled by his voice. The wind whipped her hair across her face and she peeled it away, tucking the long, golden strands behind her ears. Her hand went to her pocket. Something flashed in her palm as she extended it toward him.

"It's a Spanish doubloon," he said in surprise.

"My friends find them washed up here all the time, especially after a storm. They think there must be a wreck somewhere around here."

"I wouldn't be surprised. The bottom of the ocean around the Keys is dotted with wrecks of one kind or another."

"Maybe your friend should come and investigate," Laura said, pocketing her treasure.

"My friend?"

"The salvage diver you told me about. Does he still recover wrecks?"

Gentry nudged loose a broken conch shell from the sand with his toe. "Ah, no, I think he's retired from treasure hunting."

"Too bad. I always thought treasure hunting would be a great way to make a living." She picked up a piece of driftwood, examined it, then tossed it back to the sea. Gentry found her amazing. Everything seemed to fascinate her, from the bit of gold in her pocket to the tiniest inconsequential seashell.

"Always seemed a bit risky to me," he said, realizing how staid and old he sounded by comparison to her youth and enthusiasm.

She looked at him in surprise, her green eyes like brilliant gems in the fading sunlight. "Don't you take risks in your job, Simon?"

He shoved his hands in his pockets as he shrugged. "Not as many as you might think. Most of the time, my job is pretty routine. Boring even."

She laughed softly. "Not many people would say that after being shot in the line of duty."

"That was the exception, not the rule," he said with a grimace.

"What made you decide to become an agent, Simon? Did you grow up thinking of yourself as Eliot Ness?" she teased.

"Where I grew up, Eliot Ness wasn't exactly a hero."

She stopped walking and turned to face him, intrigued. "Where did you grow up?"

"In a little town in the backwoods of Tennessee. People around there still called FBI agents 'revenuers.' My grandmother was shocked when I told her I was joining the Bureau. Until the day she died, she insisted to her friends and neighbors that I was a Fuller Brush salesman. That, at least, was a respectable occupation."

Laura smiled. "She sounds like quite a woman."

"That she was. When I was twelve, about the time my sisters were getting all those raging hormones that drive everyone crazy, I decided to go live with Gram. She'd been alone for over forty years, she certainly didn't need a boy with a nose for trouble landing on her doorstep, but she took me in just the same. I never went back home."

"Your parents didn't mind?"

"They didn't live that far away. They saw me all the time. Besides, they had six other kids. One less was probably a relief," he said without resentment. "Living with Gram was probably the best thing that ever happened to me. I didn't know it at the time, but she had a very profound influence on me. She was one of the strongest, bravest people I ever knew, with a deeply instilled sense of justice that was black and white—no shades of gray. She could be tough," he said ironically. "Real tough."

"But you needed that," Laura said with an insight that surprised him.

He grinned. "Yeah, probably."

"So how did you come to join the FBI?" she asked curiously. In wordless agreement, they turned and started back toward the house.

"I was recruited out of law school. I'd lived in a small town all my life, and I guess I was still young enough that the idea of danger and intrigue appealed to me."

"Why did you never marry?"

Silence, and then, "I did."

Laura's footsteps faltered. She gazed up at him in astonishment. She'd just assumed—stupidly, of course, that he was single. Instantly, her gaze darted to his left hand.

Simon saw her glance and said, very quietly, "She died."

The look on his face made her want to cry. In sympathy, yes, but also because now she understood why he didn't want her, why he couldn't love her.

"I'm sorry," she said hoarsely.

He shrugged, but the dark intensity in his expression contradicted the casualness of the move. "It was a long time ago."

"Were you married for very long?" Laura couldn't help asking. Now that she knew part of his history, she felt compelled to learn it all.

"Two years. Look, it's getting late. We'd better head back."

He started toward the house, but Laura caught his arm. He stopped and glanced back, his expression guarded.

"Did you love her very much?"

His shuttered gaze held hers for one suspended moment. "Yes," he said, and then turned and walked away.

Gentry poured the last of the coffee down the drain as Laura gathered the remnants of their hasty meal from the table. Dinner had been tense and quiet, with the earlier conversation still hanging heavy between them. When he'd reluctantly told her about his coming meeting that night, the tension had thickened even more. But he couldn't just leave her—not again—without an explanation.

He glanced at Laura's silent form as she bent to her task. A silky curtain of hair fell across her cheek, and impatiently she shoved it back, a gesture with which he was becoming familiar. She looked up and their gazes collided.

"I want to go with you tonight," she said quietly.

"That's impossible."

"*Why?*" She spread her hands on the table and leaned toward him in silent appeal. "I could be your backup, Simon. I know how to handle a gun. I write about this sort of thing all the time. I've researched—"

"You still don't get it, do you?" His brows drew together as he glared at her. "This is not some neat little plot you've conjured up for *Vicki Love.* You may be like her in a lot of ways, but rushing into a situation you don't know anything about is reckless and dangerous." When she opened her mouth to argue, he cut her off angrily, his teeth clenched. "Listen to me. There is a very good chance that whoever tried to kill me last night knows you were with me. You walk out that door, you place your life on the line. You aren't to leave this house at all. Do you understand? I don't want you going back to Key West until this whole thing is over.''

"When will that be?" she asked, lifting her chin a notch. Her eyes glittered dangerously, a look that made Gentry nervous for some reason.

"Soon," he said as he picked up his gun from the counter and tucked it into the waistband of his jeans. "With any luck, it'll all be over soon.''

Chapter 10

A mosquito zeroed in on Gentry's neck, whining in his ear as he stopped in the feathery shadow of a palm tree and scanned his surroundings in every direction. He could hear the muted sounds of music and laughter one block over on Duval Street, and somewhere in the distance, a dog barked. But it was quiet here. Quiet and calm and very dark, with a warm southerly wind tripping across his face and the moon hanging low in a star-banked sky.

For fifteen minutes Gentry remained cloaked by the shadows as he watched the house at the end of Whitehead Street and waited, but he detected no movement of any kind, except for the breeze whispering through the trees.

At last he himself moved, slowly, deliberately, still with great caution. He drew his gun and started toward the house.

The gate squeaked, sounding very much like a woman's scream in the deadly silence of the yard. The lush canopy of leaves shrouded the thin starlight, throwing the lawn into an eerie, deep purple shade. Slipping from shadow to shadow,

Gentry moved stealthily toward the house, pausing now and then to listen.

A black cat shot across the path in front of him. Gentry jumped, then cursed under his breath as he stepped onto the porch.

His right hand moved to his left arm to swipe away another mosquito. As he looked down, a tiny red beam moved across his arm and toward his heart. The instant he recognized the laser sight, he dived toward cover.

With a loud *thwack,* the bullet buried itself in a tree trunk directly over Gentry's head. With his own pistol brought to bear, he edged back into the shadows, trying to get a fix on the gunman. Crouching, he began circling the yard.

He moved warily, pausing to listen, then pressing forward. His own heartbeat sounded loud in his ears as adrenaline pumped through his veins. He moved silently through the bushes, a part of him almost enjoying the hunt. Somewhere in the darkness, someone waited to kill him. But Gentry wasn't quite ready to die.

A twig snapped behind him. He stopped and whirled but it was too late. An inch to his right, he heard the unmistakable click of a pistol being cocked a split second before he felt the cold metal of the gun barrel touch his temple.

"Stick 'em up, Gentry."

Stunned, Gentry turned slowly, until he directly faced the killer. He said in a wooden voice, "It was you all along. You're the leak."

"Give the man a gold star," Greenwood said in a voice that was fraught with deadly resolve, a voice that no longer matched the fresh, boyish countenance that could have come straight from a college yearbook. "Now, I'm afraid I'm going to have to ask you to drop your gun, ole buddy. Nothing personal."

For a moment the alternatives flashed like a teleprompter through Gentry's mind. His finger tightened on the trigger of his own pistol, but the metal aimed at his head told him the most he could do at this point was buy some time.

He relaxed his grip, and the gun fell to the ground with a disquieting thud.

"I never would have suspected you, Greenwood. I thought you were one of the good ones, one of the few people in this world I could count on. How did he get to you?" he asked quietly.

A spark of moonlight flashed off the FBI-issued SIG-Sauer—exactly like Gentry's own—as Greenwood moved to kick away the twin. "Money, what else? One million dollars. That's more than you and I would ever see in three lifetimes. It was an offer I couldn't refuse." His face took on an almost defensive look as Gentry studied him relentlessly. "Hell, you probably would have done the same thing if you'd had the chance."

"I'm sure it eases your conscience to think so."

Greenwood shrugged, an infuriatingly casual motion. "For a million dollars, I can learn to live with myself. Besides, what's the real difference between them and us except politics and a hell of a lot more money?"

A question Gentry had pondered at length, but now he answered without hesitation. "There is the matter of honor."

Greenwood gave a low, harsh laugh. "Spare me your noble sentiments. They don't mean much when you're staring down the wrong end of a gun, now do they?" He shook his head slightly in disbelief. "You made it too easy, Gentry. I'm surprised at you. When push came to shove, you forgot your own rules. What was it you used to tell me that summer at Quantico when we first met? Watch your back and trust no one. You must have told me that a dozen times."

"You have a good memory. Maybe you can remember exactly when you decided to sell out." Gentry could hear the thunder of his own pulse in his ears as his mind raced ahead. No longer was his enemy an enigma, but a man he had trusted and admired. A man he had laughed with and drunk beer with. A man he'd considered a friend.

The summer Gentry had first met Greenwood at Quantico, the Bureau's training center, he'd recognized his brilliance and his eagerness, but even then there had been an edge to the younger agent that had worried him. But not for long. Greenwood had proven himself time and again. He'd saved Gentry's life once. The irony of that image hit him full force now as he stared into the face of his savior and his executioner.

Greenwood smiled, still looking for all the world like the all-American boy next door. He cocked his head, studying Gentry intently in the pale light. "This whole espionage business is a load of crap, Gentry. Haven't you figured that out by now? The boys in Washington sit on their fat asses, smoking their Cuban cigars and drinking their Russian vodka while they send us out to thwart the enemies of democracy. It's no more than a game to them, a huge, global chessboard with absolutely no rules, except the ones that serve their own purpose. And you and me, Gentry, are no more than automatons who bow and scrape and serve their capricious wills. So you know what I decided one day? If I was going to be a pawn, I was going to be a highly paid one."

"And you're being paid to kill me, is that it?"

"Among other things."

"Did you kill Lester?"

"Lester was a pawn too. Unfortunately, he tried to play both sides of the board, both ends against the middle. You have to be good to do that. And I'm damned good, Gentry. I owe it all to you—"

"MacKenzie's paying you. I know that," Gentry cut in sharply. "But if I'm going to die, I want to hear you say it. I want to know how he intends to smuggle out the plans. You owe me that much, Greenwood."

The grin flashed again, quick and bright. "Wouldn't be polite to kiss and tell, now would it, Gentry? Tell you what. I'll give you a hint. Saturday night, my friend. Saturday night, in plain view of all."

Gentry's mind clicked rapidly ahead. Saturday night. The International Art Auction. High rollers from all over the world jetting in and out. Yachts sailing into international waters. A charity function with the eyes of the world on it. And the prearranged sale of one or more paintings. A plan so simple, it would work brilliantly, and right under their noses . . .

"The microdots are hidden in the paintings," he mused softly.

"At least your mind's still quick," Greenwood commented.

"Which paintings?" Gentry asked sharply.

"It's not going to matter to you one way or another—"

He had barely voiced the last word when Gentry lunged, making a grab for the gun. His hand chopped at Greenwood's arm, and the gun discharged a bullet into the ground at their feet. Their arms locked in a death grip as the pistol made wide arcs in the air.

Pain shot up Gentry's injured arm like a blazing arrow but still he hung on. Greenwood's elbow jabbed at his stomach, making contact before Gentry could step away, but still he didn't let go. His other hand came up to close around Greenwood's throat as the two men struggled in a deadly embrace. Then Greenwood's knee jerked upward and connected with Gentry's groin. The air left his lungs with a painful roar. His head spun dizzily as he fell backward into the shadows.

The pain was excruciating, blinding, but the soft swoosh of air near his ear as a bullet whizzed past had him rolling away, trying to struggle to his feet. But the younger man was already standing over him, the pistol aimed at his head.

"You're getting too old for this business, Gentry," he said with only a slight quickening of breath. He shoved a lock of hair from his forehead as he glared down at Gentry. "You should have retired from the field a long time ago. Now it's too late."

He held the gun at arm's length, his finger tightening on the trigger. Unconsciously Gentry braced himself, but when the shot came, it came from a different direction, and the sudden explosion reverberated through the darkness, shocking both of them. A red circle formed on Greenwood's chest. He looked down, his expression puzzled. The gun slipped from his hand, and then, as if in slow motion, he pitched forward to the ground.

Gentry lunged for the gun, rolled to a crouch and aimed at the shadows, all in one fluid movement. But what he saw stunned him, took away his breath. The gun lowered, and he merely stared at her for a long, emotion-packed moment.

She must have approached during the fight because he hadn't heard a sound, and obviously, neither had Greenwood. There had been no telltale footfall, no rustling leaves, no snapping twigs. There had been no shriek of panic, no giveaway scream, no terrified sobbing.

What there had been was stealth and purpose. Silent and capable stalking. Quick assessment and even quicker action. What there had been was—skill.

She was good, Gentry thought in a sudden burst of admiration. Like a professional. She was swathed in black—leggings, sweatshirt, scarf—that blended with the night, made her one with the shadows. A pale wash of moonlight spilled across her face, bathing her in a strange, ethereal glow. With the gun still pointed at Greenwood's lifeless form, she looked like an avenging angel, a saintly specter not quite of this earth.

Gentry's breath tightened sharply in his chest, and for a moment, her silent profile held him trapped. Shaking his head slightly, as if to break free, he knelt beside Greenwood and checked for a heartbeat, surprised to find the rhythm faint but steady.

"He's alive," he called softly.

There was no reaction from her, not even so much as a soft sigh. She didn't budge an inch. Gentry glanced up, probing her face in the weak light. The scene still playing in slow motion, he got up and walked toward her. The outstretched hand gripping the gun now shook violently. When he reached her side, he gently pried her fingers from the metal.

"It's okay," he said softly, wrapping his arm around her shoulder, shielding her from the grisly view on the ground. She trembled against him, her shoulders first, then her whole body as both of his arms came around her. Her breath escaped in tiny little sobs that made Gentry close his eyes and hold her even tighter. "It's okay," he whispered again, stroking her hair with the palm of his hand.

He pulled back slightly and smoothed the hair from her face as he stared at her. "You saved my life."

Her lovely eyes were wide and liquid as she stared at him, still with that same look of horror. "But I shot him. He may die—"

Her voice cracked dangerously, and Gentry grabbed her shoulders, giving her a firm shake. "He would have killed me if you hadn't shot him. Now, come on. Let's get the hell out of here."

She resisted the tug on her arm, held back even as he urged her to follow. "We can't just leave him here. We have to help him—"

"Like hell we do. We have to help ourselves right now. There may be others. We'll call an ambulance as soon as we're a safe distance away. Now, come on."

Like a zombie, Laura let him pull her through the darkness, half dragging her at times until they were out on the street.

"How did you get here?" he demanded in a whisper, her hand still gripped tightly in his.

"The K-Kellys' BMW. Over...there. I followed you." Her teeth were chattering so badly, she could hardly speak. She pointed her finger at a darkened alleyway across the street.

"We'll take it," Gentry decided. "Hell, I've already stolen a boat and a Jeep. May as well go all the way. After this mess is over, it'll take me a week just to return the stolen vehicles," he muttered.

But his irony was lost on Laura. Cold and numb. That's how she felt, she thought dazedly, like someone exposed too long to the elements. She wondered if, like frostbite, the excruciating pain would come later. She had almost killed a man—

Don't think about it, she ordered herself. Think about getting into the car. Think about buckling the seat belt. Think about Simon *still alive* getting into the driver's seat beside you. Think about—

Oh, God, think about anything but a stranger lying bleeding back there in the darkness—

They were streaking through the darkened streets, following a maze of alleys and side streets. Laura thought herself familiar with Key West, but within moments she was hopelessly lost, her sense of direction gone haywire. It didn't matter, though. She was with Simon. He would take care of everything. He would help her through this night. He would make her forget—

He expertly pulled the car to the curb near a pay phone, set the parking brake and got out. He punched in a series of numbers, spoke briefly into the receiver, then hung up. Within seconds, the phone rang and he picked it up.

Laura sat in the car and watched him. While he talked, his gaze roamed the street and their surroundings with a practiced, vigilant eye. His features in the stark light were dramatically etched. She could see the lines of weariness on his face, the agitation in his movements as his hand went up and swept through his hair. But there was something else in his eyes—a cool, calm acceptance of everything that had happened tonight and a sort of quiet excitement that was perhaps the most frightening aspect of all to her.

"Did you call an ambulance?" she asked anxiously, the moment he'd climbed back into the car.

"I called a friend." His voice was terse as he turned to face her. "He'll clean up—he'll take care of things."

"But—"

"Laura, believe me, he'll take care of him. We want Greenwood alive. At least until he can talk."

Greenwood. So that was his name. Somehow putting a name to the faceless shadow made the horror all the more real. *Greenwood.* He'd been a child once, someone's son. Perhaps he was a husband now, a father. Dear Lord—

"Are you all right?" Simon asked quietly, touching her hand briefly.

She placed her palms on either side of her face as she let out a deep, shaky breath. "I still can't believe it. It's like a dream, like it happened to someone else. Is...this the way it always feels?" She clasped her hands together tightly, trying to stop the trembling.

"You've got the shakes," he said sympathetically. "It'll pass. What you need is a good, stiff drink."

She swiped the back of her hand across the moisture on her cheek. "I'm afraid I'm not handling this very well." She tried to laugh but it turned into a sob. "This is not at all the way Vicki would react. She'd be cool and calm—" *Like you,* she silently added.

Simon's hand tangled in her hair as he said softly, "Welcome to the real world, honey."

His voice seemed to open the floodgates. Tears flowed freely down her face. "I was so...scared. I'm still...scared. I'm not...very strong...after all."

"Do you think being afraid makes you weak?" He brushed the back of his hand across her cheek, wiped away the tears with his thumb. "Only a fool doesn't feel fear. You were afraid, and yet you did what you had to do. You saved my life. You're a very strong woman, Laura."

She took a deep, shaky breath. "I couldn't let you die," she whispered. "No matter what I had to do."

Her eyes fluttered closed as he bent closer and brushed his lips against hers in a kiss so light, so feathery, she might have thought she imagined it. Except it rocked her all the way to her toes.

I love you, she thought in wonder, and knew that for the first time in her life, she meant it. At that moment, having stared mortality in the face, the future ceased to matter. Being with him at this moment was enough. Having him safe and alive was everything. If the pain came later, after he was gone, she'd face it then. But somehow she knew it would be worth it.

Almost as though trying to dispel her revelation, Simon said, "We're not through yet, I'm afraid. We have to meet someone first." He bent forward quickly and brushed her cheek with his lips. "Hang on, honey. With any luck, it'll all be over soon."

He shoved the car into gear, released the brake, and the black BMW shot into the darkness like a racehorse loosed from the starting gate.

At least a dozen blurry, bloodshot eyes squinted in the general direction of the door as Laura and Simon entered the sleazy waterfront bar.

"Are you sure this is the place?" Laura asked, hanging back slightly when he would have led her inside.

"This is it," Simon said with an apologetic grin. "Try to think of it as soaking up a little local color."

Laura gave him a doubtful look as they wove their way through the rickety-looking wooden tables and straight-backed chairs to a darkened booth near the back. A woman wearing a black G-string, stiletto heels and an expression that wavered somewhere between sultry and sorrowful, bumped and gyrated her way along the wide bar that also served as a stage.

A song about a dangerous man blasted from the speakers as smoke swirled around the dancer's legs so thick, it might have been a stage prop gone awry. But it wasn't. At least half of the patrons propped at the bar dangled cigarettes from their slackened lips; the other half let their smokes smolder in overflowing ashtrays near their drinks.

Most of the customers were men, and their eyes were all over Laura. She clung to Simon and felt the reassuring pressure of his arm around her waist as he guided her toward the back and a private booth. As they passed in front of the bar, the dancer gave Simon a sizzling smile and an animated grind, but he appeared not to notice as he stepped aside and let Laura slide into the hazy booth first.

Within seconds a waitress sauntered toward them, slapped a couple of napkins on the table, then leaned forward, displaying her ample bosom for Simon's perusal as she took their orders.

"Two bourbons. Better make them doubles," he advised, and Laura saw his gaze slip downward to the low cut of the woman's halter top. For the first time since she'd pulled that trigger, she felt her pulse leap to life. She wrapped her arm through Simon's and pressed herself closer to his side. The waitress's smirking gaze sized her up and down before she turned and sashayed back toward the bar.

When the drinks arrived, Laura picked hers up and downed half the contents in one, long drink. The fiery liquid exploded in her stomach, tightening her throat painfully as she coughed and gagged.

Simon reached over and removed the glass from her hand. "Take it easy on the rotgut. The stuff they serve in here could kill a sailor."

"You've been in here before?" she rasped, her throat still burning from the shock.

"Not one of my prouder accomplishments." He grinned deprecatingly, but the smile disappeared as his eyes were drawn to the door. Her gaze followed his, and she gasped slightly. The man who had just entered had undoubtedly the most handsome face she'd ever seen. A camera would adore him, she thought absently, letting her gaze sweep over him. He had thick, golden brown hair, bronzed skin and the most extraordinary crystalline-blue eyes.

His presence in the seedy bar seemed incongruous and out-of-place; at the very least he belonged in one of the more trendy places on Duval Street or Mallory Square. But the heads that shifted toward him gave him no more than a cursory glance before turning back immediately to the dancer, who was slowly sliding her way down a pole protruding from the center of the stage.

The man ambled up to the bar and said something to the surly-looking bartender. The bartender threw back his head and laughed long and hard, continuing as he did so to wipe a glass with a towel he'd just used to clean a spill on the bar. Beside her, Laura felt Simon tense.

The newcomer turned and swept the bar with a careless gaze. His eyes met Laura's for one brief moment, and a look of appreciation flickered in the light blue depths. Then he turned toward the stage and deliberately folded a bill lengthwise before tucking it snugly inside the dancer's G-string.

A few moments later he approached the booth facing Gentry and Laura. Up close, his looks were even more striking, but as Laura gazed up at him, she felt no more than a stir of curiosity.

"Evening," he said politely. "Welcome to Nick's Place. I'm Nick Corey," he said, bypassing Simon to extend his hand to Laura. She took it uncertainly, her gaze flickering to Simon.

"Why don't we cut the chitchat?" Simon said roughly, lifting his drink to pull down a long swig. He set the glass back down on the table without batting an eye. "We have a lot to talk about, Corey."

"So it would seem." For the first time, the smile left Nick's face, and he looked serious. "Let's go back to my office." When Simon would have thrown some bills on the table, Nick stopped him. "It's on the house. It's the least I can do after the night's work you've done."

Laura and Simon followed Nick through the smoky bar into a dimly lit hallway. Nick extracted a key from his pocket and unlocked an intricate-looking security system. He flipped on the light and closed and locked the door behind Laura and Simon.

Laura stared at the office in amazement. Posh and elegant, it seemed more suited to an office in Trump Tower than in a seedy bar in Key West. Brown leather sofas and chairs were strategically placed on top of thick, mushroom-colored carpeting, and a polished walnut desk and credenza occupied one corner, along with a state-of-the art computer system. The walls were decorated with framed enlargements of underwater scenes of divers holding up what appeared to be bricks for the camera's eye.

Nick touched a button on the wall, and a panel swung open, revealing an impressively stocked bar complete with flashing crystal. "I keep the good stuff in here," he said, pouring brandy into large, iridescent snifters. "Your boy's still alive," he said, handing Laura and Simon the glasses. "We've got him tucked away safe and sound."

"Thank God," Laura murmured, drawing both men's gazes as she took a tentative sip of brandy. Her hands trembled so badly, the amber liquid sloshed against the sides of the snifter. She set the glass down on a table. "Do you have a washroom? I mean, besides out there...."

He nodded his head toward a door. "Right through there," he said, and his tone was oddly gentle.

When Laura had disappeared into the bathroom and closed the door behind her, Nick motioned Gentry to a chair, and he sat down behind his desk.

"How much does she know?"

"More than I wanted her to," Gentry said, frowning at the swirling liquid in his glass. "She knows I'm FBI, that I'm on the trail of a spy and that the operation down here has been shot to hell."

"Does she know about MacKenzie?" Nick asked casually, tilting his glass to his lips.

A muscle in Gentry's cheek began to throb. "No. If she suspected I was after him, she could blow me right out of the water."

Nick lifted his brows in surprise. "Come on. I don't believe she'd do that for a minute."

"Believe it," Gentry said harshly. "She can't find out. We're too close. I can't afford to tell her."

"You can't afford not to."

"What do you mean?"

"Any fool can see she's in love with you. What's she going to do when she finds out the truth?"

"I'll deal with that later," Gentry said grimly, setting down his glass to steeple his fingers under his chin.

"So what do you want from me?" Nick asked, frowning.

"I need your help, Nick. I'm on my own on this one. If he got to Greenwood, there's no telling who else he might have bought off. I can't trust the Bureau anymore."

"Hell, I never did trust the Feds," Nick said ironically. "You should have joined the Company a long time ago, Gentry, especially after your guys botched that Miami job."

"If I recall correctly, if you cowboys hadn't blundered in where you had no jurisdiction, the Miami operation would have gone down just fine."

"Oh, well, we'll never know, will we?" Nick said with a careless shrug. "So tell me what you need this time."

"This is strictly off Company time," Gentry warned.

"Fine by me. The Company doesn't own me. I'm an independent businessman," he said with a reckless grin.

Gentry quickly explained the situation to Nick. "I need you at that auction on Saturday night. For obvious reasons, I can't make my presence known there. But I'll be there, in the background. I want you to be my eyes and ears. We have to find those paintings before they leave MacKenzie's possession."

Nick hesitated for a moment, trailing a finger around the edge of his glass. He slanted a look at Gentry. "What's in it for me?"

"I'll owe you one."

Nick reared back in his chair, locking his hands behind his head as he grinned at Gentry.

"Just like the good old days, Gentry?"

"Yeah. Except we're both older. And I'm feeling a hell of a lot meaner."

"God help us," Nick muttered, lifting the brandy to his lips and draining the glass.

As soon as they walked into the house, Simon headed for the phone and Laura headed for the kitchen. She poured herself a stiff drink, downed it and poured another. Cradling the glass in both hands, she carried it with her outside, and perched on the low stone wall encasing the terrace.

There was a scent in the air, a sweet heaviness of exotic spices and night blooms. The lush opulence smelled of whispers and shadows and dangerous secrets.

The hand that lifted the glass to her lips still trembled. With a muttered oath, Laura tossed back a quick swallow, blinking rapidly as the stinging liquid brought tears to her eyes.

She wanted to be numb again. She wanted to forget what had happened earlier. She wanted—

A strong hand reached out and removed the glass from her hand. The frosted light sparked fire in the cut crystal as Simon set the glass on the wall beside her. "That won't help, you know."

She lifted her gaze to meet his. His eyes were so clear, like a shower-rinsed sky. She wanted to lose herself in those eyes, drown in those silvery pools.

She let her gaze drop, reaching a finger to trace the side of the glass. "You know what I've been thinking?"

"Nothing good, I can see."

"I've been sitting here thinking how very easy it is to take another human being's life. Just like that—" She tried to snap her fingers, but her thumb and finger rubbed harmlessly together, refusing to obey her command. She looked up at him. "Just like that, and he's gone," she whispered helplessly.

Simon grabbed her shoulders, his fingers biting into her skin. "Listen to me, Laura. You shot a man who was trying to kill me. If you're going to knock yourself out thinking about what you did, then think about the consequences if you *hadn't* shot him. I'd be dead now. Would that make you feel better?"

She gasped as the gray eyes probed her face, no longer clear and soft, but hard, steely, angry. "Of course not—" she began hesitantly. "But Simon, how do you live with it? Please, tell me, how do you forget?"

"You don't forget."

He spun away from her and moved to the other side of the terrace, staring out into the misty night. His fingers moved to plow the inevitable trail through his hair as he mouthed a silent curse.

When had things gotten so complicated? he asked himself bitterly. In a few days' time, maybe sooner, she would slip out of his life like a dream, and he would let her. He could do nothing else because what she was feeling now was what he lived with every day of his life. The lives he'd altered haunted his dreams, but he'd chosen his path long before he'd ever met her. There could be no going back. Hell, he wasn't so sure he'd do anything differently anyway, and he was too damned old to change now.

Better to let her go now than to start allowing himself to think about what might have been.

"Simon?" Her fingers touched his arm lightly, but they seared a path all the way to his soul. Her scent tantalized his senses, and her face in the moonlight was unearthly perfection. There was nothing he wanted more than to wrap his arms around her, let her pull what strength she could from him. But that wouldn't help, he realized. Touching her would only compound his problem.

"Do you ever get lonely in that shell, Simon?" she asked softly.

Startled as always by her perception, he turned to stare at her. "I've never thought too much about it one way or the other," he said briskly.

"I think about it all the time," Laura confided, her fingers tracing absently up and down his arm.

Gentry tensed, willing himself not to think about the acceleration of his pulse. "You, lonely?" he asked incredulously. "I don't believe it. You could have anyone you wanted. With just a snap of your fingers, men would fall at your feet."

"Even you?" Her heavy-lidded gaze trapped him with intensity, with sultry heat.

"Don't you know?" His voice was a dark, husky whisper as he touched the golden strands of her hair with fingers that trembled. "I already have."

"Then prove it." She weaved slightly toward him as one hand crept up his shift front. "Stay with me tonight, Simon. Make love with me. Make me forget."

His hand closed over hers, tightening his grip for a moment before carefully releasing her. "That's the whiskey talking. It wouldn't be very heroic of me to take advantage of you in this condition, now would it?"

Her other hand slid up to toy with one of his buttons. "But as we both know," she began in a seductive voice he knew wasn't her own, "you're no hero."

"And you seem intent on proving that," he said roughly, shoving her hand away. "God, Laura, stop it!" Desire thudded inside him, hot and strong, but he forced himself to take a step back from her.

"Aren't you even going to kiss me?" she asked in disappointment.

"This is all wrong," he said, spreading his hands up as if to ward off her attack. "You'd hate me in the morning."

"It's already morning. And I don't hate you, Simon. Far from it."

"What we're going to do," he said firmly, "is get you into the shower."

"That sounds promising," she said with a slow smile.

"*Alone*. You'll feel like holy hell in the morning if we don't get you sobered up before you go to sleep."

"Well, I'm certainly not going to beg for it," she said coolly, tossing her head regally as she turned and started for the door. Her steps were cautious and exaggerated, the movements of someone who no longer had complete control of her faculties. She threw Gentry one last look over her shoulder. "You know something? I should've let Greenwood shoot you."

Gentry ignored the comment as he followed her through the door, grabbing her elbow when she would have tripped over a rug. She merely threw him a withering look as she opened the door to her bedroom, not bothering to challenge him when he followed her through. Her fragrance—a fragrance he'd come to know so well—permeated the room with subtle dominance.

The bathroom was lavish with a huge, sunken tub, strategically placed mirrors and a shower stall built for two. He reached inside the stall and turned on the cold water, carefully keeping his eyes averted as Laura stripped behind him.

But, dear Lord, what the whisper of dropped clothing could do to a man's resolve. He leaned his head against the cool surface of the glass doors and closed his eyes. He felt his heart pounding all the way in the pit of his stomach as he struggled to keep his eyes closed and averted from her. But her scent was already clouding his brain. And her voice as she whispered his name—

Then she stepped into the shower and her scream brought his gaze flying back to her. "It's freezing!"

"That's the idea," he commented dryly.

He quickly turned away but not before he'd gotten a glimpse of golden skin and long, bare legs. Hell, how much was a man supposed to take, he thought weakly, his gaze inadvertently finding her silhouette in the mirror across the room.

Laura stood under the icy jets of water, feeling the shock vibrate all the way through her body. But in a moment her head began to clear and her own resolve sharpened. She turned on the hot tap until the shower become steamy.

"Simon, I forgot the soap. It's there on the vanity. Will you hand it to me?"

When he would have handed the soap over the stall to her, she opened the door and stood before him, water streaming down her body. His expression was that of a man who had just had the props knocked from under him. He cursed, letting the bar of soap slip soundlessly to the thick carpet at his feet.

Laura stepped forward and curled her fingers around a fistful of his shirt. She tugged, but he was already inside the shower, muttering dark oaths and heated promises as he jerked her into his arms.

Chapter 11

"You're so damned gorgeous," he gasped, sliding his hands up and down her shivering body. Her skin was warm and wet and pliant beneath his fingers. Her head fell back wantonly as he devoured her throat, then moved downward, letting his tongue ride over the sensitive peaks of her breasts. Her fingers locked in his hair, pulling him to her, arousing him to desperation by the simple act of submission.

And Gentry let himself go. He could think of nothing but how soft her skin, how warm her whispers, how deep her desire. The need was raging, consuming. He lifted his mouth to hers, his tongue penetrating with hard, demanding thrusts that were met and matched by her own.

She leaned back against the ceramic tile wall, her fingers fumbling urgently at the buttons of his shirt. When they were undone, she shoved the dripping fabric down his arms and he shrugged out of it, flinging the shirt to the floor without ever removing his lips from hers.

His hands were everywhere and so were hers, first moving restlessly over his shoulders and arms, then flattened against his chest, then busy once more at the snap and zipper of his jeans.

"Oh, God, hurry!" he demanded, pressing her back with his hips, grinding against her in a hot, urgent preview of what was to come. His breath was coming too quickly, his pulse thundered in his ears as the hot, steamy water cascaded over them.

He cursed the resistance of his wet jeans, but her hands were there pulling and shoving, caressing and stroking until the act of removing his clothing became an erotic act of foreplay.

He closed his eyes, letting her hands consume him. With her, he could be clean again, whole again, young again. She could ease his guilt, wipe away the regrets—

Oh, it had been her from the moment he first laid eyes on her. Her hair, her legs, her voice. It had been her . . . her . . . her . . .

He drew away for a moment, gasping for breath as he stared deep into those green depths that pulled and tugged and lured him into the swirling waters. She was lightning and thunder, rain and wind, a tempest of passion that he could not control. She tasted like wine, sweet and potent, and deceptively dangerous. She wrapped one leg around his, curling her body into his in seductive surrender.

His hand moved to her breast and she sighed. He kissed her again and she begged softly for more. He pulled her to his body and she melted against him.

It was like a dream, an impossible wish, a prayer finally answered. He no longer cared about tomorrow, about duty and honor and country, concepts easily shoved aside. There would be regrets, undoubtedly. There would be remorse, accusations and more guilt. There would be hell to pay when she found out the truth, but for now, this moment, he had her. It was enough, more than he'd ever dared hope.

Oh, the thrill of it! If it had been Vicki who had daringly begun the seduction, it was Laura who weakly reeled from the consequences. He filled her with sensations, with tastes and scents and feelings.

His tongue carried the sharp bite of whiskey and danger and passion into her mouth, arousing her to a fevered excitement.

His body felt warm and hard and slippery beneath her restless hands, his skin smelled faintly of after-shave and the night wind, darkly alluring, intensely exciting.

And sounds...! The feverish litany of her name whispered against her throat, the heated promises breathed against her lips and the sound of her own heartbeat pounding in her ears.

She sampled water droplets from his skin with her tongue, slid her body against his warmth until the friction began to build both within and without. And all the while, the hot jets of water pelted their bodies, adding to the frenzied urgency of the moment.

His mouth on hers sparked a passion that threatened to engulf her. His hands at her breasts spread the fire all the way through her. His fingers sliding against her thighs shot the flames deeper, deeper within her. Expertly he positioned her, and then he was inside her, and her whole body ignited.

This was it, she thought weakly, gasping his name over and over. *This* was what she had so long been searching for. *This* was what she had been waiting and wanting without knowing why.

But not just the passion. Not just the fire. The holding and being held, the unselfish giving and the greedy demanding, the sharing and taking. It was being consumed and consuming, wanting and needing and being fulfilled in every possible way. It was two people becoming one for a brief, glorious moment—one body, one mind, one soul. It was soaring together, higher and faster and farther than ever before, staring deep into each other's eyes as the pinnacle was sought and reached, and sharing the wonder as the universe exploded around them.

Breathless and spent, Laura's knees buckled. Slowly she slid downward against the slippery tile wall until she was sitting on the floor of the shower. Gentry made no move to hold her. Instead, he reached to turn off the taps, then sat down himself, his own knees none too steady.

Silence, except for the drip of the faucet and their own ragged breathing. Gentry leaned against the tile, head back, legs sprawled in front of him. Modesty had deserted him at the moment, and so had his strength.

He knew the romantic thing to do would be to scoop her up and carry her off to bed, make love to her again, slower, with more finesse this time. But right now, he wasn't sure he could make it to the bed himself without crawling. His legs still trembled from the fierceness of their passion.

"Simon?"

"Umm?"

"Was that the encore?"

It took him a minute to realize what she meant, and then he laughed a low, wicked laugh. "What if I told you that was just the warm-up?"

"Oh my goodness."

At her tone, he laughed again. "Don't worry. The way I feel right now, that may well have been my final performance."

"Somehow I doubt that," she said softly as their eyes met and clung. They weren't touching, but they might as well have been. The heat radiating between them was an almost tangible thing.

"So do I," Gentry said with feeling, reaching for her hand as she scrambled to her feet. With a quick, decisive move, he pulled her to him, tumbling her across his lap. She lay in his arms, staring up at him with eyes that were incredibly soft and hazy and very, very sexy.

"Lady, who *are* you?" he asked in wonder.

She reached up and brushed a damp lock of hair from his forehead. Her fingertips trailed down his cheek, feathered across his lips as she whispered, "I'm not sure I know anymore."

"What's your real name, Simon?"

Some moments earlier they had relocated to the king-size bed, Laura had applied a fresh bandage to Simon's arm, and now they were tucked cozily between the white, satin sheets. Simon lay on his back, arms folded behind his head as Laura snuggled against him, her fingertips trailing lazily down his stomach. She could feel the hard muscles of his abdomen contract beneath her touch. His eyes were closed, but she saw his brows draw together briefly in a sensual wince.

"The less you know about me right now, the better," he murmured.

"Better for whom?" She raised herself on her elbows to stare into his eyes. "We've showered together, Simon. We should have no secrets between us. If you can't trust me by now, you never will."

Gentry sighed, resigning himself to the conversation. "We've been through all this. You know I can't tell you any more than I already have. And that's too much."

She rested her cheek against his chest, feeling the steady rhythm of his heart beneath her. "That's the story of my life, you know. I always want what I can't have."

"Don't we all," he said softly, and something in his voice made her glance up, but his eyes were closed again, the expression on his face veiled.

She clasped her hands together on Simon's chest and rested her chin on them. She stared at him for a long time, her thoughts a jumbled mess inside her head.

"Simon?"

"Umm?"

"Who is Nick Corey?"

"He's a friend. Someone I met a long time ago."

"He's the salvage diver you told me about, isn't he? The one who discovered a Spanish galleon? What's he doing running a dive like Nick's Place?"

"I don't know, Laura. Maybe he likes the clientele."

"Maybe it's his cover," she suggested softly.

He lifted one lid and regarded her calmly. "Cover for what?"

"I don't know. FBI. CIA. You tell me."

Both eyes were open now, but his expression still remained undaunted. "I never said he was an agent."

"You didn't have to. Why else would you have gone to see him?"

"All right," Simon acquiesced grudgingly. "He does the occasional odd job for the CIA."

"You mean he's a mercenary?"

"I'm not sure he'd be flattered by that term," Simon said dryly. "He does have principles, such as they are."

"He only works for the good guys you mean," Laura surmised.

"If you can make the distinction."

"Do you trust him?" she asked, disregarding his sarcasm.

"Yes. As much as I do anyone right now. After tonight, that's not a whole hell of a lot."

"Simon?"

He didn't answer her this time, merely raised his brows at her query.

"Why does this case mean so much to you? Your cover's blown, your life's in danger. Why not let someone else take over?"

"There is no one else," he said, shoving himself up in bed until his back rested against the headboard. Laura sat up, too, waiting for him to continue. "He's *mine,*" Simon said at last. "I've been waiting three long years for this. If I don't do it now, he could get away with all this, and someone I care about a great deal would never be free. I can't let that happen. I owe her—"

"You *are* doing this for her," Laura said softly.

"She and her husband are living out of the country right now, under assumed names. But as long as this man goes free, her life is in danger. He knows she's the only one who can pin anything on him right now. He's tried to kill her twice. He won't stop until he succeeds ... unless I stop him first. I can't fail. Not again."

Laura frowned. "What do you mean 'not again'? You've done everything you can. You've risked your life. What more can you do?"

"Whatever I have to."

"It's not just this case, is it?" she whispered, as she stared at the stark truth in his eyes. "You're obsessed with solving every case. Why?"

"Because it's the only thing I can do. For her."

Laura knew instinctively they were no longer talking about his witness, the woman with no memory, but of someone else, someone much more significant because she was dead. It was hard to fight a ghost, Laura thought, her throat tightening with fear. Maybe impossible.

"What was her name?" she asked softly.

"Caroline." The room was dark, shadowed by moonlight, but Laura could see the bleak expression in his eyes and her heart ached for him. For herself.

"What happened?"

"She died because of me, because I got careless."

Their eyes met briefly and he glanced away. Laura could feel the warmth they had shared slipping away, and she wrapped the sheet around herself, sensing that he no longer wanted their closeness.

"When it happened, I swore that I would never put anyone else in that position. That's why I have to get away from you, as fast as I can. I have no right to be here with you."

She glanced at him in alarm. "I gave you the right just a few minutes ago. I'm not worried about the danger—"

"That's not what you said earlier," he said harshly. "Have you forgotten what happened so easily? We both could have been killed. The longer I stay here, the more danger I'm putting you in. Sooner or later, I'll have to leave. Sooner would be better."

"For whom?" she whispered again.

His gaze met hers in a silent challenge. "For you. I can't make you any promises."

"I haven't asked you for any," she said simply.

"But you do ask. Every time you look at me, you ask." The bitterness in his voice dissolved to tenderness. He lifted one hand to tuck a strand of hair behind her ear. "You deserve better than this, Laura. Better than me. If things were different—"

"Don't," she whispered. "Things aren't different, and I learned a long time ago that commitments don't mean that much anyway."

He pulled her to him, wrapping his arms around her as she lay on top of him. His lips moved in her hair. "Are you sure about this, honey? The last thing I want to do is hurt you," he said huskily, but even as he voiced his concern, his body was moving against hers, responding immediately to the intimate contact.

She wound her arms around his neck and pressed herself tightly to him, fanning the already leaping flames. Her gaze met his in a very soft challenge. "Who says I'm the one who'll get hurt?"

He cupped her face with his hands as his lips brushed hers, then skimmed across her cheek to nuzzle her neck. "Maybe that's what I'm most afraid of," he whispered hoarsely.

Chapter 12

A stripe of sunlight angled across Gentry's face. He muttered a curse as he threw an arm over his eyes. He rolled over, reaching for the sheet, but the satin slithered off the end of the bed before he could grab it.

"Damned nuisance," he muttered, raising himself up on one elbow while he rubbed the stubble of his chin with the other. He'd fought that damned satin sheet all night while it slipped and slid all over the bed. So much for glamour, he thought dryly, but he had to admit there had been something deliciously decadent about the feel of satin beneath his back while Laura had—

He frowned suddenly as his gaze moved to the other side of the bed. Where was she anyway? His heart bumped in momentary panic, then settled again as his eyes lit on the open terrace doors.

He found a fresh pair of jeans in the closet, slipped them on, then stood in the open doorway, his arm propped against the frame as he stared at the aquamarine wash of waves pounding the shore.

The breeze was stiff today. The giant fronds of the coconut palms dipped and swayed to the rhythm of the trade winds. Sunlight skipped and sparked off the water as the tide rose and sank. And in the sea, the metallic threads in her pink swimsuit like streaks of fire, Laura was swimming like a dolphin.

He stood watching her for a long time, drinking in the sight of her lithe, golden body moving effortlessly through the water with sure, powerful strokes. She was terrific, with the grace and symmetry and power of a natural athlete. And beautiful. God, how one woman could be so beautiful and giving and sexy—it made him ache all over again, just watching her.

And he couldn't stop watching her. He could spend the rest of his life watching her. He could die a happy man watching her cut through the waves like an Olympic champion, watching her dip her hair into the water and trail her fingers through the long, glorious strands, watching her raise her face to the sun and laugh from the pure joy of a beautiful day.

He drew his breath in sharply. How long had it been since he'd taken the time to enjoy anything so simple and innocent as sunlight on his face, as a walk on the beach, as holding hands with someone he loved—

Whoa, wait a minute, he ordered himself sternly. That kind of thinking was dangerous. There was no room in his life for the simple things, not anymore.

But lately...

Lately, he'd undertaken the dangerous and depressing pastime of reflecting. He wondered, sometimes after he'd gone to bed, the remnants of his TV dinner thrown in the garbage, if his life might have been fuller had he remarried a long time ago, had children who would be half-grown by now.

Instead he was past forty, alone and doubting very much whether the end really did justify the means.

Grimly, he pushed himself away from the door frame and wandered down to the tiny strip of beach. He sat down on the sand and watched Laura frolic in the waves. She saw him and raised her hand in greeting, laughing delightedly when a wave knocked her off balance.

She came running through the water, sunlight dancing along the golden flecks in her sleek suit. The cut was daring, dipping low at the neck and riding high on her thighs. The wet fabric clung to her body, molded her curves in a way that sent his pulse pounding. She stood before him, raising her arms to push back her hair. The innocently provocative gesture tightened her stomach muscles even more and emphasized the alluring roundness of her perfect bosom.

Gentry felt his own stomach muscles tightening convulsively as he stared up at her. Their eyes met and locked, and she smiled down at him, slowly, knowingly, as she knelt, planting her arms on either side of him. Their gazes were suddenly level, their lips mere inches apart. Water dripped from her hair onto his chest and arrowed down his stomach.

"Did I happen to mention," she began in a low, breathless voice, "that you were sensational last night? Each..." she brushed his mouth with hers "...and every..." her tongue outlined his lips "...single...time."

His lips fastened on hers, moving over her mouth in a sensuous back-and-forth prelude. With one fingertip, he rimmed the neckline of her swimsuit, barely skimming the gentle rise of her breasts. Heat blasted through him like a rocket leaving the launchpad.

"I can't believe I still want you so badly," he murmured against her mouth, echoing her exact thoughts. "After last night, I can't believe there's anything left—"

She pushed him back on the sand, kissing him long and hard until they were both gasping.

"Let's get in the water," he said urgently, his hands moving over her, touching, kneading, probing.

"You shouldn't get your arm wet again," she breathed against his mouth, her own hands busy.

His grin was slow and easy. "Don't worry," he said in a husky murmur. "I don't plan on getting in that deep. At least not over my head."

But as her tongue plunged inside his mouth, Gentry knew he was already a drowning man.

"You know, if you close your eyes, you could almost believe we're on vacation," Laura said dreamily, as she shifted to a more comfortable position in the lounge chair beside the pool.

Gentry threw her a glance she missed. The sun on his chest did feel good, though. Really good. He pillowed his head on his arms as he let his gaze drift over Laura. His gun lay on the table between their chairs, a graphic reminder that this was no picnic, no summer romance. "I don't take vacations," he said curtly.

Laura lifted herself on her elbow and glared at him. "Ever?"

"No."

The terse reply made her wince. "You do have a dark side, don't you, Simon?"

Their gazes met. "Don't we all?"

"Maybe." She picked up her iced tea and sipped. "Tell me about this man you're after. Do you know his name? What he looks like?"

"I know everything there is to know about him."

"Then why don't you just arrest him?"

Gentry shrugged uneasily. "It's not that simple. He has connections. I told you last night, we've never been able to pin anything on him."

"Then what makes you so sure you have the right man?" she asked logically.

"You sure are nosy, woman," he groused, wishing she'd change the subject.

"Well, I am more than moderately involved, you know."
She set down her glass and swung her legs over the side of
the lounge as she eyed him sagely. "I know all this has
something to do with Jake."

There was a strange, empty feeling in Gentry's chest as he
said, "What if it does? What would you do?" He strove to
keep his tone neutral.

"Are you saying he *is* involved, Simon?"

His gaze flickered for a split second, but he didn't drop it.
He looked her straight in the eyes. "No. I'm not saying that.
I'm asking what your reaction would be if you found out he
was under investigation."

She frowned. "I have a feeling we're playing semantics
here."

Gentry sat up and faced her. "Just answer the question."

"All right. Then I guess I'd have to decide where my loyalties lie. He's been very good to me, Simon, and it would
be difficult for me to believe he'd ever do anything really
wrong. Now you answer *my* question."

"Which is?"

She paused, staring up at him with eyes that were enig-
matic, full of mystery. "Was that question personal or professional?"

Gentry's smile was grim. "A little of both, I'm afraid."

His answer seemed to satisfy her. She changed the subject. "What happened last night with that man . . . Greenwood?" She hesitated over the name as though having difficulty putting voice to it. "He was supposed to be on your
side, Simon. What happened?"

Gentry shrugged. "He went bad. It's the worst thing that
can happen in our business, like a dirty cop. We don't like
to admit it, but it happens."

"No wonder you have a hard time trusting people," she
said softly. "If you trust the wrong person, you could get
killed."

He gave her a long, steady look. "Exactly."

In his mind, he pursued his quarry, a series of endless shadows that blended and merged until the names and faces became indistinguishable. But it didn't matter because he knew they were the enemy. They had to be stopped. He couldn't fail again, so he ran and ran, chasing shadows, until his heart felt as though it would burst from his chest.

"Simon? Simon, wake up."

Strong, nimble fingers grasped his shoulders and shook him. The dark fog lifted as he opened his eyes. The velvety eyes staring down at him were shadowed with concern and fear and some deeper emotion he would not let himself believe—

"What time is it?" he asked abruptly, propelling himself upward like a tightly wound spring. He turned to her. "Do you have any idea what time it is?"

Laura sat up beside him, pushing her fingers through the tangled strands of her hair. "I don't know. After midnight I guess. . . ."

But he'd already turned away, mumbling to himself. "Where's my watch? Where's my damned watch?"

"It's on the nightstand. You put it there before you took a shower—"

"And I didn't even think to put it back on," he cursed, searching the nightstand for the watch. "That's great, just great." He picked up the watch and peered at it in the moonlight. "Almost one-thirty. Damn!"

"Simon, what is the matter?" she asked softly, touching his arm with a tenderness that touched the deep, hidden places in his heart.

His deception gnawed at him, ate away at the very foundation that had been the essence of who he was for too many years.

In another time, another place, he might have been relieved to know he still had a conscience. But now, it was merely a hindrance to him, a worrisome burden to carry as the task before him drew nearer.

Laura reached to smooth back a strand of hair from his forehead, and he recoiled from her touch. The hurt in her eyes was swift, as though the thrust of a dagger had met its mark. She withdrew her hand quickly.

Gentry cursed himself again, unable to meet her eyes as he sat up in bed and swung his legs over the side. He drew on his pants and restlessly paced to the window, parting the slats to stare out at the moon-drenched sea.

The beat of the waves tore at his nerves. He needed to be doing *something,* anything. Time was wasting, and here he was, cocooned in some tropical retreat, drifting through the days and nights in the arms of a woman he could never hope to—

Damn, what a mess, he thought, tunneling his fingers through his hair. The desire to open up to her, to tell her the truth about his mission was an incessant throbbing in his temple. But he was so close now. *So damned close.* And God help him, he still needed her help.

Behind him the bed creaked as she shifted her weight. Her footfalls were as light as fairy dust—he only sensed her presence a mere second before her arms slipped around his waist and she cradled her cheek against the bare skin of his back.

Her open submission to him never failed to amaze him, to stir him; her touch never failed to excite him. Her fingers locked together over the tense muscles of his stomach as he willed himself not to react. He'd taken too much from her already; somehow accepting her comfort seemed the worst crime of all.

Her lips touched his back, igniting the fire already smoldering in the pit of his stomach. He closed his eyes, testing his willpower to the fullest extent of his strength. He had to talk to her. Now. Tonight. He had one more deception, one more thing he needed to take from her—and then maybe, just maybe, they both could be free.

"Simon, what's wrong?" she whispered again, her breath fanning the sensitive skin at his neck. "What were you dreaming about?"

Her cheek nuzzled his back, an oddly soothing sensation. Her fingers loosened their hold and negligently caressed his stomach, his rib cage, his back. In spite of his self-recriminations, his body responded to her touch, like a match to tinder.

"Tell me about her, Simon," she urged, her voice husky-sweet and seductive, a voice that could—like Circe—lure the strongest man from his course. "Tell me about Caroline."

A silent chill settled over the room, where earlier their soft whispers and sighs had warmed the night with a blaze of passion. There was a distance between them now, a chasm that widened and deepened until Laura feared it might never be bridged. She longed for him to turn and take her in his arms and tell her she was the only woman who had ever mattered in his life.

But it would be a lie, and that she could not take.

Simon stood with his back to her, one hand propped against the window frame as he tilted his face toward the starry night sky.

"We met in law school. After I joined the Bureau, she went on to work in the D.A.'s office in Washington. She was strong, beautiful, very committed. She thought she could save the world. My aspirations weren't quite so lofty, but she made me feel like I could make a difference. She had faith in me, trusted me, and I failed her in the worst way possible.

"There was a man, a mafioso, whose son I helped send to prison. The boy was killed inside, and the old man blamed me. He sent a hitman to Eleuthera, where Caroline and I were vacationing."

Laura's breath sucked in sharply at the matter-of-fact recitation. Simon had lived the dark, shadowy underworld in which she glamorized *Vicki Love.* He played the games she'd always thought of in terms of adventure, excitement, intrigue. But looking at his ravaged face now, she realized what a brutal world it was, and the games that were played there were played for keeps.

She shivered suddenly and reached for her robe. Belting it around her, she leaned against the window frame as she asked softly, "What happened? She got in the gunman's way?"

He spared her only a brief glance as though he didn't quite trust himself to look at her. "I was never the target. Murdering my wife was his ultimate revenge. An eye for an eye."

"Simon, I'm so sorry." The platitude sounded so inadequate, so meaningless. Laura said helplessly, "You . . . saw it happen?"

"We were walking on the beach, watching the sunset. It was the first time both of us had been able to get away since before we married. I was too relaxed, complacent. I let my guard down."

"But you had no way of knowing something like that would happen. How could you know?"

He ignored her question as he continued to talk in a voice carefully devoid of emotion. "One minute we were walking along, talking about what we would have for dinner that evening, and the next moment she was lying at my feet." Gentry closed his eyes as the memories gushed forward. It was funny because he could hardly even remember Caroline's face after so many years. But he recalled vividly how the blood had bubbled from the bullet hole in her chest, how she'd felt in his arms with her life ebbing away, how the warmth had drifted from her hand long before he had stopped holding it. "It was all my fault," he said numbly. "She trusted me, and I failed her."

Laura turned her head and stared bleakly out the window. So many things were clearer to her now. Simon's obsession, not just with this case, but with every case was his own way of avenging Caroline's death. *She thought she could save the world.* Because he blamed himself for her death, he'd taken on her noble ideals, tried to right all the wrongs single-handedly so that his life had purpose, meaning.

"What happened to the man who ordered the hit?"

His gaze touched hers briefly. "He died."

Gooseflesh prickled the back of Laura's neck as she stared at Simon's stoic features in the moonlight. "That's why you have such a hard time trusting people," she said perceptively. "Because you don't want anyone trusting you." His brooding gaze swept her briefly, then turned back to the window. She said softly, "What about the woman who lost her memory? Your witness. You trusted her. You let yourself care for her."

"That was a mistake," he said coolly. "But I never let those feelings get out of hand. I knew there was no future for us. She was in love with her husband. The decisions I made were based solely on her safety."

"And what about us, Simon?" With one fingertip, she traced her reflection in the glass. "What about a future for you and me?"

He sighed heavily, as though the weight of the world rested on his shoulders. "I've never lied to you about how I feel," he said at last.

"Maybe not," she acknowledged, tilting her chin slightly in unconscious defiance. "But maybe you're lying to yourself. I think you could love me, Simon, if you let yourself."

His eyes were bottomless, soulless. "But I don't want to love you."

"You've made that abundantly clear," Laura said with a flash of anger.

"Laura—"

"Don't," she said helplessly. "Don't try to make me feel better because you can't. And don't say anything you don't mean because I can't stand lies."

"All right," he agreed, his own tone frosty. His gaze fixed on her with chilling intensity. "Then don't ask me any more questions."

"I have just one more," she said, wrapping her arms around her waist. "What can I do to help you solve this case?"

Something flickered in his eyes, some indefinable emotion she couldn't quite decipher. It might have been hope or relief or even distrust. With Simon, she could never really tell.

"Why would you want to help me?" he asked doubtfully.

She lifted her chin. "Because when you walk out that door, there's a good chance you may never come back—for whatever reason. I'm not going to live with regrets. You're not the only one who's ever been hurt, you know. But I was willing to take another chance with you. You're the one who'll end up with the regrets, Simon, not me."

His gaze captured hers, as if measuring the truth of her words. Slowly he said, "Better regrets than guilt."

Dawn was falling, shifting the patterns of light outside the window of the bedroom where they still sat, hunched over Laura's precise drawings of the MacKenzie mansion. Earlier Simon had told her his suspicions about the auction being used to smuggle out the microdots, and he'd asked her for a detailed layout of the house, still evading her questions regarding Jake's involvement.

As a lonely child that first summer in Key West, Laura had been over every inch of that house, devising games and spinning fantasies to while away the long hours of solitude. From memory she scrupulously sketched every nook and cranny, every door and window for Simon's intense study.

"Jake's hired extra security to patrol the grounds," she said, bringing Simon's gaze up swiftly to meet hers. He wore an odd look of speculation for a moment, as though he'd forgotten her presence. "Some of the paintings to be auctioned are quite valuable and because of all the comings and goings, the alarm system will have to be deactivated. But guards will be posted at all the entrances."

Simon's brows were pulled together in concentration as one finger stroked his chin. "Where will the paintings be kept until auction time?"

"They'll be moved by armored vans from the warehouse sometime today. Jake's cleared out the library, and they'll be stored in there and brought out one at a time according to their place in the catalog. The auction itself will take place in the salon, which adjoins the library."

Simon traced a line on the drawing with his fingertip. "These French doors lead directly into the library, isn't that right?" At her nod, he said, "If I could somehow create a diversion—"

"I can do that," Laura offered quickly. "I'll be there anyway. I could slip away. No one knows the house and grounds better than I do—"

"Absolutely not." Impatiently, Simon picked up her pencil and tapped it against the sketches. "The lock won't be a problem," he continued, as though the matter had been completely settled. "All I'll need is a couple of minutes at the most."

Laura grabbed the pencil from his hand, forcing him to look at her. "I can do it, Simon. I want to help you. You can't walk in there without backup—"

"God, Laura, get serious! There is no way I'm going to let you anywhere near that house tonight."

"What do you mean, you won't let me?" She had gotten off the bed and was standing arrow straight, her eyes blazing with a combination of anger and determination. "You can't stop me," she said furiously. "I have a right to be there. Besides, Jake's expecting me."

Simon rose from the bed and grabbed her shoulders. "To hell with Jake. The man I'm after has killed at least once. He won't hesitate to do so again when he realizes he's trapped. I don't want his next victim to be you."

"And I don't want it to be you!" Her voice rose on a note of desperation. "You can't ask me to stay here and do nothing to help you! Just let me create the diversion you need to get into the library, and then I'll leave again. I won't even have to enter the house. As soon as I've given you the time you need, I'll be out of there. I'll come back here and wait for you."

Her eyes glittered with angry resolve, but Gentry could see the fear there, too, determined as she was not to show it. She was so strong and brave. So beautiful and so damned trusting. She was the kind of woman a man would die for, Gentry thought suddenly, the kind who would haunt a man's dreams when dreams were all that were left to him.

Closing his eyes briefly, he pulled her to him and she came willingly. His arms tightened around her, strong and possessive. "You're a very dangerous woman, Laura."

"Not to you," she whispered against his neck. "Never to you."

Then suddenly, she was clinging to him, her own arms fastening around his neck to draw him nearer. "I'm afraid for you, Simon."

"It's all right," he said, trying to smile. "Nothing's going to happen to me. I'm the good guy, remember?"

She drew back and looked into his eyes. "I don't want you to go."

"Please don't ask me not to," he said, because suddenly he knew if she kept looking at him like that, he'd do anything she asked. He'd give up the hunt...and he'd never be able to look himself in the mirror again.

"I wouldn't ask that of you," she said softly. "I would never make you choose. But I wish this night was over. I wish it was already tomorrow."

"Only the very young can afford to wish away their lives like that," he told her lightly. "The days go by quickly enough as it is, sweetheart. Don't wish for tomorrow."

He buried his face in her hair as the guilt swamped him because he knew there would be no tomorrow for them. If he lived through tonight, by tomorrow she would know everything, know that he had lied to her, used her, deliberately deceived her. And if he didn't make it out of this, well—in either scenario, he felt his life rushing headlong to its conclusion. The years of loneliness stretched before him, bleak and cold, like a slow, lingering death.

He lowered his mouth, taking hers with uncharacteristic

gentleness. He held her close, not desperately this time, but as though she were something fragile and elusive.

"Simon . . ." She sighed as her hand reached up to stroke his cheek.

"My God, how beautiful you are," he whispered. There was a pain somewhere inside his chest, in a place he would have sworn there was nothing. He felt a surge of feeling there now, an overflow of emotions and desires. It hurt, he discovered, and then wondered why that should be so. He wanted her, and he could feel her own desire trembling through her, and he knew that only moments from now, she would be lying in his arms. So why did he hurt?

"I love you," she whispered against his lips.

"I don't know what to say." He swallowed, gazing deep into her eyes. "Laura—"

"Don't lie and say you love me," she pleaded, sensing his hesitation. "No lies, remember?"

His hand smoothed back her hair with infinite tenderness. "I can't be anything but what I am, Laura." He kissed her hand again, one finger at a time. She didn't move, only stared at him with her heart in her eyes. "You know what I am, and yet you're still here."

"For as long as you want me."

Till death do us part, he thought with bitter regret. But whose death would it be that rendered them asunder? Hers?

He put his hands to her face, capturing her in the most gentle of embraces. He touched his lips almost reverently to hers, and felt her tremble.

"I want you," he said intently.

"Take me," she said simply.

He lifted her then, sweeping her into his arms, but not in a rush of uncontrollable desire. Not in a blaze of passion as the other times had been. He held her as a man would hold the woman he adored.

And when he laid her on the bed, he began to make love to her. . . .

Chapter 13

The MacKenzie mansion sparkled like a brilliant gem as a row of limousines, conveying the elite guests invited to the senator's charity art auction, wrapped around the tree-lined block. The mellow glow of the street lamps fired the dazzle of diamonds and sapphires and sequins adorning the women, and the perfume that scented the air was that of money, and plenty of it.

From his hiding place near the south side of the house, Gentry peered through the thick foliage and tried not to remember the look on Laura's face when he had left her. She had fought him until the end, but he had finally persuaded her—threatened her actually—to stay behind and wait.

But the danger aspect aside, he'd had his own personal reasons for not wanting her here. When MacKenzie fell, he wouldn't go down gracefully. Gentry wanted to spare Laura that scene. And, too, if truth be told, he didn't want her to see his part in all this. This morning, after they'd made love, he'd begun entertaining the dangerous fantasy that maybe

she would never have to know about him, that maybe they
could start over, with a clean slate.

Don't think about that now, Gentry, he admonished
himself sharply. *You've got a job to do, so do it.*

From his position he could see the sentry posted outside
the French doors leading to the library. According to Laura,
MacKenzie's office connected to the library, where the
paintings would be stored until auction time.

The guard was huge, with hulking shoulders and mam-
moth hands. Gentry couldn't see the man's weapon, but he
had no doubt he would be heavily armed, and, judging by
his size, he wouldn't be easy to take out. At least not quietly.

He glanced at his watch and noted the time. Somewhere
inside the house, Nick Corey, with his last minute invitation, would be circulating, making his own rounds of quiet
observation. It had to be tonight, Gentry thought, feeling in
the pit of his stomach the nervous excitement that accom-
panied every assignment. That this happened to be the most
important case of his life did nothing to alleviate the tension. This was his last chance.

He rested on his heels, scanning the upper levels of the
house. Several of the bedrooms had private balconies, but
none of them were easily accessible and all of them were well
lit. As he weighed the possibilities, a sound intruded on the
night. His head whipped up abruptly. A boat was roaring
toward the nearby dock at full throttle, then suddenly the
engine was cut. Quite distinctly, he heard the soft thud of
the fiberglass hull bouncing off the rubber guards as the
boat pulled up to the dock. And then all was silent.

He smelled her perfume before he saw her. She was almost directly in front of him before he recognized her, but
the golden splash of hair down her back, the tall, lithe grace
of her body draped in a dramatic black cape, the soft, seductive drawl of her voice as she spoke to the guard were all
unmistakable—she looked like a vision straight from the
pages of *Vicki Love.*

Gentry's first urge was to spring from his hiding place and strangle her before she got herself killed. Just what the *hell* did she think she was doing?

He was furious to find that his hands were trembling as he pulled his gun and prepared to defend her. But just as he was about to move, a spotlight draped her in brilliance. A guard on the roof had witnessed her arrival and trained the light on her as she walked toward the sentry at the library doors.

He could probably take them both out, Gentry decided, but Laura had placed herself directly in the line of fire. He edged back into the bushes, seething at his helplessness and her foolishness.

Her laughter rang out as clear as a bell as she approached the guard, letting the black cape slip down her arms to reveal a creamy expanse of shoulder and neck, left bared by the strapless black gown she wore. Her throat glittered with a choker of diamonds blazing with color as she moved in the spotlight. With an exquisitely feminine movement, she tossed her hair over her shoulders and laughed again.

"Would you mind turning off that light?" she called up lightly. "I know I must look a fright." She fussed with her hair for a moment and smoothed the satin cape as she stared up at the hulking guard.

The spotlight angled across the man's face, and Gentry could see his eyes—small and dark and beady—and they were all over Laura. His knuckles whitened into fists as he imagined smashing them into that ugly brute's face, watching the blood spurt from his already flattened nose.

After a moment the spotlight went out, and Gentry saw the guard on the roof move away. His gaze went back to Laura.

"Would you mind doing me a favor?" she asked a trifle breathlessly to the guard at the library's door. She let the cape slide farther down her arms. "I couldn't get my boat tied off, and if it drifts away, well...it's not really mine, you see. I borrowed it, and I would just die if anything happened to it. Could you help me?''

From his vantage Gentry couldn't see her face, but he had no difficulty imagining the curve of her lips as she smiled, the sweep of her thick lashes across her cheeks, the rise and fall of her breasts—

Damn her, he thought with a twinge of reluctant admiration. She was too damned good at this. The big ape looked as though he was ready to throw her down on the ground and rip off what little remained of that dress.

"I'm not allowed to leave my post," he said stoically.

"Oh, but it would only take a moment. And I would be so grateful…" Her voice trailed off demurely, as she moved closer and traced her finger along his arm.

He cast an agitated look around him. "All right. But we have to make it quick."

"Thank you," she said with exaggerated relief. "It's the black boat. You can't miss it. I'll just wait for you here."

As soon as the guard was out of sight, Gentry leapt from his hiding place and grabbed her. She gasped and whirled.

"God, Simon, you scared me half to death!" she whispered furiously.

"What the hell are you doing here? I told you to wait at the house."

She rolled her eyes expressively. "You're wasting valuable time, Simon."

"Here." He reached inside his jacket pocket and withdrew the keys to the BMW. "It's parked in an alley a couple of blocks over. You'll find it. Now, get the hell out of here."

"But—"

"Do it." His tone was low and deadly and brooked no argument.

With an annoyed sigh, Laura plucked the keys from his hand. "You could have at least said thank you."

Gentry bent swiftly and kissed her hard on the mouth. "Thank you," he whispered. "Now, get out."

"Single-minded pig," she said without rancor, then turned with a smile and melted into the darkness.

Without missing a beat Gentry snapped open the lock on the doors with a pocket knife and stepped inside.

A small, brass lamp burned on a table near double-paneled doors he knew opened into the salon. Directly across the room another door opened into what Laura had told him was MacKenzie's private office. Gentry crossed the room and put his ear to the wood. His hand closed on the knob and jiggled it slightly. The door opened without a squeak.

As quietly as mist, he slipped inside, then threw up an arm to shield his eyes as a brilliant blast of light targeted his face.

Laura stepped into the foyer and offered her cape to the butler. "I'm afraid I've forgotten my invitation," she said with an apologetic smile.

"That's quite all right, madam. The senator's expecting you."

He turned away without further ado, and Laura crossed the foyer to the salon. She stood at the back, tugging at her long, black gloves as her gaze scanned the room. Rows and rows of velvet-padded seats took up most of the floor space, but the glittering crowd mingled at the fringes of the room, talking and laughing and sipping the inevitable champagne while they waited for the auction to begin. Across the room, a man stood reclining against the wall, arms folded across his chest as he glared at her in cold disapproval. Nick Corey. Laura would have recognized him anywhere.

He started across the room toward her, but just then the library doors swung open and Senator Jake MacKenzie walked out. A collective awed hush fell over the crowd as he took the podium and said into the microphone, "Ladies and gentlemen, if you'll be kind enough to take your seats, the auction will begin."

There was the general rustle of satin, the shuffle of feet as everyone took their places. Senator MacKenzie surveyed the crowd, smiling slightly. "I hope you're all feeling generous tonight." After the smiles and soft laughter faded away, he turned serious, his blue eyes earnest. "I don't have to remind you that the money collected here tonight will go a long way toward feeding and housing the homeless of our country. I don't have to remind you how fortunate we all are when so many people all over our great nation don't even have the basics—food, shelter, clothing. I don't have to remind you that while our children are at home, safe and warm in their own beds, other children are on the streets literally fighting for their lives. I don't have to remind you of any of those things because I know that, like me, you have a deep, abiding love for this country. Ladies and gentlemen, the buck stops here tonight. So let's get started."

The crowd sat quietly, mesmerized by his words, his powerful persona, his indefinable charisma. Even though she'd seen him give dozens of speeches, even though she knew he was not the man everyone perceived him to be, Laura still felt herself respond to his velvet coercion. He knew how to move an audience, she marveled. No question about it.

A pressure on the small of her back startled her. Laura gasped and whirled. Nick Corey's handsome face stared down at her, the blue eyes cool, assessing.

"What the hell are you doing here?" he whispered furiously. "Does Gentry know you're here?"

"I'm supposed to be here," she whispered back. "And who's Gentry?"

Nick's mouth thinned as he grabbed her elbow and steered her out of the salon. "We've got to get you out of here."

"Why? I came to help," she said, trying to struggle unobtrusively against his hold.

"And just what do you think *I'm* doing here?" he asked through clenched teeth. "This is no place for amateurs."

"I'm hardly an amateur," Laura said, slipping so easily into her Vicki Love persona, she hardly realized she was wearing it. "Simon needs me, and I'm not leaving until I make sure he's all right. Besides, it might look suspicious if I left before my paintings are auctioned."

Nick gazed down at her, a flicker of admiration in his crystalline eyes, and a curious flash of something across his features that looked almost like envy. "When things get hot around here—and they will get hot—you think he's going to want you around? You won't help him, believe me. You could prove to be a fatal distraction."

Laura tried to flinch away, but she knew his words held the ring of truth. An image flashed through her mind, a picture of Simon lying in her arms, his blood covering them both as his life slowly ebbed away. What would it be like to watch someone you loved die, to feel so helpless and useless and guilty? For the first time since Simon had told her about Caroline, Laura understood exactly what he had gone through all these years, why he had made his career the all-consuming force in his life. A job couldn't die in your arms. A job couldn't leave you behind to face the long, agonizing nights alone. A job required commitment, guts, determination—but it didn't demand your soul.

If Simon died because of her, she wasn't sure she'd be able to live with herself.

"I'll go," she said simply, realizing that that was all she could do for now. And she had turned to do exactly that when the auctioneer's voice caught her up short. *The Knight* had just been announced, and Laura couldn't resist the temptation to take one last peek inside. As the satin drapery was lifted from the painting, a gratifying murmur of oohs and aahs drifted from the audience.

Laura stared at the painting, awed for a moment herself. From this distance, the flaws were invisible and the knight's resemblance to Jake was astonishing. He looked regal, dauntless, righteous—all the qualities Laura had tried to achieve but failed. Or so she'd always thought. The painting she saw now was breathtaking perfection.

And it wasn't hers. The revelation swept over her with dizzying speed. That painting was not hers.

Nick said urgently at her ear, "You agreed to leave, remember?"

She turned, her eyes wide with shock. "Nick, that painting..."

His gaze swept toward the front of the salon, then back to her as he shrugged impatiently. "So? It's someone's idea of a sick joke."

"What do you mean?"

"In case you haven't noticed, Senator Jake MacKenzie is hardly a knight in shining armor," he said dryly.

"But that's not my painting," she whispered desperately.

"Congratulations. Now let's go."

He took her elbow again, but Laura shook it off, unmindful of eyes this time. "*The Knight* is my painting, but *that* one's not. Don't you understand? It's a fake, a forgery. For some reason—"

A light dawned in Nick's eyes. "I understand," he interrupted quietly. Then he smiled. "Perfectly, as a matter of fact. Get out of here, Laura. I think the fireworks are just about to start."

Laura turned back for one last glimpse of the painting. The bidders seemed to be mostly women, she noticed, except for a dark-haired man standing against the wall. His eyes fastened on Laura for a moment and he smiled ever so slightly. She had the unpleasant sensation, an ugly feeling that the man had somehow violated her. She whirled to face Nick again, but he was nowhere in sight.

The butler stood at the door, however, her cape draped artfully across his arm. She took it from him and fastened it into place. "Good night, Charles," she said in resignation.

He bowed slightly as he opened the door for her and she stepped out into the night.

Once away from the mansion, Laura abandoned caution. Slipping out of her heels, she ran along the sidewalk, keeping to the shadows as much as possible. The black satin cape billowed behind her like a dark specter in rapid pursuit.

She had already passed the alley before she noticed the black BMW. Backtracking, she glanced warily over her shoulder, making sure she hadn't been followed. The street was eerily silent, the alley dark and gloomy. The hairs on the back of her neck prickled with awareness as she approached the car.

Something shuffled in the darkness. Laura whirled, her breath catching painfully in her throat. With a loud *meow,* a scrawny cat leapt to the top of the wooden fence edging the alleyway. He crouched there, amber eyes glowing in the dark.

Laura let out her breath with a shaky laugh. "You scared me half to death, kitty," she scolded softly. "Twice in one night." The cat eyed her balefully for a moment, then with a graceful lunge, vanished to the other side of the fence.

Laura turned back to the car and with hands that were still shaking, fumbled with the key in the lock. Across the alley the movement of her own shadow on the side of a whitewashed building tripped her heart all over again. Cursing softly, she stared for a moment at her own distorted silhouette. And then behind her shadow, another one appeared. For a split second all she could do was stare at the shadows in fascination, as though watching a drama unfold on a movie screen.

And then, as she opened her mouth to scream, flesh-and-blood hands closed around her throat.

Chapter 14

Colored squares of light floated before Gentry's eyes as he squinted and tried to refocus yet again.

"Can't you turn that damned light off?" He shifted his position, feeling cold metal touch the back of his neck.

"Quiet."

The one word command was all he'd heard since he'd walked into the trap a few minutes ago. The bright light had been trained on his face so that he had gotten only brief impressions of his surroundings, couldn't determine how many men were in the room with him.

Only one way to find out, he thought with grim determination, but before he could make a move, the office door swung open and someone else came into the room. Gentry could see nothing, but he could sense the added tension, the almost tangible fear in the man standing behind him.

"Welcome, Mr. Hunter," said a deep voice somewhere behind the light. "Or should I call you Agent Gentry? In either case, I've been waiting for you."

"Not as long as I've been waiting for you, MacKenzie."

"At long last we meet." The voice lowered. "Turn off the light."

The spotlight was doused immediately. In a moment Gentry's normal vision returned, and he cased the room with a detailed glance. The office was small, with floor-to-ceiling bookcases on two sides and a barred casement window on another. An oil painting stood against the bookcases.

Behind a massive oak desk at the other end of the room Senator Jake MacKenzie sat in a high-backed leather chair that reminded Gentry very much of a throne. Behind him two bodyguards stood sentry, their massive shoulders and necks dwarfing their heads.

"Who knows how long we might have strung out our little game? But now you've gone and made it personal, Gentry."

"It's always been personal," Gentry said, eyeing MacKenzie with open disgust.

"But you committed the cardinal sin. You took something of mine." His voice was deceptively calm as one steady finger stroked the delicate stem of a champagne glass sitting on the desk in front of him. When he looked up, the blue eyes were ice-cold, deadly and completely sane. "No one, *no one* steals from me."

He pushed the glass aside and got up to walk around the desk, then stood leaning against it as a half smile played at his lips. "Sit down, Gentry," he offered politely, gesturing toward the straight-backed chair directly opposite the desk.

"I'm not tired, thanks."

"Maybe Ricco can persuade you that you are."

One of the men behind MacKenzie grinned, displaying the uneven rows of tiny, sharklike teeth. He opened his jacket just far enough to reveal the Colt Python shoved inside a shoulder holster.

Gentry sat.

"Perhaps we'd better have your weapon," MacKenzie suggested. "I'm sure you know the routine. No sudden moves and all that."

When he hesitated a fraction too long, Ricco drew the .357 Magnum and aimed it directly at Gentry's heart.

"Don't be a fool, Gentry. You know the rules. As long as you're alive, you still have a chance, albeit a slim one," MacKenzie said with a smile. "Drop your gun to the floor. Buy yourself a little more time."

Gentry eased the SIG-Sauer from his pocket and slipped it to the floor. The other goon came forward and stooped with a grunt to pick it up. He laid it on the desk behind MacKenzie, but the senator shook his head. "You know I detest guns. Too unpredictable." His hand dipped lazily into his tuxedo jacket and withdrew a pearl-handled switchblade. He pushed a button and the blade whipped out.

"I'm sure in your line of work, you're only too aware of the advantages of a knife over a gun. You have no control over a bullet. Oh, you can aim for an arm or a leg, try your damnedest to miss a vital organ, but still..." His words trailed off, as he slid the blade back and forth between his thumb and forefinger. "A knife can go as shallow—or as deep—as you desire. The pain can be prolonged for hours, days."

MacKenzie straightened and began pacing across the thick carpet as he continued to talk. "You're a dying breed, Gentry. A counterespionage agent in a world that no longer needs nor tolerates spics. If you continued with the Bureau, you would no doubt be reassigned as so many of your comrades already have been. You'd be a rookie again at—what? Forty-one, forty-two? You stayed in the game too long, Gentry. You've outlived your usefulness."

"I may be a dying breed, MacKenzie," Gentry said calmly. "But so are you. The sleaze factor went out of vogue with the last administration. The American people won't tolerate the likes of you much longer."

In a lightning move MacKenzie spun and knelt beside the chair. With one hand, he grabbed a handful of Gentry's hair, and jerked back his head, exposing the throat while one of the bodyguards pinned Gentry's arms behind him.

The blade flashed in the light as the long, wicked point made contact with his neck. Gentry felt the slight sting as the blade pierced skin, then the slow trickle of blood down his throat. The pain was light compared to the torture in his arms, but his stomach rolled sickeningly. He'd seen someone die once who had had his throat slashed. The gasping for breath, the sickening gurgle in the chest, the endless flow of blood—

As if to perpetuate the image, MacKenzie said softly, "I'm going to cut you, Gentry, very slowly, very precisely, in dozens of places, until you beg me to kill you. And I will. I will, Gentry. I'll be merciful, I promise you. All you have to do is answer my questions."

"I'm not the only one on to you," Gentry said, trying to quiet the muscle in his cheek. "You can kill me, but you'll never be free. Your reign is over, you son of a bitch."

The blue gaze slashed him with scorn. "You still don't get it, do you? You're all alone in this, Gentry. You are the last piece of evidence against me. All the records you so carefully prepared are gone, destroyed. Your pitiful little operation down here has been condemned by your superiors. Everyone involved is *gone*, Gentry. You and Atwater are the only ones left who know, and I wouldn't count on his help if I were you. He's nothing more than a washed-up old man who'd sell his mother's soul for the price of a bottle of bourbon. You should thank me for sparing you that same destiny."

"It seems to me you've forgotten one little detail," Gentry said coolly. "There is a witness."

MacKenzie sighed deeply. "Ah, yes. The lovely Cassandra, the witness who has no recollection of seeing me exchange incriminating information with her cousin. The witness who didn't recognize me when we came face-to-face the night her cousin died. The witness whom you have tucked away in London with her husband, Jarrod.''

At Gentry's shocked look, MacKenzie merely smiled. ''Oh, yes. I know she's in London. It's only a matter of time before my people locate her and eliminate the last shred of evidence against me.''

''Not the last,'' Gentry said evenly, taking great satisfaction in the flash of uncertainty in MacKenzie's eyes. The senator lifted one brow, and Gentry grinned. ''Greenwood's alive.''

''Impossible. We would have known—''

Gentry laughed. ''We may be a dying breed, but we still have a very effective network. You're a dead man, MacKenzie.''

Again the elegant brow lifted. ''Perhaps. But I have my own network. I can be out of the country with a fortune on a moment's notice. You, on the other hand, are not so lucky.''

The knife pierced again, and this time the blade sliced deeper. The sting sharpened to pain, and the blood flowed freely. From the salon came the sound of applause as painting after painting came to the block. MacKenzie smiled. ''Hurts like hell, doesn't it? That's just the beginning, Gentry. And we have all night. I'll put in an appearance now and then at the auction, just to keep the masses happy, but the real fun will be in here.

''Now, for the questions I promised you. I want to know Cassandra Chandler's current name. I want to know her exact location. And before this night's over, you'll give it to me. But first . . .'' He paused, carefully wiping the bloodied knife blade on a white silk handkerchief. ''Did you touch her?''

''Cassandra?'' Gentry asked innocently. ''She's a married woman, MacKenzie.''

''You know damned well who I'm talking about.'' He shoved the cleaned edge of the blade against Gentry's bleeding throat. ''Did you touch her?'' he screamed, and for just one second, Gentry saw the flash of madness in those baby blue eyes.

Gentry smiled. "Yeah, I touched her."

"Damn you!"

MacKenzie sprang to his feet and stalked to the desk, then whirled, flinging the knife toward Gentry. It stabbed the floor between his feet.

Gentry arched an ironic brow. "Nice throw."

"You'll pay dearly for that," MacKenzie said between clenched teeth, and Gentry knew the senator wasn't referring to his last comment. MacKenzie's nostrils flared white. "The price is the whereabouts of Cassandra Chandler."

"There's nothing you can do to me that would make me tell you that."

"No?" MacKenzie nodded to one of the guards, and he moved across the room to open the door. Laura stepped inside.

Gentry's breath caught in his throat as he stared at her. She stood there, looking dazed as her eyes darted around the room. The strapless black dress she wore had to be the shortest one Gentry had ever seen, and for a moment, every pair of male eyes in the room had one common focus. Then her gasp of horror brought them all up short.

"Simon! Oh, my God!" She tried to rush to him, but a huge arm shot out and restrained her. "Simon—"

"I'm okay," he said quietly, trying to reassure her with his eyes.

Laura spun to face Jake. "What happened?"

"He and I had a slight disagreement," Jake said calmly. "I don't know what he's told you, but the man's a government agent, Laura. He's trying to frame me, trying to save his own skin at my expense."

Laura's heart plunged in terror as she stared at Simon's blood-soaked shirt. Once again she started toward him. Once again the bodyguard who had followed her into the room subdued her.

And suddenly, as she looked from Simon to Jake, everything began to fall into place for her. In fact, she realized now that her subconscious had been flirting with the truth for days, but she'd pushed it aside, trying to ignore the implications. Jake was the man Simon sought, and he had known it all along, even from their very first meeting.

She'd accused him of using her once, but she could never have imagined the full extent of his deceit.

Her tormented gaze swung around as MacKenzie advanced toward her. He stabbed the air in Gentry's direction with his finger. "How could you let that man touch you? You were mine!" he screamed.

"I'm not a possession!" Laura countered defiantly. She straightened her shoulders as she faced Jake MacKenzie eye to eye. At that moment Gentry knew he had never admired her more, because she wasn't just facing a man, she was facing an important part of her past that had been a lie, a fantasy.

"You were the one he wanted all along," she said in a whisper-soft voice. "It was never me."

"Of course not," MacKenzie sneered. "He's a fanatic, Laura. He'd do anything to bring me down. Including using you. Look at this." He pulled something from his pocket and shoved his palm toward her. "Do you know what that is? A listening device, a bug he put in my phone the day you let him into my home. How do you feel about him now, my dear?"

From across the room Gentry saw MacKenzie's mental knife meet its mark with keen precision. He'd known the exact moment when Laura had felt the first glimmer of doubt, and his heart had sunk. Now, she turned to meet his gaze.

"This man's sole raison d'être for the past three years has been my destruction," MacKenzie ranted. "You don't actually believe he has a conscience, do you? He wanted *me*, Laura. The shortest route was through you. If you don't believe me, why don't you ask him?" he ordered.

Gentry saw Laura flinch and he cursed softly. The destruction of her trust in him was the hardest thing he'd ever had to witness.

"Ask him what his real motive was in sleeping with you," MacKenzie continued. "Ask him, damn you!"

"Simon—" Her eyes pleaded with him across the room.

"You don't even know his real name," MacKenzie smirked. "Try Gentry."

Laura's gaze faltered at the name, but she didn't look away. Gentry's own words were rushed as his eyes issued an appeal. "The man's a murderer, Laura. A traitor. He had to be stopped. Surely you can understand that." But the explanation sounded hollow even to his own ears.

"See?" MacKenzie said almost gleefully. "I'm telling you the truth, and he's done nothing but lie to you. I was willing to share it all with you, everything, and you threw it all away because of *him*." He practically spat the words at her. To Gentry he said, "Now's your chance to prove yourself to her, Gentry. You tell my boys here everything I want to know, and once I'm safely out of the country, I'll order her release. Her fate is in your hands. I'll be waiting for the call." He nodded his head to the guard who had brought Laura in. "Take her to the yacht."

"No!" She tried to fight her way to freedom but her hands were quickly manacled behind her back.

Across the room, she saw Simon free one arm and strike out wildly at his captors. There was the sound of crashing furniture, then the duller sound of metal meeting flesh. And then she heard no more as Jake MacKenzie shoved her outside and closed the door behind them.

Gentry's head throbbed with pain as he slitted one eye and looked around. He was lying on the floor, facedown, where he'd fallen from the blow to his head. The two goons hovered over him, arguing over which one would do the honors on him. The one called Ricco muttered absently as he swiped at the blood streaming down his face. Just to the right of Gentry's head, the pearl-handled switchblade was still impaled in the floor.

His fingers inched toward the blade as he tried to keep the rest of his body completely still. If he could just grab the knife before they realized he'd regained consciousness—

Suddenly the door burst open with such force, it slammed against the wall. Without hesitation Gentry plucked the knife from the carpet and rolled to a crouch. Ricco had already drawn his gun, but the man in the doorway fired, and the weapon flew from the thug's hand. Ricco screamed and collapsed to the floor, nursing his wounded hand.

"Against the wall, both of you. Hands up, legs spread. Do it!" When the other guard hesitated, his hand wavering over his weapon, Atwater said calmly, "Make my day, creep."

"Oh, brother," Gentry muttered, rolling his eyes heavenward.

Sam spared him barely a glance. "Are you going to sit there all night, Gentry, or would you like to disarm these two idiots?"

Gentry stood and snapped closed the knife blade. "Hell, Sam, I didn't know you still had it in you," he said appreciatively, crossing the room to collect the guards' weapons. "Where's Corey?"

"Right here, Gentry." He walked into the room, preceded by a short, dark-haired man with a pencil-thin mustache. "Here's your buyer—" Nick gave him a shove, and the man stumbled forward "—and your evidence..." At Nick's nod, two men carried a painting inside the office and set it down beside the one already there. They looked identical. "All rolled up in one very tidy package. And remember, Gentry, you owe me."

"It's Laura's painting," Gentry muttered. "He duplicated her painting."

"And you can thank her for recognizing the fake," Nick said. "If she hadn't been here, they might have gotten away with it right under our noses. She's some woman, Gentry."

"You don't have to tell me that."

"Where are you going?" Nick asked, as Gentry started across the room.

"He's got her," he said grimly.

"MacKenzie? Hell, Gentry, do I have to do everything?"

Gentry spared him a killing look. "You okay with them?" he asked Atwater. Gentry was already halfway out the door before the older man had time to answer.

"I haven't felt this good in years," Sam said gruffly. "Pension or no pension. You know what they say. Old FBI agents never die," he paraphrased, his gaze narrowing on the two thugs across the room. "We just get meaner."

"You've given me hope, Sam," Gentry said over his shoulder.

"MacKenzie knows he's cornered," Atwater called. "He'll be more dangerous than ever...."

Gentry laughed.

Laura strained against her bindings, but to no avail. Her arms were tied behind her back and secured to the back of the chair in which she sat. Across the stateroom Senator Jake MacKenzie was busily emptying his safe.

For the several minutes they had been aboard the yacht, Laura had watched Jake, studied his godlike face, and wondered why she hadn't seen the truth years ago. Jake MacKenzie was a power-hungry, egotistical man, but the fact that he'd been kind to her, had cared about her when no one else had, had blinded her to the obvious.

"Why did you do it, Jake?" she asked softly.

He glanced up and shrugged, then went back to his work. "The excitement, the challenge, the danger. I did it because I could get away with it," he said simply. He paused for a moment with a stack of money in one hand. "Do you remember that summer I came home from Vietnam, all the ceremonies held in my honor, all the parades, all the speeches? None of that meant anything to me. It was the excitement and danger I experienced in Nam that was the real high, that out-of-control, living-on-the-edge rush. I wanted more of it, Laura. But nothing ever came close. Not sports, not sex, nothing. Until this."

"You sold out your country because you wanted excitement?" she asked incredulously.

"The money hasn't been bad, either," he said, waving the stack of bills in the air. He laughed dangerously and tucked the money into the satchel to join the other stacks already inside. "You know what the real high would have been? Knowing what I know as I took the oath of office to be president of the United States. And you could have been there with me, but your boyfriend's changed all that. You do have the worst judgment when it comes to men, my dear."

"I'm starting to realize that," she said meaningfully.

"Of course, good ole Clark, in his own way, really did love you, but he was weak, Laura, too easily manipulated. He could never have made a woman like you happy. You should thank me for saving you."

Laura stared at him in shock. "What are you talking about?"

"I'm the one who started the rumors about Kendall. I'm the one who slept with your maid of honor the night before your wedding. Afterward, the silly little fool was more than willing to do anything I asked her. Including lie to you, her best friend."

Laura sat stunned, reeling from his words. Would there ever be an end to the lies and deceit, the manipulations? Because of her an innocent man's reputation had been ruined. Simon had once told her that she trusted too freely. At that moment, she felt she would never trust again.

Simon. Gentry. Whatever his name, his was the most painful betrayal of all. He'd lied to her, used her in order to get to Jake. He had never wanted her, only what she represented. She was no more than a pawn to either man.

"What are you going to do with me?" she asked coldly, using every inch of her willpower to keep the fear from her voice. Never, never would she give him the satisfaction.

"I had planned to take you with me," Jake said. "But, you know, the thought has occurred to me that this could all blow over. As soon as I give the word, your hero back there will be history. But before he goes, if he cares about you at all, I'm sure my men will be able to extract certain bits of information from him that will help me...eliminate the last of the evidence against me. Except for you, of course." He shrugged regretfully. "You can see my dilemma, I'm sure. I'm afraid this is the end of the fairy tale for us, my dear."

"You don't have to kill him!" Laura cried urgently. She didn't question her defense of Simon; she only knew that, regardless of what he'd done, she didn't want him to die. *Please, God, not that.* She closed her eyes on the silent prayer, then said, "You can go anywhere in the world and start over, Jake. All that money, the diamonds you showed me—you can live like a king! For God's sake, don't add murder to your crimes."

"Too late," he said with a brilliant smile. He snapped the satchel closed and lifted it from the desk. "Defending him to the end, is it? How sweet. Is it really love this time, Laura?"

"Yes," she whispered, trying to quell the rise of emotions in her throat. "If you ever cared about me at all, you won't do this."

"It's him or me," he said with a disarming smile. "I choose me. You, I'm afraid, will have to meet with an unfortunate accident, which my men will see to, of course. It's really too bad you have such a penchant for swimming alone...."

"You'll never get away with this, Jake."

He paused at the door and looked back at her, shaking his head sadly. "My dear heart, I can get away with anything. Haven't you figured that out by now?" He cocked his head at the sound of an engine starting up. "Ah, there's the chopper warming up. In another lifetime, my love . . .'' He saluted her briefly, then turned to exit through the door.

Someone was waiting for him in the doorway. Laura thought at first it was one of the guards coming to get her, but suddenly Jake was slowly backing into the stateroom. Simon followed him, his gun aimed at Jake's chest.

Cornered, Jake cast about frantically for a weapon, then flung the satchel at Simon's hand. The gun flew across the room. And as Jake lunged for the pistol, Simon lunged for him.

There was no grace in the fight. No wary stalking or appraising or measuring from either of them. The moment their bodies collided the struggle became a deadly fight to the finish.

Jake collapsed back on the desk and Simon dived after him. His momentum carried them both off the desk and they rolled to the floor, their blows connecting with sickening precision. Jake fought desperately, like a wild thing cornered who had nothing to lose and everything to gain. Simon fought coldly, with deadly purpose.

Laura shivered at the look in Simon's eyes. She marveled that she had known this man's passion, his gentleness, but the warrior who fought before her was a complete stranger to her.

With the edge of his hand, he applied a vicious chop to Jake's neck, but Jake moved at the last minute, weakening the blow. He countered with a swift jab to Simon's stomach, and Laura saw pain explode through him, heard a string of words like nothing she'd ever heard before, and then he landed a punch to Jake's face, and the senator's elegant nose disappeared in a flash of blood.

The blow seemed to weaken MacKenzie's spirits. He made another unsuccessful strike at Simon, who'd taken full advantage and followed his opponent to the floor, pinning him down and immobilizing him. The fight was over.

Simon looked down at him for a few seconds as both men struggled for breath. Something flashed in his hand, and

Laura saw that it was a knife. She screamed as he clicked it open.

"Simon, no!"

He spared her barely a glance, but it was enough to make her quiver in fear at the look in his eyes. Once, while on safari in Africa, her party had happened upon a lion who had just killed a gazelle. There had been a terrifying moment when the beast had looked at them with challenge and rage and possession before he turned and coolly ripped into the still-warm flesh. That same look was in Simon's eyes now.

The knife flashed silver in the light as the point touched Jake's face. Simon turned it, so that the flat edge of the blade slid down the flawless skin. Jake gasped and tried to flinch away, but Simon's hand closed around his throat.

"You took something of mine, MacKenzie."

He said the words calmly, but the knife flipped over with deadly precision. The blade marked the skin, and a thin stream of blood arrowed down the once perfect face.

Jake howled with pain. For just a heart-splitting second the point flirted with his throat, and then, disgusted, Simon snapped closed the blade and stood. Jake doubled up, clutching his face. With one eye still on him, Simon reached for his gun.

From somewhere on deck a series of shots rang out, piercing the night with the warlike sounds of death and destruction. The lights in the stateroom flickered, then went out altogether as though someone had turned off the powerful generator. From the stunned blackness came the distinct sound of labored breathing, of scrambling feet. Something brushed against Laura's legs and she screamed. The lights flashed on briefly, time enough to illuminate Jake MacKenzie heading toward the door.

Simon's hand closed tightly around the knife handle. Then he turned, and began slicing through the ropes binding her hands.

When Laura was free, he grabbed her wrist and jerked her up. "Hurry up! We've gotta get out of here. All hell's breaking loose."

She needed no further encouragement. She ran beside him, their footsteps flying along the darkened corridor and up the metal stairs to the main deck. A volley of shots whizzed past their heads, and Simon pulled her down on the slippery deck, shielding her body with his.

In the screaming darkness, their eyes met briefly. "I've got to get you out of here," he said grimly.

"What about you?"

"My job's not done yet."

But even as he said the words, the *whop-whopping* flutter of the helicopter drew their gazes upward.

"Jake," she whispered, unmindful of Simon's dark gaze as her own eyes remained glued to the flashing lights. The helicopter rose steadily in the night amidst a shower of bullets. Sparks flew in the darkness where metal met metal.

Oblivious to the gunfire still peppering the deck, Simon stood and took aim as the helicopter swung around and headed toward the open sea. Laura covered her ears as his gun spit in rapid succession.

The helicopter continued to rise out of range. The lights winked with taunting precision against the blackness of the sky. Simon aimed one last time, a desperate shot. The bullet hit the fuel tank, and the helicopter exploded into flames. Then, nose first, the burning chopper dived toward the sea.

The fireball lit the sky as brilliantly as sunlight. Slowly Laura got to her feet and stared at the trail of burning debris littering the surface of the water. She was hardly aware of the gunfire on deck fading away. The shouts behind her barely registered as she numbly watched the fiery remains of an illusion dissolve before her eyes.

Beside her, Simon said softly, "It's over." He put a comforting arm around her shoulders and tried to draw her close.

Dimly aware that the deck had suddenly become crowded with armed agents and Jake's captured goons, Laura pulled herself away from him as she stared him straight in the eye. "Yes, it is over. It's all over. So don't you touch me. Don't you dare touch me again. I am not your possession."

He glared down at her in the moonlight, his face grim with exhaustion. "What the hell are you talking about?"

Her gaze blasted him with icy scorn. "How do you even have the nerve to ask me that?"

He ran a weary hand through his hair. "I guess I didn't stop to think what this might do to you. I'm sorry. You looked up to him, you respected him. I know that. But surely now you can see what he really was. You have to understand why I did what I did."

"I understand that you used me to get to him."

Gentry controlled the urge to grab her and shake some sense into her. The violent night had left him shaken and slightly sickened. MacKenzie could have hurt her, killed her... all because of him. He stared at her helplessly. "He was a murderer," he said at last. "He very nearly killed you. What would you have had me do?"

"I don't know," she said honestly. "Anything besides that stupid, macho, eye for an eye scene in his stateroom. You didn't do that for me. You did it for your own egotistical satisfaction. You used me to get to him. 'You took something of mine, MacKenzie,'" she mimicked as her eyes blazed with their own fire.

When he would have reached out for her, she backed away from his touch. "I was nothing more than a pawn to the both of you, a way to get to one another. Neither of you cared about me. You're no better than he was, Simon—Gentry—whatever the hell your name is."

She stared at him for a moment, her eyes flashing a challenge, daring him to deny what they both knew was true. In the silence that followed her accusation, Gentry became acutely aware of the silence all around them. He glanced up and met the avid gazes of his fellow agents, each staring at

him in differing measures of respect, admiration, and...
disbelief. He could almost hear their mental calculations.
The man with ice water in his veins was heatedly arguing
with a beautiful woman in plain view of a dozen witnesses.

"Don't you have anything better to do?" he asked grimly.

Sam Atwater stared at him for a moment longer, then
said, "He's right. Round 'em up, boys. We've got a full
night of interrogation ahead of us."

Embarrassed by the scene, Laura allowed Simon to take
her arm and guide her away from the crowd, into the deep
shadows of the deck. She couldn't see his expression, but she
knew his dark gaze was on her, compelling her to look at
him.

"Maybe you're right," he said softly. "In a lot of ways,
I am no better than MacKenzie. I knew for a long time I'd
lost my perspective on this case, but I couldn't quit. I
couldn't fail. It was more than just a quest for justice. What
it finally boiled down to was him... or me."

She'd heard Jake say almost the same thing. The thought
sickened her now. "You never cared for me at all, did you?"
she asked bitterly, staring into the darkness. "I was part of
your plan all along. Is that the only reason you fished me
out of the water that day, so you could get closer to Jake?"

"When I first met you—" he broke off, struggling for
words, "—you took my breath away," he said with uncharacteristic eloquence.

Laura remained unmoved. "I'm supposed to believe that,
after tonight?" She clung to her anger, clutched it to her,
held on for dear life, because without it, she knew she would
be lost. "I trusted you."

"And I warned you not to," he said with devastating
simplicity.

"I asked you point-blank if Jake was involved," she cried
angrily. "Why didn't you just tell me the truth? Why did
you have to use me like that? I would have done anything for
you. Why couldn't you just have trusted me?"

He grabbed her arms, his anger bursting forth like a caged thing finally free. "I can't afford to trust anyone. Can't you see that? Because if I do..." His words trailed off as their eyes met in the moonlight.

Laura finished softly, "Because if you do, you might fall in love again. You might be hurt again. Oh, I understand, Simon. I understand you so well." She paused, her own anger suddenly melting away, leaving only an empty, hollow feeling of despair. "You're running scared, and I feel sorry for you because when you finally stop running, you may just find there's nothing left for you."

She started past him, but he caught her arm. "Laura—"

"Don't," she whispered. "You can't give me what I want. At least let me be the one to walk away."

His hand dropped from her arm. She turned, and did not look back.

Chapter 15

Washington, D.C.

Gentry stood staring out the window watching the rain pound against the glass. He'd been back in Washington for nearly two weeks, and it had rained every damned day. Jesus, would the sun never shine again?

He turned away from the window and paced restlessly across the worn carpet. Atwater sat at a long, metal table, briefcase opened in front of him and a pair of bifocals perched on his nose. He looked at Gentry over the rims.

"Will you stop that infernal pacing? You've done nothing but pace since we got back from Florida twelve days ago. You're driving me nuts."

Gentry shoved his hands into his pants pockets as he glared down at Atwater. "Yeah, well, you're not doing a whole helluva lot for my disposition, either. How many times do you have to tell that story about 'saving Gentry's ass'? To hear you tell it, you could have taken out the Iraq army single-handedly."

Atwater snapped closed the lid of the briefcase and removed his glasses. "What's really eating you? You go

MacKenzie. The brass at the top are licking your feet and trying to cover their butts. You're a hero, man. What more do you want?''

"I don't know," Gentry muttered, turning back to the window. He leaned a shoulder against the frame as he watched a 747 streak to a landing. He'd never felt less like a hero. "It doesn't feel the way I thought it would feel. It's like I stayed at a party too long because I had nowhere else to go. Do you know what I mean?''

Atwater scooted back his chair and came to stand beside Gentry. "It's her, isn't it?'' When Gentry's guilty gaze collided with his, Sam said, "You're worried about seeing her again, about whether or not she still blames you. Two years is a long time, Gentry. I'm sure she's had plenty of time to realize you were acting in her best interests.''

Gentry stared at him for a moment without comprehension. Then he said, "You mean Cassandra Chandler?''

Atwater's bushy white brows soared. "Of course. Who'd you think I meant?''

The phone on the table rang once, sparing Gentry from an answer. Atwater lifted the receiver and listened for a couple of seconds, then hung up.

He glanced up at Gentry. "Their plane's landed. Security's bringing them straight here.''

Gentry merely nodded and turned back to the window. But when Cassandra and Jarrod Chandler entered the room, he'd been staring at the door for several minutes.

His first thought was that she looked even more beautiful than he'd remembered. Petite and delicate with blond hair curling around her shoulders and huge blue eyes, Cassandra Chandler clung to her husband's arm as they walked into the room. Jarrod Chandler's height made her appear even more diminutive. He bent and said something to her, and both of them looked across the room at Gentry. And they were smiling.

"Well, you did it,'' Jarrod said, crossing the room quickly to shake Gentry's hand.

"You never gave up," Cassandra said, as she clasped Gentry's hand in both of hers. "I don't know how we can ever thank you."

Gentry smiled. "I think you just did. So how does it feel to finally be home?" he asked quietly.

Cassandra smiled up at her husband and their gazes locked. "I've been home for two years, Gentry."

Home.

Gentry gazed around dispassionately at the narrow confines of his apartment. He'd never given his surroundings much thought, much notice before, but now the heavy oak furniture—hand-me-downs from various family members—the old leather sofa that served as his bed as often as not, the unadorned walls, seemed gloomy and impersonal. No pictures, no mementos, no paraphernalia from an interesting, full life. Just a place to hang his clothes. A place to sleep—when he could.

He laid his gun on the dining room table and crossed the room to the window, raising the blinds, but the heavy curtain of rain blocked the light. Fixing himself a bourbon, he sat down in the armchair near the window and opened the paper as he sipped his drink.

MacKenzie's downfall still dominated the front page. The internal investigation into the Bureau—the bribes, the payoffs, the nebulous dealings of some of the powers-that-be—would take months, years maybe to sort out. The nightmare was far from over. There would be hearings, trials, endless statements and depositions. But at least his witness was home, safe and sound. At least he hadn't failed her.

And now he was home, relieved of assignments for the next four weeks. A severe reprimand for disregarding orders, the section chief called it. Atwater told him later to think of it as a vacation. Enjoy it.

But he didn't take vacations, Gentry thought with increasing gloom. Not since...

Automatically, he tried to turn his thoughts away from the past, but this time the images were persistent. He closed his eyes as his mind drifted back to that day so very long ago.

What he hadn't told Laura about that day, what he had tried never to admit even to himself was how angry he'd been at Caroline for dying. He'd trusted her and she'd left him.

Fourteen years. That's how long he'd buried the rage and called it guilt. That's how long he'd been obsessed with that one moment in time. That's how long he'd carried this blackness inside him. Fourteen years…one third of his life, lost forever in the ashes of his own despair.

Finally letting himself face the hurt, Gentry faced his past now as he'd never done before, and saw it for what it was— a misguided man's attempt to save himself from the pain and heartache of losing someone else he loved. Someone he might come to love even more than he had Caroline. Someone he needed and who needed him.

Someone like Laura, he thought with an ache that reached all the way to his soul.

He'd been wrong to live in the shadow of the past, wrong to live in fear of the future. Because in the end, all that really mattered was the brief, shining moment that was *now*. Everything else was only a memory. Or a wish.

He knocked back a long swig of bourbon and grimaced slightly as he wondered what to do. The case was over now and he could do whatever he wanted for the next four weeks. He'd faced the past and he was free.

To do what? he asked himself grimly. Free to go to Laura? He sat there for a moment torn between an almost irrational urge to go to her and the persistent doubts that told him he shouldn't.

Would she even want him anymore? he thought with a flash of uncertainty. She'd seen him kill a man she had cared about for far longer than she'd even known Gentry. In one way or another, he'd shattered all her dreams, her fantasies that were so much an essence of who she was. She'd put her trust in him, and he had repaid her by using her, putting her own life in danger for the sake of his obsession.

There was no reason in the world to justify his going to her now except one. He loved her. Loved everything about her, her bravery as well as her fears. Her boldness as well as her shyness. Her confidence as well as her insecurities.

He loved everything about her, but did he love her enough to trust her not to leave him? Did he love her enough to put himself on the line, to face rejection because she might not be able to forgive him? Did he love her enough to face whatever answer she might give him and go on with his life?

Uncertainty twisted like a knife in his gut. For so long he'd relied on no one but himself. For fourteen years he'd lived for no one but himself. Was there room in his life for someone else? Would she understand the importance of his job, the long hours, the calls in the middle of the night? Or would she grow tired of him and walk away...?

Gentry surveyed his dismal surroundings one last time as he contemplated the evening ahead of him. A gloomy apartment, an empty bed and a long, lonely night.

The coming hours seemed portentous somehow, a tragic little preview of the rest of his life.

Laura sat on the tiny square of beach and traced a huge heart in the sand with the pointed end of a piece of driftwood. Her gaze scanned the sea. The water was so blue today, she noticed absently. A shimmering turquoise blue with hardly a change in tint where sea met sky. In the early morning quiet a soft breeze tinkled through the wind chimes somewhere behind her and gently rippled the loose bangs across her forehead. Idly she shoved them back.

She took a deep breath and sighed. Had it really been only two weeks since Simon had left? Every morning she had awakened with the same thought. Simon was gone, and there wasn't a damn thing she could do about it. Simon was gone, and it was his choice.

He was already back in his own world, with its shadows and lies and games without rules. He hadn't trusted her enough to trust him. By now, he had probably forgotten all about her. After all, he hadn't called. He hadn't written. And he'd left Key West that day without another word of love. He'd somehow conquered his demons when he'd faced Jake, and now he was whole again. Now he no longer needed her, she thought sadly. Not the way she needed him, with her body and her soul and her heart. Especially her heart.

At least one good thing had come from the whole sordid mess, Laura decided. When the story first broke, her mother had tracked her down at the beach house. When she'd first seen Crystal trudging down the beach, carrying her Chanel pumps in one hand, Laura's first thought was that her mother had come to blame her for everything. The backlash of gossip in Washington had embarrassed her, humiliated her. But Crystal had shown surprising concern for her daughter's well-being.

"You could have been killed," Crystal had whispered, and the shimmer in her eyes had looked genuine.

It wasn't a fairy-tale ending by any means, Laura reflected. Her mother had stayed for two days, as long as either of them could stand the awkwardness, but at least it was a shaky start, a rocky beginning when everything else in her life had seemed to be ending.

Just this morning she had written the final episode of *Vicki Love*. The beautiful agent, the perfect woman, had outlived her usefulness. If Laura had learned anything in the past few days, it was that she could rely on her own wits. She still had fears. She still had insecurities. She was far from being a perfect woman, and she never would be. But she could live with her faults now, accept her weaknesses; and already the glimmer of an idea for a new heroine—one with flaws—was flickering around in her mind. When she returned to Washington, she'd begin work on it, but Laura knew she was postponing her trip home, and for a good reason. The temptation to locate Simon was still too great.

She could even accept the fact, without blaming herself, that Simon hadn't loved her enough to stay. But accepting it didn't make the pain go away, she reflected dejectedly. She wasn't sure anything could do that. Except maybe time. And she had a lifetime of that.

Inside the traced heart in the sand, she scribbled the letters LAURA LOVES—

"Is that fill-in-the-blank or multiple choice?"

Her head whipped around at the voice behind her as she struggled to her feet. "Simon! What are you doing here?"

He shrugged, looking suddenly at a loss. "I've been asking myself that question ever since my plane landed an hour ago. I—" He broke off and shrugged again. "There were some loose ends down here that needed tying up."

"Oh." The tiny light that had flickered to life inside her died at his words. Laura tried to fight down the overwhelming disappointment she felt.

"So how've you been?" he asked casually, but his eyes were curiously restless as they scrutinized her face.

Laura frowned slightly. "Fine. And you?"

"Oh, just great." He shifted his gaze, scanning the horizon with a wariness that seemed to come so naturally to him.

Laura studied his silent profile, trying to calm her pounding heart. He was dressed casually in jeans and a cotton shirt, and the faint shadow of beard on his face gave him a dangerous, reckless air. It reminded her abruptly that he *was* a dangerous man.

"About that night…" he began uncertainly. He brought his gaze back around to hers, and Laura felt her heart sink at the darkness, the bleakness of his look. "I'm sorry you had to be involved. I'm sorry you had to see everything."

"I'm sorry you felt you had to do it, Simon. I'm sorry you felt you couldn't trust me. You could have, you know," she said softly. "I would never have betrayed you."

"I couldn't be sure . . . I mean . . . you knew him all your life. You cared about him."

In spite of the raging emotions inside her, she managed to say in a nearly normal voice, "But I loved you. I still do."

She saw a myriad of emotions flicker through his eyes— a little doubt, a little fear, and hope, so much hope, it made her ache to look at him.

"You don't know what you're getting into," he said hoarsely. I'm hard to get along with, Laura. I spend long hours at work, I get phone calls in the middle of the night, there would always be secrets I couldn't explain—"

"Maybe I wouldn't ask you to," she said simply.

"*All* women ask," he said ironically, sweeping his hand through his hair.

A flash of anger sparked in her eyes. "I'm not all women, Simon. I'm the one who happens to be in love with you. I've missed you," she whispered. "Bad temper and all."

For the first time, she saw a hint of amusement in his eyes. "I've missed you, too."

"And?"

He frowned slightly. "And?"

"I want to hear the rest of it. I need to hear it."

"You drive a hard bargain, don't you?" he grumbled, but his eyes were smiling. "All right. I . . . I . . ."

Laura cocked a brow and glared at him, and he grinned. "I love you," he said simply.

Without hesitation, he opened his arms, and without hesitation, she walked into them.

"Welcome home," he whispered.

Her hand reached up to touch his roughened cheek as her gaze adored him. "Simon, there's just one thing I have to know."

The wariness returned to his gray eyes, turning them to smoke. "What's that?"

"What *is* your real name?"

A grin touched his lips as his head lowered toward hers. "My name is Richard. Richard Gentry."

"Nice to meet you, Richard," she whispered, just before his mouth claimed hers.

* * * * *

A romantic collection that
will touch your heart....

to Mother with Love '93

Diana Palmer
Debbie Macomber
Judith Duncan

As part of your annual tribute to
motherhood, join three of Silhouette's
best-loved authors as they celebrate the
joy of one of our most precious gifts—
mothers.

Available in May at your favorite retail outlet.

Only from 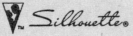 *Silhouette*®

—where passion lives.

ƬINTIMATE MOMENTS®
Silhouette®

Silhouette Intimate Moments is proud to present:
The SISTER, SISTER duet—Two halves of a whole, two
parts of a soul.

Mary Anne Wilson's duo continues next month with
TWO AGAINST THE WORLD (IM #489). Now it's Alicia's
turn to get herself out of a dangerous bind—and into
the arms of the kindest, sexiest man she's ever seen!

AMERICAN HERO

You have spoken! You've asked for more of our irresistible American Heroes, and now we're happy to oblige. After all, we're as in love with these men as you are! In coming months, look for these must-have guys:

In COLD, COLD HEART (IM #487) by Ann Williams, we're looking at a hero with a heart of ice. But when faced with a desperate mother and a missing child, his heart begins to melt. You'll want to be there in April to see the results!

In May we celebrate the line's tenth anniversary with one of our most-requested heroes ever: Quinn Eisley. In QUINN EISLEY'S WAR (IM #493) by Patricia Gardner Evans, this lone-wolf agent finally meets the one woman who is his perfect match.

The weather starts to heat up in June, so come deep-sea diving with us in Heather Graham Pozzessere's BETWEEN ROC AND A HARD PLACE (IM #499). Your blood will boil right along with Roc Trellyn's when he pulls in his net to find—his not-quite-ex-wife!

AMERICAN HEROES. YOU WON'T WANT TO MISS A SINGLE ONE—ONLY FROM

INTIMATE MOMENTS®

10TH
Anniversary

Celebrate our anniversary with a fabulous collection of firsts....

The first Intimate Moments titles written by three of your favorite authors:

NIGHT MOVES   Heather Graham Pozzessere
LADY OF THE NIGHT   Emilie Richards
A STRANGER'S SMILE Kathleen Korbel

Silhouette Intimate Moments is proud to present a FREE hardbound collection of our authors' firsts—titles that you will treasure in the years to come from some of the line's founding members.

This collection will not be sold in retail stores and is available only through this exclusive offer. Look for details in Silhouette Intimate Moments titles available in retail stores in May, June and July.